For a late friend,
an art teacher,
and my lovely wife

I

"We who were living are now dying
With a little patience."

-   T.S. Eliot, *The Wasteland*

One

He was born in darkness.

All the boy had ever known were damp, cold walls, dripping with moisture and smelling of spoiled milk. His home was steel wires and concrete floors, surrounded by shelving, which housed tin cans of foreign materials. *Paint* and *tools* were what they were called, but he didn't fully understand their uses. He didn't understand much of anything. And neither did the others.

There were three more, each of whom, raised by the shadows of their concrete home – only ever allowed to touch the cold earth and colder steel, and seldom each other. Two of the others were like him, and one was different; one was a girl.

The boy, called Number Two, often thought of the girl. She was the fourth to sprout, a taproot who found life far below the foundation of their estate and rose through the pockets of concrete, wedging a crack, splitting the surface in a bloom of soft white illumination. Her face glowed through the cellar in which they were born. She was warm. She was everything.

Two didn't know how long he'd been alive.

He knew little of the concept of time but understood that in the future, he would leave his home of darkness and bring light to an even darker world.

The boy was destined to save a dying planet he'd never set foot upon. He'd never witnessed a December sunrise or watched the moon wade through the night sky. He knew nothing of the world he was fated to salvage.

To pass the time until the day he would eventually leave his cage, the boy fixed his mind on what he knew. He thought of the sound of water droplets, which fell at a metronomic pace, splashing softly, just faintly enough for him to hear, on the concrete between his and Three's cages. He thought of the sound of the others' breathing, and how when Four slept, she often cried out in a feeble whimper which made Two want to pull apart the steel wires that surrounded him. He thought about the door up high, the portal. He thought about the painful yellow light that invaded his home every time the portal opened. He thought about what came through the opening – about *who* came through.

Papa.

The man beyond the door was powerful. He possessed knowledge that the four could only hope to one day attain. Papa knew how to bend light and manipulate machine and was nearly as powerful as God. In fact, he was a disciple of God. Papa spoke with the Lord and received words and messages, which he often shared with the four. It was God who told Papa about the prophecy – that one day, the children would bring light to the world of sin. Now it was Papa's job to help prepare Number Two and the others.

Two thought of the man nearly as often as he thought of Number Four – *nearly*. The girl was constant, like the dripping of water in the corner of the room. She reminded Two that he existed in someplace, in some point in time, and wasn't just a part of some heavenly mission. She helped Two understand that he had blood coursing through his wiry body. She infected his thoughts, even though they barely spoke, even though they hardly did anything at all other than listen to the rise and fall of each other's chests.

Two scratched the inside of his brittle thigh and surveyed the room. The boy's leg had been housing an itch since his last private message with Papa. He tried not to think on it, but the deed proved difficult. Every time the water splashed against the concrete in the corner of the room, it acted as a reminder that something was not right.

Two looked at Three's cage, hoping it would distract his mind from the itch. Beyond the steel wires of the opposing cell lay another boy, one who had been affected during the last portal opening. During that visit, Papa shared a message with the four before leading Three down the hall to the holy room to share a separate, private message with him. Since that time, Three had an ill effect of his own, seemingly worse than Two's itch. His body had been perfectly still for some time since. Every time Two thought of his itch, every time the water dropped to the floor and made a tiny, audible *splash*, he thought of Three. Two wondered when his friend would move again.

Two

Every Thursday night, Oliver Brady worked security at the Clyde County Power Plant. He held the night shift on Friday and Saturday as well, though he never felt like he was doing much work of any kind. For the most part, Oliver just sat in a small office, about the size of a broom closet, staring through the windows and jotting down notes in the plant's logbook. At the top of every hour, Oliver would leave his station and walk the premises, keeping a watchful eye for troublemakers, though he seldom saw any.

Clyde County covered a rural mass of three towns across southwest Missouri – those being Plainsview, Napoli, and Saint Clara – each of which had a population of less than nine hundred people. The number of livestock spread across the county far surpassed that of the human population, which meant there wasn't much source for crime. It seemed one was more likely to be struck by lightning than robbed or wronged by someone from Clyde County. And the people who lived there loved that fact.

The lack of criminals was an interest Oliver shared with the County's residents. He wasn't one to work in law enforcement – if you could call security detail at a county power plant *law enforcement* – just to abuse his power and enforce the long arm. He only worked there for his weekly trio of nights because he needed a second source of income. Oliver was a thirty-nine-year-old man who lived in a small town with limited employment opportunity, and a teenage daughter who solely relied on him. His day job at the Napoli Feed Store would never cut it alone. Hell, having both jobs provided just barely enough to survive, but Oliver and his daughter were always able to make do.

Another reason Oliver enjoyed the peace and quiet of the town and the plant was because the security officers weren't authorized to carry a weapon, though he was certain that most of the others broke that rule. In fact, a fellow nightshift worker, Paul Wayne, often boasted the Colt handgun he hid beneath his waistband. Oliver disregarded the others and followed protocol, only carrying the issued flashlight and cell phone. The flashlight was meant to help spot vandals or thieves, and the cell phone was meant to dial 9-1-1. If an officer were to witness any criminal activity under the yellow beam of his or her flashlight, they were supposed to, according to the employee handbook, verbally address the wrongdoers to deter the criminal activity.

Oliver sometimes considered the handbook's rules to be quite absurd. There was a long list of what the officers were authorized to do, as well as the mandated procedures for their shifts. It seemed like a lot of nonsense, because all the staff ever did was sit in an office and occasionally walk the fence line. If Oliver had to guess, he'd say that most of the officers didn't even adhere to the patrolling procedures. He imagined most of his coworkers just filled out the logbook as if they patrolled. Oliver couldn't do that. He followed the handbook, despite thinking the rules were a bit asinine. Most of the trespassers he came across were bored teens anyway, hopping the fence to explore the plant's entangled maze of steel and concrete. The kids usually scattered like roaches when he shone his light on them. There were only a few occasions when Oliver actually had to use the cell phone, the most recent being a man attempting to strip the plant of some of its copper.

This particular Thursday night was the usual drag. Oliver sat alone in the security office, staring through the window at a pad of concrete, illuminated by the brilliance of the power plant's countless lights. *Friends* reruns played on the fifteen-inch flat screen to his side, but the dutiful officer never watched. He only powered the television for background noise, so that the silence of the latest hours of the night and earliest hours of the day didn't drive him mad. He also used the TV to help keep himself awake, though coffee and cigarettes performed the job more proficiently.

The time was nearing four in the morning, meaning Oliver only had about two hours left before his relief came, but even closer was his next patrol. In ten minutes, he'd have to make from his weathered chair and walk the perimeter of the plant. He really didn't feel like moving. He was tired – the kind of tired that accompanies the small hours of the morning. Every night, around this time, Oliver became incredibly drowsy. When he first took the job, he figured he'd adapt, but later found there was no getting used to the schedule. Whatever, that's what the coffee and the cigarettes were for.

Oliver looked at the clock once more. It read 3:56.

"Ah," the man groaned to nobody but himself. "Alright then."

Oliver fumbled from his chair, his joints creaking all through the process. A Marlboro Red snuck between his fingers. He opened the door and lit the tobacco beneath the late August moon.

Just another patrol.

Three.

A soft wind crept through the compound. The air blew warm and mild, but still caused the aging choir of steel to groan. Oliver listened to the plant sing as he ran his hand along the chain-link fence that encompassed the looming towers. On the other side of the wire was the faint sound of highway traffic, likely tractor-trailers making their haul to or from St. Louis. An hour from now, on his last patrol, another sound would be added to the melody of the Clyde County night: the rooster call of the first locomotive leaving the Saint Clara train yard. That train horn was one of Oliver's favorite sounds, as it meant that relief was just around the bend. He'd hear it soon.

Oliver's hand against the fence made a rustling sound as he walked. His head craned from side to side, searching for any trespassers as he made his patrol, but all he saw were the dark, pillowing stacks of concrete and twisted metal that he knew so little about. The night, alive as it might have been on the opposite side of the fence, was dormant inside the compound. The plant creaked and moaned, but its noisy existence was artificial. The ever-present mass of the building made Oliver feel incredibly lonely sometimes. There were some nights while strolling aside the enormous construction that he felt he was the only man in the universe. This warm August patrol was one of those.

Oliver held his flashlight in the opposite hand to that which touched the fence. He flicked the light from side to side as he walked, half out of boredom and half out of respect to searching for criminals. His hazel eyes followed wherever the light beamed, darting back and forth like a sort of tennis match. He imagined himself the Federer of security officers, even though his joints often ached and he was far from athletic. Oliver rubbed a hand through his scraggly, reddish-brown head of hair. He was also less handsome, he thought. The officer chuckled a moment, falling into the stage of tiredness where everything ends in a laugh. In that moment, he was his own personal comedian, envisioning himself, a lifelong farmhand from rural southwest Missouri, turned feed store clerk and security guard, a Goddamn professional athlete.

Oliver laughed again, but his moment of joy was cut short by an alarming sound near the building. A quick, rattling noise echoed across the compound and nearly caused the security officer to leap over the fence. In an instant, Oliver was back to his senses, listening as the noise subsided to the regular creaking and groaning. Trying to keep calm, he panned his flashlight towards where he assumed the noise originated and began to move at a jog towards the building.

As Oliver approached, more noises began to sound. The rattling picked up, as did Oliver's pace. His Irish Setters, though soft-toed, slapped heavily against the pavement, rivaling the noise made by the unknown culprit he pursued. His breath grew heavy, his lungs and legs unaccustomed to sprinting.

When Oliver was about twenty feet from the building, only separated from the brick and mortar by the rounded edge of what he thought to be a decommissioned surface condenser, the sound was at its loudest. The security guard slowed his pace and gripped the issued cell phone, hoping the trespasser wasn't going to be hostile. Crouched slightly and pressing his body against the steel, he heaved for oxygen.

"Who's there?" Oliver shouted from his hiding place between breaths. He winced at the sound of his own voice. It didn't sound like him. The sprint and the anxiety seemed to have pulled the strength from his vocal cords.

The rattling sound stopped momentarily, but there was no reply voiced. Oliver considered what to do next and inhaled. He couldn't delay much longer. Praying that the trespasser wasn't another copper thief, or worse, Oliver darted around the corner, beaming his light towards the source of the ruckus.

"I said, who's there?" shouted Oliver as his light shone upon a flight of concrete stairs which led to a double-doored entryway. The beam then flicked down to a dumpster where raccoons began to scatter, running as frantically as the security officer had run just moments before.

Four

The rusted, single-cab Ranger twisted through the winding roads of Clyde County, headed back towards Oliver's two-bedroom home in Plainsview. The driver rubbed the tired from his eyes and examined the new sun, which was casting blood-red needles of light over the fields on either side of the lane-less pavement. He took this route every single weekend, and still, he found it beautiful. Oliver didn't think that would ever change.

The service in the truck was poor, shifting to static from time to time, but Oliver found the white noise almost comforting. The alarming buzz helped him keep his eyes on the road, like a hidden messenger saying, *stay awake, Oliver.*

"Well, it's another fine mornin' here in Clyde County, and you're tuned inta KWX 97.5, The Bull," proclaimed the man on the radio. He spoke in a high-pitched, southern twang of an accent, sounding just like everyone else in the county.

"Yessir, the Good Lord's done blessed us today," said another man, in more of a baritone. "Gonna be bright and sunny *all day*, so get yer hats out and dust off those sunglasses. I know the last few days've been—"

Oliver tuned out the radio as he turned a bend in the road. On the side of this particular crook of pavement was a field which housed an ancient white oak, whose limbs were vast and trunk was large and grayed with age. The tree stood near the edge of the blacktop. Being so old, its roots must've stretched through layers of soil and spread underneath the very road that Oliver navigated. This oak was his favorite sight along the route home, but the mass of limbs and leaves wasn't what made him tune out the radio station as he screeched to a stop. It was what he saw pinned to the bark, about six feet from the base of the trunk.

The Ranger's hazards came on as the old truck kicked up dirt along the soft shoulder. Oliver, sweating, found his cell phone.

Hey Hon try and find a ride to school. If you cant thats alright too. I wont make it back in time for you to take the truck. Sorry. Explain later.

Five

Deputy Van Daniels was parked on the shoulder of State Highway Z shooting radar when he received the dispatch, ordering all nearby officers to report to County Road 21, about ten miles south of the Clyde County Power Plant. Now the deputy was parked next to a dust-covered Ford Ranger, the lights atop his squad car flashing but making no noise. He radioed in to dispatch, stating that he was the first officer on the scene and that he would begin cordoning off the area.

The overweight deputy sweated as he stood from his cruiser. He wasn't really sure what the proper procedures for the situation were. His job, up to this point in his career, consisted of pulling people over who were speeding towards Arkansas, or in the opposite direction towards St. Louis. The officer's job was strictly to issue tickets and earn the county some money, but now he was supposed to handle what appeared to be some sort of crucifixion. Jesus, he didn't want to fuck this up, but was scared – certain – that he would.

"Mornin' officer," the man who sat on the bed of the Ranger said. His legs were dangling and swinging back-and-forth, which made him look childlike.

"G-good morning," Van stuttered, not quite sure what to say. "You Mr Brady, I reckon?"

"Sure am, but Oliver is just fine."

Oliver popped up from his seat on the tailgate. Van watched as his boots made a crunching sound against the earth, then looked at the tree. Goosebumps invaded the deputy's arms, even though the sun was warm and beat against his ivory skin. He shook the sweat from his palms and adjusted his belt. The latter motion was simply a nervous tick, as his pants fit snug around his bulging waist.

"So tell me Mr Brady, how'd you stumble upon …" Van didn't know how to describe the scene. "… this?"

Oliver looked at the tree and furrowed his brow. "Well," Oliver began, "I work the night shift up at the Plant. Security detail. Was on my way back home this morn when I pulled around this here bend. I always look at the tree when I pull around, see? I enjoy it. It's my favorite sight on my way home. And, well …" Oliver, exhausted from second-shift, stopped what he was saying and looked at the scene once more. "Well, you just can't miss that."

Van rubbed the bleeding sweat from his forehead with the back of his arm. In an instant, the perspiration was back. The sun and the scene bore down like a judge and jury.

"Mmhmm." The deputy nodded. "You sure can't."

Both men looked towards the oak, neither saying a word. The bark was thick with hundreds of years of age, and the limbs were countless, full of memory. Van pondered how many years had the tree been standing in that very spot, stretching towards the sky and watching as life passed it by. The tree had witnessed many years of crops growing in its field-home, as well as the construction of its lane-less road neighbor, and then watched still as traffic breezed by, carrying men like Mr Brady to and from work. Perhaps the tree saw lovers take a picnic beneath its branches, or even make love near the base of the bark. Van didn't know the past, but what he was certain of now was that the tree had been desecrated.

He looked to the base of the oak. Hanging about six or seven feet above the grass below was a boy. His body was naked, save for a loincloth stained brown with dirt, and his arms were outstretched like Christ's on the cross. There were no stakes through his palms, but instead, his wrists were roped and tethered to two branches. Crows picked at the boy's skin and cawed at the officers, threatening them to leave their meal alone.

"God," Van said under his breath, "he can't be no older than thirteen."

"Nope. Can't be."

The boy had a head of long, dark hair falling to his shoulders, and the youthful face of an adolescent. His skin, scarred and crusted with dried blood, was as pale as the moon. Van wanted to look away from the sight but couldn't. It was as if the boy, or the tree which housed him, had a magnetic force. Van wasn't sure why he couldn't pull his gaze from him. The pudgy officer wasn't sure of a lot of things, but knew he wanted to be on the other side of the highway, shooting his radar. He didn't want to be looking at this dead boy. Things like this, crucifixions, weren't supposed to happen in places like Clyde County.

"What do you make of this, Officer?" asked Oliver.

Van finally looked away and replied with a shiver. "I have no idea, Mr Brady."

"Please, call me Oliver," he rubbed his eyes and began to point. "Did you see that? Up on that boy's head?"

Van looked again towards the tree to examine the child once more. Atop the child's head, resting like a crown, was a manmade weave of thistle and thorns. There was dried blood in a pattern of streaks, running down the boy's forehead, pooling in dark red patches near the corners of his hollow, milky-white eyes.

"Jesus Christ," Van blurted out before he could catch himself. In the back of his mind, the officer asked the Lord's forgiveness for taking His name in vain. He was sure that God would understand the misstep, seeing the circumstances.

Six

Francine and Keith Banks were sitting at the breakfast table, eating a late morning meal when the phone rang. Keith, reading the morning paper and nursing his coffee, looked at his wife and raised his eyebrows. Francine groaned and stared back at her husband, who seemed more distant every day. She wore a tired expression, one that showed she'd given up on trying years ago. Laundry could be packed in the bags under her eyes. That is what became of a wife living life with a man she didn't love.

Ring ...

Ring ...

"I guess I'll get it." Francine scowled.

She stood from her kitchen chair, intentionally bumping the table with her hips, rattling Keith's coffee cup at the opposite end. He looked over the top of his paper, through a pair of thin-rimmed eyeglasses. The silent contortion of his face said, *really Francine?*

"Hello. This is the Banks' residence," Francine said into her end of the landline.

"Francine?" a stiff, southern accent bellowed through the phone. "Is this Francine Banks?"

"This is she."

"Wife of Keith Banks?"

"Yes." Francine eyed her husband, who was rifling through the back pages, uninterested in the call. "May I ask who's calling?"

The voice on the opposite end of the line coughed and cleared his throat. "I'm sorry ma'am. This is Sheriff Jay Farnswell, with the Clyde County Police Department."

Francine looked again at her husband, a mysterious concern finding her face. "Why are you calling?" she asked. "You understand that we live in Rolla?"

The sheriff murmured something on the other end of the phone, inaudible to Francine, then began, "Yes, I know that ma'am," his voice still stiff. "You see, I'm sittin' here with our county's medical examiner, and – well …"

"What is it, Sheriff?"

"Are you standin' right now, Francine?"

"Yes."

"You might want to sit down."

Francine, again, looked at Keith. This time he peered back, over the top of his pages. The eyes behind his square glasses looked stoned, disengaged. He was miles away.

"Just come out with it, Sheriff."

A moment later, the phone fell from Francine's hand and collided with the floor, making a crashing noise as it skidded across the tile. Keith nearly jumped from his chair. The coffee, in his hand now, swirled around the brim of the cup. Once the liquid settled, he set the cup back down, nervous he might be startled again.

"Jesus, Francine," Keith said in a low voice. "What was that about?"

Francine slumped to her knees, arms spilling out towards the closest countertop, in search for support. Her gray eyes, haunted, having been unloved for a long time, filled up with tears. "They found him," she said, her voice trembling. The words barely found their way from the woman's lips.

Keith set the paper near his coffee cup and shot to his feet. "Found who?" he interrogated, but his eyes and face gave away that he already knew who Francine was talking about. Still, he needed to hear her say it, so when she kept silent, he asked again. "Who, Francine? Who did they find?"

Keith's voice was but a quiver. Francine looked up from her spot on the floor. She was tiny, shrunken by reality, shrunken under the burning gaze of a man she once loved. The emotion of the unreal moment was almost too much to bear. Francine could feel her heart screaming in her chest. Her body contracted, searching for air to breathe. Keith ran to her side and knelt beside her. His arms found their way around her body. They were locked in a warm embrace, both of them dampening from a combination of tears and sweat. They hadn't held each other like this in years.

"Our boy," she finally said. "They found our boy."

Seven

When Oliver returned home, he found his daughter asleep on the couch, her back-pack on the floor and her Chuck Taylors spreading dirt on a throw pillow. Normally, shoes on the couch would have caused Oliver to stir, but not this day; not after what he had witnessed. He was just happy to see the sixteen-year-old lying there, wisps of strawberry hair falling over her closed eyes, chest rising and falling in a careless, midmorning slumber. She was beautifully alive.

Oliver, unable to take his eyes off his daughter, watched the girl sleep. He kicked his boots off near the door and noticed her roll onto her side. The whole drive home, he hadn't been able to stop thinking about the tree and the boy. His mind was spiraling, connecting the images of the dead child to his own life. How many times had he taken moments like this one – these little moments that seemingly meant nothing – for granted? He wondered, how many times he had come home from work on a Saturday or Sunday morning, and walked right past his sleeping daughter, failing to even acknowledge her existence. The thought made Oliver shrink into his skin.

"Dad," she said, her voice soft and raspy from napping. "You're back."

She escaped the cushion's clutches as Oliver made his way through the living room. He lumbered to where she stood and wrapped his bearlike arms around her, being sure to squeeze as tight as he could. The breath in her lungs poured out in an exaggerated gasp.

"I love you, Becca," Oliver said. His eyes began to swell, but he forced his emotions into the pit of his stomach. Now wasn't the time to break.

"Um ... okay. I love you too," Becca said in return, a bit confused by the interaction.

Oliver didn't share his feelings often. It was obvious to him now that he'd been neglecting to do so for the majority of his daughter's life. He wondered, *am I a bad father?* The answer was an obvious *yes*. Why else would an embrace and shared affection seem so foreign? The bear-hug he laid on his daughter might have made her think he was an imposter, an alien, impersonating her father. He needed to love her more.

"Sorry I made you miss class," Oliver said, rubbing his hand along the new stubble on his face. The hair had sprouted overnight. He would shave later. If he wanted, he could grow a decent beard, but the color would make him look twenty years older. The last thing he needed was a head of red hair with a heavily salted beard below it. He'd look ridiculous, more so than he already thought he looked.

"You say that like I'm upset," Becca responded and laughed, which forced Oliver to crack a chuckle of his own. He didn't laugh enough with her. "What hung you up anyway?"

Oliver considered the question. He wondered if he should tell her the truth or not. A boy, crucified on a tree, wearing a crown of thorns around his bleeding scalp while birds made a meal of the body. It was not really an early morning conversation topic. The boy wasn't a conversation topic for any time of day. *Better I keep quiet*, he thought, crippled with his exhaustion from the past eighteen hours.

"Eh, nothing," Oliver lied and rubbed his daughter's head.

She squirmed and cried, "Dad!"

Oliver laughed. "I'll tell you later. Let me nap for a couple of hours then I'll take you to lunch. If I'm not up by noon, come wake me, okay?"

"What if I'm hungry before then?" Becca groaned and pulled her bottom lip into a frown. She was adorable. Simply looking at her made Oliver wanted to burst. God, he'd wasted so many moments.

"Then just wake me up when you're hungry. How's that sound?"

Becca smiled. "Better."

"Goodnight, baby girl," Oliver said, making his way to the kitchen to grab a glass of water.

Once in his bedroom, Oliver removed his security uniform and fell to a heap at the foot of his bed. His body felt heavy like it might collapse the queen-sized frame, though he weighed only about two hundred pounds.

As was Oliver's habit after his night shifts, he rubbed his eyes, seeing constellations when he pulled his palms away. Images of the boy continued to flash through his mind. On the edge of his bed, he continuously replayed the morning's turn around what used to be his

favorite bend in the road. The child's frail, outstretched arms, shoulders looking as though they were about to pop from their sockets, marched through Oliver's memory. The boy was so incredibly thin. His pale skin looked as if it might rip apart at the seams where his ribs protruded. His legs, which hung limp and were riddled with bruising, were so thin Oliver couldn't believe they would have even supported the boy's slender frame, had he been standing and not hanging from a tree. And the young face, the face of a child whose life was taken too soon, was stuck in the front of Oliver's mind. He kept seeing the bloodstained forehead and thin cheeks, and the makeshift crown which entangled his long hair. All of these images plagued Oliver, but what stuck out the most were the eyes, soulless and milky white, as empty as the Dead Sea. Like a black hole, they pulled Oliver into them.

Oliver shivered away the chills he felt and again pressed his palms into his eyes – a pair that would hopefully never see whatever it was that boy had seen. He didn't want to think about the child anymore but found the task of steadying his mind incredibly challenging. It was like having an anxiety attack and someone telling him to calm down. Impossible. Still, he tried his best to think of anything else. He thought about working the feed store, as well as the plant, and even some of his old jobs. He recalled traveling and riding horses across the Montana plains when he was young, but everything eventually faded into an image of the boy's face. After every memory,

those eyes returned. When they did, Oliver couldn't help but transition to thoughts of Becca, which actually seemed to help.

One of his favorite memories of her was when she was just a little girl, bouncing through a puddle, wearing a pair of overalls that swallowed her entire body. The shoulder straps would always fall to one side or the other, and the bottom of her pants had to be cuffed several times above her shoes, but his little girl loved to wear them, so that's what Oliver dressed her in.

Her mom, Lela, would always laugh and look at Oliver with arched eyebrows. She'd say, "Oli, what have you got her in? You didn't put her in the outfit I picked out?"

Never failing, Oliver would respond by helplessly raising his hands and saying, "I don't know what you're talking about."

Oliver, still on the foot of his bed, looked to his nightstand. There, underneath the bedside lamp, stood a picture of the three of them. Oli was on the left, and Lela was on the right, each of their hands holding one of Becca's, whose arms were stretched high, like a television evangelist's. In his current moment of lost remembrance, Oliver fixed his eyes on Lela, the only woman he'd ever loved. He looked at her long blonde hair and soft button of a nose. He looked at her toothy smile and her calm blue eyes, which more than contrasted his. She was so beautiful, inside and out.

The picture on the nightstand formed a black hole of its own. Oliver couldn't look away. The image of his family, now just the fog of a memory, threw him over the edge. He was spiraling into the abyss

now. On the edge of his bed, body sore and tired, mind wrecked, Oliver wept himself to sleep.

Eight.

The highway trek back to St. Louis was long and arduous, made worse by having been up through the night. Manfred kept hearing the rumble strips shock the rubber tread of his Town and Country. Each time his tires met the bumps, the roadside alarms pulled his eyes back to the pavement, but it was a dangerous line to walk. Manfred smacked his cheek, widening his eyes as a pulse of energy erupted through his body. The feel of his face in that moment was different. He was usually clean-shaven, but by now his cheeks had started to produce the beginnings of a jet-black beard. A razor would be taken to them as soon as he arrived home.

Through a fatigued haze, Manfred watched the world breeze by. Beyond the glass of his tinted windows was always either a canopy of thick Missouri forest, crop fields, or prairies housing fat grazers. The beasts would huddle together in any shade they could find, usually beneath the shelter of windbreaks. Manfred wasn't certain which sight he preferred, as all proved equally dull.

Nothing came through the radio. Manfred didn't much care for the twangy sounds of the music that dominated the stations of the Missouri South. Really, he didn't much care for any type of music, save a nice symphony piece, but they weren't going to play that on the local radio, so the soft hum of the highway was what he tuned in to. The constant buzz of passing traffic that accompanied his own engine's growl was actually quite tranquil. He fought off the desire to fall asleep

and listened. He watched the trees go by, and the fields go by, and off of every exit, he watched the vinyl siding of the snake-oil churches go by.

The churches were Manfred's favorite sights along the lonesome stretch of highway that spanned St. Louis to Clyde County. He liked to laugh at the old chapels of varying names like First Baptist Church, First Methodist Church, and Cowboy Christian Church. The echo of his laughter erupted through the open air of his minivan. It was a pleasant moment, just for himself, all by himself.

Manfred didn't find the churches funny because of their names, nor did he find them funny for what they worshipped. In fact, he worshipped the same thing. What he found funny was how blind and mislead every single pastor, and every single person who attended the services was. The fools were all wasting their time. They were sheep people – ten percent tipping imbeciles who could do no better for the world than asking strangers to come and live like them. They couldn't possibly understand the Lord at the depth that he, Manfred John Phillips III, understood Him.

Manfred scoffed in his driver's seat at the very thought. For he, the captain of his slate gray Town and Country, which cruised up the highway at a brisk sixty-five miles per hour, was in direct contact with God. He was a disciple, placed on the Earth to carry out the work of the world's Creator. And he always came through. Manfred always succeeded in his missions.

The previous night was no exception. It was a difficult duty. He had never had a child die before, so the experience was fresh and new, a little exciting even. When he first realized the child had passed, Manfred wasn't certain how to discard of him, but after spending some time in meditation, the idea came like a light from above. It was clear then that Manfred had to sacrifice the boy. He needed to do so because the child was weak, not truly belonging to the prophecy. That was the only explanation for his body failing him. The boy wasn't really one of the four, but was of the flesh of the Earth. Manfred had to make a display of the weakness, which mirrored the world's weaknesses. He needed to send him back to the place he belonged, and he had to do so somewhere he'd never be caught. Clyde County was perfect. The police force was small and ignorant of their duties. The outsourced detectives that would surely come would find nothing but cold dead ends. They would find no prints and there'd be no reason to assume Manfred was to blame. There'd be brief investigations but they'd give up almost instantly, having about as much information as when the child first went missing. It would be like searching for a needle in a needlestack. It was a perfect crime, though Manfred didn't see his work as such. He knew that it was something bigger – something divine.

The Earth could not continue to spin, and society would never progress if Manfred didn't carry out his work. He knew that if he ever stopped listening to the Lord, hell would open upon the world, at a faster rate than it already was. Manfred was like a gatekeeper, a barrier between the unseen worlds and the Earth which he and the sheep inhabited.

Manfred passed by a sign for Jack in the Box, and his belly rumbled with hunger. As he pulled off at the exit, the servant of God speculated, just how many other gatekeepers existed across the Earth. Surely he wasn't the only one. He couldn't possibly be. There had to be a man or woman like him in every corner of the Earth, all of whom received signals from God, telling them where to go and who to take.

Manfred smiled at the notion that he wasn't alone in his mission.

Nine

Downtown Napoli, Missouri consisted of a single two-lane strip of road that extended a stretch of about a mile and a half. Crowding the sides of the road were mom-and-pop shops of assorted variety, all of which showed their age. The peeling wood and cheap sidings were rotting off of the bones of their foundations, weighted with dirt and grime that would, till the world collapsed, go on unwashed. There was the Napoli Grocery, where consumers paid a dollar or two extra for basically everything. Tim Edwards' Hardware for the handyman in everyone. A thrift store which smelled like wet cardboard, and on top of its used clothing, sold fudge and a small selection of handguns. Gram' Tilley's Antique Shop, which never saw customers but somehow always stayed in business. The feed store, which helped keep livestock and stable-animals in good health. And in the center of the two-lane strip was a town square, where there stood a courthouse, though there were never any legal processions to be held. Off of the town square was a system of roads, like tributaries, branching off to the tiny residential trailer homes and farmland.

Nestled on the banks of one of the tributaries was the Clyde County Police Station, a fairly large building when compared to the surrounding establishments. It was late morning, nearing Saturday afternoon, and in the lower levels of the station stood a medical examiner, the county sheriff, and six of the county's twelve deputies, one of whom was Van Daniels.

They stood in a cold, sterile, blue-lit room, staring down at the body of a dead child. It was twelve-year-old Robert Banks. Those in the room were nervous, having a conversation about what to do with the boy, what to say. Each voice reeled with anxiety, rattled by the scene and the suggestion of the county sheriff, Jay Farnswell.

"I'm not sure I can go through with this," Deputy Van blurted, tugging on his belt. "It just don't seem right. We're officers of the law."

His outburst pulled the eyes of the others upon him. Fellow deputies and the sheriff glared, as did the medical examiner, Gerald Collins – an old white man with feathers of white hair and perpetually cold skin. Those who stared, overflowing with discontent, clearly didn't have the same stance as Deputy Van.

"Now, now, Van," began Gerald, in a raspy voice which always seemed to be grumpy. The medical examiner could've discovered he'd won the Power Ball and his reaction would've sounded as though a hammer had dropped on his foot. When he talked, Van watched as the skin, like dried leather, tightened around the examiner's face. "You've got to think about the bigger picture."

"What the fuck does that even mean?"

The old man narrowed his eyes and opened his mouth, but was interrupted by Deputy Williams.

"It means you have to think about the repercussions of letting this shit get out," she said. Her green eyes were fierce, and her brunette hair was pulled back in a bun so tight it looked artificial.

"Think about everything that's going to come to our little county here if we let news of what really happened get out. Reporters. Detectives. Anti-religious fanatics. You name it."

Van stared blankly at the woman, unable to believe what he was hearing. Deputy Williams intimidated him and always had. Sometimes he thought about fucking her, but mainly he thought about her shrill voice and sharp eyes, which always seemed to look at him in hate. That gaze could boil water, and currently, Van began to sweat under it.

"Well," the stiff, calm voice of Sheriff Jay eased through the room, "the detectives are comin' either way. And the reporters too. But what we want to avoid is a prolonged investigation."

The leader of the bunch stretched the word *prolonged* out in emphasis of what that investigation might entail. He, like the others, didn't want strangers snooping around and turning up the soil of their quiet little town. The main issue for Farnswell, Collins, and the deputies was that the crime scene was an act of blasphemy against the Lord. The sheriff didn't want the world to come in and make a display out of their town. He didn't want outsiders slandering, or constant news reports making their religion out to be a joke, or worse, a cult. All Farnswell wanted was to maintain peace and quiet, keeping the media circus cuffed. He wanted life to stay the way it had always been in Clyde County.

Argument sparked again, in the leave of Farnswell's melodic overtones. It was back-and-forth until Sheriff Jay spoke once more.

"Here's what we're gon' do. We're stickin' with the story that we found the boy on the side of ole' Farmer Hamilton's field. We found him right there, about a mile or so south of that tree. There wasn't no crucifixion. There wasn't no religious bullshit. None of that. And I know no one else saw it 'cause I didn't get no other calls. We just found him layin' there, on the side of the road. Got it?"

Van eyed the sheriff. Jay Farnswell, a big man standing about six-foot-three, with a head of neat brown hair and a calm demeanor, was always someone who Van respected greatly. But now – now the sheriff was taking a different shape. Van watched as Farnswell mutated into a stranger. The others began to take the same form. Van didn't feel comfortable even standing in the same room as them, especially Gerald Collins. The old bastard looked other-worldly, like an insect who had crawled to the surface of the Earth from a sewer. Van thought a better name for the medical examiner would be Gregor Collins.

"What are we to tell the boy's parents, Sheriff?" interrogated Van. "What are we going to tell the detectives and the reporters when they come? He's been missing for over nine years. Gerald said it himself. You think people have forgotten the news stories? Do you think—?"

"Oh shut the fuck up, Van," the sheriff cut in. "We ain't tellin' 'em that the boy didn't die. We ain't sayin' that we didn't find him. It's not like we're tryin' to cover it up *completely*. We're just not sharin' the bit about all that religious bull shit. The hangin'. The crucifyin'. Understand? Or are you too dense?"

Van stepped back. He had never felt smaller than he did in this moment. Pawing for his belt, he watched the eyes of the other deputies burning upon him like a spiteful jury. No, it was worse than spite. It was shame that he saw.

"W-well," Van stuttered, his voice sounding strange, "what about Brady? Oliver Brady. The man who found him. What do you think he's going to say?"

"Oliver Brady from the feed store?" Jay laughed and threw his hands up in the air. "I'll speak with him. Me and him go back. He'll play along. And if he don't, who gives a damn? Do you think there's gon' be any credibility in his story? A single father who works seven days a week and don't sleep? Who is *still* talking about his wife? His mind ain't wired right. He could've just been seein' things. Just makin' shit up. Projectin'. You see?"

Van shivered. The reality that they were going to deny what really happened began to set it.

"No one is comin' to my county," Jay continued, "and tarnishin' the good name of the Lord. No one is gon' say that little boys are gettin' crucified and strung up on trees. You got that? I don't want reporters lingering here for weeks and pulling up the roots of our little town."

Silence filled the room. Van looked around, listening to the gentle hum of the overhead lights. He wanted to be anywhere else. "I just don't see this working out," admitted the overweight deputy, in a tone of defeat.

"Well, you're just gon' have to work with us, Van." The sheriff's voice warmed. He came to Van and placed his palm on the deputy's shoulder – a calming gesture. "Do you want people comin' down here and disrespecting our town, and worse, our Lord and savior? Do you? 'Cause I know I don't."

Van shook his head. "No, I reckon I don't."

"Good." The sheriff smiled. He turned and grinned at the other deputies. "Now, I'm gon' call the boy's parents. I'm gon' tell them what happened, what *really happened.*" He winked at Van. "I want them to come down and see the scene, identify their kid and hear the story from us, before any of them city-boy-detectives come and stick their grimy fingers in everything. Now, it's gon' be a shit storm comin', but we're gon' get through it and get back to normal. Just gon' be a week or two tops. Let's *all* stick to our story, and were gon' be fine."

The chorus of deputies and the medical examiner nodded their heads. Van wasn't a part of this. He just stood there, fumbling his thumbs over one another, sweat soaking the collar of his brown uniform. He couldn't comprehend what was happening. All the deputy could think about was the boy, and whoever went through the work of stringing the kid up.

Deputy Van faintly recalled the news reports some nine or ten years ago. The boy's baby pictures were plastered all over the television screen for about four or five days, before the story went dry, and another crisis emerged. Van wondered how the parents must have felt at the time, and how they'd feel when they hear Sheriff Jay's voice, lying to them. Van felt sick. They wouldn't even know Farnswell was lying. They would believe every word that slipped from his tongue. Why wouldn't they?

The thought of the parents, having lost their baby so long ago, troubled Van. He couldn't imagine what it must have been like for them, having to cope with the loss and learn how to live with the knowledge that their child might have still been alive somewhere, in the care of an abductor. Over time, had they forgotten the child? Had they numbed themselves to a point where the memory of their boy didn't bother them anymore?

Van wondered how the parents would react once they realized that their boy had been alive for the past nine years. That knowledge seemed more devastating than if Robert had just died as a baby. God, the situation was so fucked up. The parents would surely crumble when Sheriff Farnswell called and resuscitated their haunting memory.

Van looked at the enormous man who he would never again respect. Farnswell believed that what he was doing was honorable, but Van understood the reality: Sheriff Jay was willing to disguise the abductor and distract detectives, just to save the face of Clyde County and their God. Grasping hold of this reality was like breathing underwater. An ocean of contrition broke over the mind of the troubled deputy. Darkened with the knowledge that a murderer was at

II

"Nature did not seem cruel to him then, nor beneficent, nor treacherous, nor wise. But she was indifferent, flatly indifferent."

\- Stephen Crane, *The Open Boat*

large, Van wondered, when would another child be taken? When would another child be sacrificed?

Ten.

It was hot, a southern Missouri summer that made shirts leach to their wearer's backs. That was exactly what Leonard Beard's white button-down did. The investigative reporter tugged at his collar and loosened up his tie, afraid that by the time he needed to be at his meeting, his shirt would be stained yellow.

On one corner of the Napoli town square, Leonard stood, rubbing his sweating forehead with a handkerchief. He stared down Montgomery Way, towards the Clyde County police station. It was eight in the morning and Leonard had arrived earlier than expected. The young reporter, age twenty-four, was scheduled to have several meetings later in the morning, the first of which was to begin at nine o'clock. He was going to interview the county sheriff, the county medical examiner, and one of the deputies over the course of the day.

Leonard was nervous for the morning's work to begin. This case, that of Robert Banks, was the first serious report he had been assigned. He was worried and had been the entire drive down, that he might spoil his one opportunity at making a name for himself in his industry. Also, he was hot – *very fucking hot*. Leonard wiped his brow once more, wishing that the case had taken place up north, in Michigan or something, where the weather's crimes weren't so severe.

Being so early, Leonard decided he'd go for a cup of coffee at Miss Margaret's Diner, which stood across the street from the police station, looking like a relic from a different age. He didn't much feel like drinking anything hot and wasn't hungry at all, but didn't know how else to pass the time. Inside the diner, the walls were painted, or possibly stained, a yellowish-white. It was an odd interior, but at least the AC worked. Hung upon the yellowed walls were pictures of farming vehicles, all of which might have been UFOs to Leonard, who knew shit about cultivating land. There were also pictures of the farmers themselves, part of the county's history. It was a quaint little place, belonging to a time where horses still drew carriages. Leonard sat at the diner's bar top and looked at one of the two waitresses, a middle-aged woman with thick wrinkles and sour eyes. She looked as old as the building itself and her nametag, written in an equally ancient font, read: **Caroline**.

"Can I help you?" she asked, voice as poisoned as her eyes. When she spoke, her thin lips pursed and exaggerated the wrinkles on her face, making her skin look like a handbag that had been left in the Arizona desert for one too many summers.

"Just a coffee please," said Leonard, offering a smile. The haggard waitress said nothing in return. She only displayed her hunched back and shuffled over to the coffee maker, which had luckily been brewing a fresh drip since Leonard's arrival.

"Here ya go." Caroline returned with a steaming white cup of dark liquid. "Cream? Suga'?"

Leonard, with an even broader smile, answered, "No, ma'am."

He let the coffee cool a moment while he surveyed the room. The diner was scattered with folks wearing overalls, and some who wore shorts over their steel-toed boots. They all seemed to be wearing ball caps, save the women, who were dressed up like they were being taken out to a morning *on-the-town*. They wore floral sundresses, their hair in buns and in curls. Every woman in the place looked like she shouldn't be with the man who sat across from her.

Miss Margaret's diner certainly housed a curious tribe. Most of the folks who shared the space with Leonard had straying eyes. There were many times, while Leonard sipped his coffee, that he caught one or another of his diner companions staring. He assumed it was because he was a young black man dressed nicely in the Missouri South. It was obvious from the moment of his arrival that they didn't get many visitors like him. Their pelting eyes weren't a bother. Straying gazes were the least of Leonard's worries. He just smiled at the folks when he found himself in contest.

Leonard continued to sip his coffee – slowly, so to not overwhelm his senses – until 8:45 a.m. At that time, the reporter placed a ten-dollar bill on the countertop, smiled at Caroline, and walked back out into the unforgiving embrace of the August sun.

Goddamn. The heat was unbearable.

Eleven.

Clyde County PD's front office space smelled like old carpet and coffee. Leonard sat in a leather chair which squeaked every time he moved. He stared at the floor, wondering why it hadn't been pulled up and replaced with tile. It was thin and ratty, originally a cream color that had been stained a brownish-beige by foot traffic. He examined and listened to the receptionist, a boring looking girl with an equally boring voice, answering calls and slapping a keyboard with a long set of acrylics.

Twenty minutes passed. Leonard waited, continuing to listen to the drone of noises, not looking at his phone. He didn't want to look unprofessional, but professionalism obviously didn't matter to the sheriff who was making him wait, even when they had a scheduled meeting time. Benefit of doubt forced Leonard to suspect that Farnswell was taken up in some affair with a criminal in a back room somewhere. Maybe the sheriff was interrogating someone, playing good-cop-bad-cop, slamming his fist against a table while smoke plumed from a cigarette on the rim of a dirty ashtray. Or maybe he was thumbing through strategies of how to answer a reporter's questions with Gerald Collins and Van Daniels. Whatever the scenario was, Leonard didn't care much for being made to wait.

"Mr Beard?" the receptionist finally said, peering over her desktop. She sounded more like a GPS system than a person.

"Yes."

"Sheriff Farnswell will see you now."

Leonard looked around, confused. Was he supposed to walk himself through the police station? "Okay," he replied, standing from his chair and hearing the leather squeak out one last goodbye.

"Down the hallway, last door on the right."

Leonard, his body growing cold from his sweat freezing in the air conditioning, followed the receptionist's directions. He tucked his notepad under his armpit and walked the hallway, glancing into the stretch of rooms along the route. They were mostly just other offices and filing rooms, each empty, except for one. It appeared to be a breakroom, housing vending machines and uncomfortable looking lounge chairs. A few deputies – one, a muscled-out man donning a crew cut; and the other, a woman with fierce green eyes – sat chatting and sipping coffee from Styrofoam cups. Each of the officers was taken by an intense silence as they watched Leonard inch by.

"Morning," Leonard instinctively said, offering a nod.

The officers nodded in return. They disappeared behind a thin wall as Leonard continued his trek to the sheriff's office. He shuffled along until he found himself standing in front of a closed door with a metal tacked sign reading: Sheriff Jay B. Farnswell.

Leonard rapped on the door three times and stood still, craning his neck to look down the hall as he listened to a series of sounds from inside the office. On the opposite side of the door, Leonard hear a muffled noise like a chair scooting across carpet, followed by the soft thud of footsteps. In the next instant, the door in front of Leonard swung open, away from the reporter. A big man with a square face and a well-kempt head of brown hair emerged in the doorway.

The sheriff eyed Leonard up and down for a quick moment before saying, "Mornin'. You're the reporter I reckon?"

"I sure am," Leonard replied, offering his usual broad smile.

The sheriff sighed and rubbed his head. "Sorry to keep ya waitin'. Was caught up in some paperwork and forgot what time it was. I'm sure ya understand?"

Leonard smiled and agreed that he did, but it was a lie. He wasn't quite sure what Farnswell meant by claiming that *he understood.* Perhaps the sheriff meant, because reporters deal with paperwork, Leonard might know what it's like to get *caught up* in it. The weight of paperwork could indeed be burdensome sometimes, but Leonard would never miss or delay a scheduled meeting for it. That was highly unprofessional. Punctuality was something Leonard would never compromise.

"Well, come on in. Have a seat," Farnswell said, showing Leonard to a chair with a large, calloused hand.

Leonard walked into the office, and Sheriff Farnswell closed the door behind him. This room was nicer than the rest of the building. The carpet was new and didn't possess a smell. On the walls were framed awards and achievements that Farnswell had obtained over his career. There was a bookshelf set up against one wall housing a collection of literature about law enforcement and other non-fiction.

Behind the desk was a large window that overlooked a golden field of wheat, which at the time seemed to be standing about four feet tall. Leonard watched the uniformed stalks sway in the sun's rays as Farnswell moved around the desk to his office chair.

"Well." The officer groaned and crossed his large arms. "Let's get on with it."

Twelve

Number Two sat upright in his cell, feeling his leg cry out in agony, begging to be scratched. The boy – who did not know the time of day, or what year, or what age he was – did in fact know that he shouldn't scratch his skin. There was a primal instinct in his head, telling him to keep his fingers wrapped around the steel wires. The cold steel of the cage created a sensation that helped keep Two's mind away from his howling leg.

Through the shadows, Two examined the now vacant cage of his cellar home. Its emptiness made Two swell up with an emotion he had never felt before. A hole was in his chest, seeming to open and close with every beat of his heart. It was a painful experience, even more so than the itch of his leg. This was the first time that Two, the boy who was born to a cage, had ever experienced loss.

Three had been there, across the room, surrounded by the thin wires of a cell, for what seemed like forever. The boys had grown close through the experience, although Two was only now realizing it. They shared a bond that not many others would ever know. Their souls were forged together by darkness, and by steel wires, by cold concrete beds, and by Papa's messages.

They were told by their papa that they controlled the future fate of the universe. He always said that they, the four, would one day command all the powers of the Earth – that they would control the clouds in the sky and the waves in the ocean because they would bring a divine goodness to a bad world. The man, their beacon of light from beyond the portal, said that his children were the last pure souls to be born to the world.

Two didn't fully understand what Papa meant when he preached and shared his ideologies. The sky was something he could somewhat imagine, but he had no idea how to conceptualize a body of water and its waves which could turn over boats and topple cities. Nevertheless, the thought of possessing the same power as Papa made Two beam. Though after realizing the pain of Three's absence, Two determined that he would only want that kind of power if he could share the experience with the others – with his friends.

Maybe, Two thought, *we could one day be powerful enough to bring Three back.*

He smiled again, a toothy grin that illuminated his shadowy home just a bit. He looked at Three's vacated cage once more. Two now understood that their time together wasn't over for good. They'd see each other again in the future, when he and the others commanded the sky and the waves, and everything else beyond their cages.

Two looked at One's cell. Though the room was pitch-black, he could see that One, who was the very first of them, was asleep. He lay on his back, making no sound save the quiet exhales of his lungs. His slender body stretched the entire length of his cage. He, who Two thought would one day be the most powerful of them all, slept as peacefully as ever. Two wondered if One felt the same hole in his chest for their missing friend. He had to. The cellmates were all bonded together as one conjoined being. It would be impossible for One to feel nothing.

On the opposite side of the room, Two noticed that Four was not asleep. She was standing at the front of her cell, fingers stretching through the slots in her wires. Her white eyes shone through the darkness and met with his. They held each other's gaze a long time, neither wanting to sever the connection. Two could see it in her eyes: she felt the void in her heart. As they looked into each other, it was as if Two could hear Four's thoughts. She seemed to be saying, *I miss him. Do you miss him too?*

Two nodded and held his eyes against her own. He stretched his fingers through the open slots of his own cage, mimicking her action. They looked into each other, listening to the ever-present drip of water in the corner of the room, thinking about Three; thinking about what awaited them beyond the darkness of their cells.

Thirteen

"Looky here, son," Farnswell said, dried up from answering thirty or forty minutes' worth of questions. "You're gettin' the same story that the detectives from up north got. The case is pretty cut and dry. The Banks boy just came and turned up on the side of the road there."

"What road again?" baited Leonard.

Sheriff Farnswell grunted and raised an eyebrow. "County. Road. Twenty. One," he said slowly.

Leonard smiled and jotted a meaningless note on his pad. He knew the road, having already written it down, but wanted to see if the officer's story would change. That's what most of his questions were designed to do, but the sheriff wouldn't budge. Nothing in his story hedged, even after countless versions of the same questions. Still, something felt off about the whole thing. The boy had been missing for nine years and then just showed up on the side of the road? He had the strength to escape his captor, and run how many miles through the woods and fields, just to die once he reached a sign of civilization? Leonard didn't buy it.

"So," Leonard began, "what are the detectives and the Clyde County Police Department doing to find the captor? To find whoever it was who took the boy to begin with?"

"Well, it ain't just us and the detectives. It's Rolla PD as well, seein' as the boy was taken from his Rolla home some years ago."

"Nine."

"Yes," Farnswell snarled. "*Nine.* Anyway, we're all collaboratin'. We're questionin' who we can, trying to see if we can dig up any information, and were accepting calls, hopin' that someone offers up a tip."

Leonard scribbled a single, comically large word on his notepad. *Hoping.* He set the pad on his lap, where the sheriff could see it. "And what are the detectives doing? Are they just *hoping* for a tip as well, or are they doing any real investigative work?"

Farnswell glared at the young reporter. Leonard smiled and retracted his negativity a bit, not wanting to stray too far onto the sheriff's bad side.

"Listen, Sheriff," Leonard said in a gentler tone. "I appreciate all of the service that men and women like you do. But right now, there's a child abductor still at large, and it just seems like there's nothing being done to find the culprit."

Farnswell uncrossed his arms and placed his palms on the desk, looking as steady as a general about to call his troops to war. "I know how it looks," the big man said. "If ya know anything about the law, then ya know that we can't do much right now. We can't just go bargin' into every house in the vicinity of where we found the boy. It's illegal. And anyway, my deputies already talked to the landowner of the farm where Banks turned up. The man showed us every square inch of his land, on both sides of the road. Believe me when I tell you, the boy wasn't taken anywhere near that farm. I don't think he was taken anywhere near this county for that matter."

"What makes you think that?"

Farnswell rolled his eyes. "People ain't like that in Clyde County."

"Like what?"

"Murderers. Kidnappers. We're a quiet people, livin' in a quiet county. That's why there are only twelve deputies under my charge. There ain't much people around here, and those who are, are the god-fearing, hardworking type. Ain't got no killers in my town, Mr Beard."

Fourteen

The sun still scorched outside the station. An unlit cigarette rested on the crest of Leonard's lips, yearning to be sparked. Feeling an emptiness when he pawed at his pockets, Leonard realized he must have misplaced his lighter. He was already frustrated, and this inconvenience added to the load.

Having felt he had learned almost nothing from the sheriff, or from the medical examiner, who he interviewed just after, irritation was setting in. The frail old man in the second interview seemed to repeat everything the sheriff had said, only in a slower, more sickly pitch. The man spoke from a phlegm-filled throat and smelled of Vaseline, which made the task of questioning him all the more difficult.

Another misfortune was that Leonard couldn't speak with Deputy Daniels, the officer who was said to have first found the boy. Farnswell shared that Daniels had called in sick early in the morning. Leonard wasn't sure if he should believe that info. It seemed like the two men he interviewed had rehearsed how they were going to answer his questions, like they were lying about something. They might just as well have been lying about Daniels. Leonard didn't know what to think, what to believe, but at least he had Van's number, complements of the receptionist.

Leonard looked around downtown Napoli, boiling from a concoction of sunshine and frustration. He cracked a wry smile, thinking about the town. He'd never been to Italy, so he had never witnessed the real streets of Napoli, but upon standing in the shithole town of 879 people, Leonard imagined the original city was a complete contrast. The place he stood was old and depleting with age. The buildings didn't have history or character, only leaking shingles and crumbling foundations. There couldn't have been much of an economy, except for farming. That's probably why the only businesses, that were still *in business*, were diners, hardware stores, and a feed store. There were several buildings along the small strip that were boarded up and lacked all signs of life. Leonard assumed these buildings hadn't had a true owner in years, maybe even decades. Some still had the faded signage from their past lives, dangling in the windows, expressing the deals that once existed. Two buildings had dirty *for-sale* signs staked out front, having found homes in overgrown weeds and sweetgrass. Leonard couldn't imagine there was a person on the planet who would want to purchase either of the properties. Perhaps the future buyer would be a hardworking, God-fearing type.

After reflecting a bit and regaining his bearings, Leonard decided he needed a lighter. It was likely that he had one in his car, but exploring some of the shops and questioning some of the townspeople seemed like a good idea. Leonard tried the hardware store first, figuring that they'd have what he needed, but when he approached the glass door, which was stained with handprints, he found the building was closed until the evening. The business operated under a strange set of hours that only a business in a tiny town like Napoli, Missouri would follow.

Leonard looked down the street again, his forehead dripping with sweat, burning into his eyes. The next best option would have to be the feed store.

Fifteen

"Good morning, Mr Phillips."

"Good morning, Ingrid," Manfred responded with a smile.

"How's he doing today?"

"Oh, he's alright," answered Ingrid, one of the caretakers of the South City Helping Hand Home. "Behaving as usual."

"Good, good," replied Manfred, melancholy because *the usual* wasn't so good at all. In fact, the usual behavior of his father, Manfred John Phillips II, was far from what society would consider normal. The man's mind was demented, withering away in fragments day-by-day.

Manfred walked down the carpeted hallways of the home, through a lobby area where more elderly folk fumbled about. They slumped in wheelchairs and over walkers, dragging oxygen tanks behind them like a fifth limb. They all chatted in their raspy voices, speaking to each other, some as old friends, and some calling out to no one in particular. One woman, a lady whose hair was very curly and whose skin resembled a dirty sponge, beamed a smile at Manfred when he walked by.

"Oh!" the woman called out. "Oh my, Vernon! It's been so long, my love. Where have you been?"

The woman thrust herself towards Manfred, wrapping her arms around him and squeezing as tight as she could. Manfred supported her tiny, aging body with ease, unaffected by her assault.

"Ma'am, I'm sorry but—"

"Oh, hush now, Vernon," she said sharply. "Just let me hold you a moment before you start up with your chatting. We'll have plenty of catching up to do, but first ..."

Manfred shut himself up. He stood quietly, his mind walking through the process of imagining Vernon. Who was he to this stranger?

A younger woman in a pair of pink scrubs hustled over and interrupted the embrace, as well as Manfred's internal questioning.

"Miss Millie?" the caretaker called. "You know not to go hugging on strangers."

Millie pulled away from Manfred. Their eyes met a moment, and in that instant, Manfred envisioned the woman's entire life. He imagined when she was younger, and in love with the man named Vernon. He imagined what her body looked like, what it felt like. He imagined what it would have been like to fuck her before she turned into a shell.

"This isn't a stranger, dear," Millie said in her sweet old voice, pulling her gaze towards the caretaker.

"Sorry, sir. Mr Phillips, right?" the caretaker asked, bouncing glances between him and the older woman.

"It's alright," said Manfred, a bit upset with himself for not recognizing the caretaker. "It's really alright."

She took Millie by the arm and pulled the old woman across the lobby, away from Manfred. He watched them disappear down a hall. The entire time, he continued to wonder about Vernon. Was the man a husband? An estranged lover? A Son? Manfred sighed and turned to walk towards his father's room. He would never know Millie's story, just as she would never know his. That was life, he thought, just a bunch of people creating their own stories – each day a page, each significant event, a chapter, until the book eventually reached its final period. Only a select few would ever read the story of that woman. Vernon was one of those minorities. Manfred could only ever browse the aisles of a library, briefly reading the spines and creating his own synopses of people's lives.

Manfred walked to the doorway of his father's room, a man whose story he knew well. He peered through the open entryway, looking upon a thin man in a wheelchair. Manny, as his father's friends and close relatives called him, was eighty-three years old, but his mind was much older. His brain aged to where it could no longer recall memories. His past was now a puzzle in constant construction. There were bits of a picture he could see, but for the most part, it was like his mind was picking up random pieces and trying them out on the board. Sometimes they would fit, but more often the pieces didn't line up, the edges didn't match, or the colors were just a bit off. Manny's entire life had slowly been carved up and divvied out into the thousand-piece jigsaw in his skull.

"Hello, Dad," called Manfred from the doorway. His voice was shaky as he thought about the severed memories in his father's head. He choked back tears and walked into the quiet room. The only sound was that of a *Jeopardy* rerun that played on the twenty-inch television in the corner.

The old man turned his gaze from the screen to meet Manfred's. The skin around Manny's eyes sagged, as did the skin around his neck. Manfred couldn't help but think his father looked a bit like a mastiff – a big one, whose jowls were so large they skimmed the grass when it walked.

"Hello, there," his father greeted and smiled. "Is it supper time already?"

Manfred shook his head. "No Dad, it's me, Manfred. I'm not a caretaker. I'm your son."

Manny groaned. "Aah, I thought it was supper time. Can you come back when it's supper time?"

The words spoken by his father were a crushing hand around Manfred's throat. Manfred frowned as Manny turned his eyes back towards the TV. He watched the old man watch his television show. Every now and then, Manny would shout something like, *what is the theory of relativity?* Or, *what is Jasper National Park?* He'd groan and ball up his fists when he answered incorrectly. Sometimes he'd smash them on the arms of the wheelchair.

This went on for a few hours, broken up by the occasional interruption from Manfred, who had moved to sit on a spare armchair, before *Jeopardy* turned to a news channel. Manfred and his father watched as a baby picture of Robert Banks, formerly known as Number Three, flashed across the screen, followed by scrolling images of Clyde County and the boy's parents. A red, rolling bar of white text along the bottom of the screen read: *If you have any information about the kidnapping and murder of Robert Banks, please call STKN's news tips hotline.*

The two men watched the story as it cycled around on itself, eventually repeating the same information but with different words and different images. The same couple of reports from the parents, and from law enforcement, repeated and repeated again. A middle-aged woman with big hair and pink cheeks sat next to a generic looking man behind a desk, labeled *STKN*. Each of the anchors blasphemed Manfred, stating his actions were horrific, abhorrent even.

Their words enraged Manfred. He fumed from his perch on the olive armchair beside Manny. He could feel his left eye begin to twitch. His feet bounced and tapped uncontrollably. For a moment, he thought about—

"Disgusting, isn't it?" a voice called from the doorway.

Manfred shot his gaze towards the uninvited voice. The invasion was by that caretaker who stole Millie away earlier. She was a young woman of caramel complexion, with a very pretty face, though Manfred saw none of these features. He looked past them, into her wretched soul – the soul of an intruder, a violator of privacy. He could see in an instant that she was tainted. What kind of bitch just barged into a room where a man sat with his sick father, wrongfully claiming that the actions of a stranger were *disgusting*?

Manfred wanted to explode, but he knew that he couldn't. He had to keep calm. Now was not the time. "Yes," he replied. "It seems they don't have the full story though."

"Not yet," she replied. "But I hope they do soon. It's pretty horrifying, knowing that the person responsible is still wandering around out there."

"Yes. Yes, it is."

The caretaker's expression was that of a ghastly misjudgment. "Did you know that the boy was kidnapped, locked up, and hidden away somewhere for *nine* years?"

Manfred arched an eyebrow. "I heard that, yes."

"Crazy," the woman said and shook away the chills. "Anyway, I was just coming by to make sure that you were alright. You know, after your little run-in with Millie earlier? She can be a little reckless sometimes."

Manfred smiled broadly. He had a sense that the caretaker had developed a sort of attraction to him. "Oh no, it's quite alright," he said slyly.

"Okay, well, if there's anything that myself or any one of us caretakers can do, just give a holler." She laughed. "Well, don't actually holler. That might scare some of the residents."

Manfred laughed as well. "I'll be sure to scream."

The caretaker giggled.

Manfred asked, "What is your name?"

"Oh, sorry. It's Brianna."

"That's a nice name," complemented Manfred, as he stroked his smooth chin with his thumb and index finger.

"Thank you." She turned to leave, but he caught her with another question.

"How late does your shift usually last?"

Brianna hesitated a moment and backed away slightly. Manfred watched as her eyes shifted and darted down the hall. He perceived that she was looking for a superior. He had her, and he knew it.

"Um, I don't know. It varies. Depending on if it's a quiet night or not."

Manfred twisted his face into a grin. "Well, maybe I'll give a holler later on then."

The caretaker shifted and said, "We'll see," before slipping away from the doorway, leaving Manfred and Manny alone once again.

Manfred observed his father, who was still eyeing the television screen. Robert Banks's face popped up again, bringing the wheelchair-bound man to tears.

"What's wrong?" asked Manfred, concerned that his father, like Brianna, thought his actions detestable.

The old man turned and looked at Manfred with sad eyes. "That boy. On the television screen there. He reminds me of my son."

Manfred choked. "Does he, Papa?"

Sixteen.

Warm water ran over Leonard's razor. He was shaving over the sink of his hotel room, wondering why it was so goddamn far from town. The Holiday Inn Express sat along a nearly empty stretch of highway, about forty minutes north of Napoli, nestled up to a McDonald's that shared residence with a Shell station. The only other accommodation options looked like something out of a slasher film, so Leonard was forced to accept the commute.

Earlier in the day, Leonard investigated all of the open shops in town. The feed store was the only place that offered him a bit of information. When he walked in, an immediate stench of grain and oats blasted his senses. There wasn't a soul in the place, other than a young woman working the counter.

"Can I help you?" she said in a churning drawl, like honey falling from her bottom lip. The sound of her voice was soothing. Leonard found himself a bit lost in her presence. She was attractive, having cinnamon hair like silk, draping in a blanket over her shoulders. The eyes which stared at him were a deep blue, and her skin would have been as white as everyone else's in Clyde County, had it not been kissed by the summer sun.

"Y'all sell lighters?" answered Leonard after taking some time to find his words.

"We have some back here, but they only come in packs."

"A pack is fine." Leonard smiled and approached the counter, looking around to examine the rest of the store. It was all just heavy burlap and paper sacks, stuffed with varying grains and oats.

"Need anything else?"

Leonard paused and eyed the girl who stood behind glass countertop, careless about his presence. Her blue eyes were distant, looking forward to closing time probably.

"Actually, yes, there might be something you can help me with."

"Really," she said. "What's that?"

"I'm here in regards to the boy who was found dead not far from here four days ago."

Her eyes brightened.

"You heard of that I'm guessing?"

"Yea, 'course. Everyone's heard of him. Been all over the TV for days and strangers have been buzzing like flies around here since he was found." She placed a rainbow pack of Bic lighters on the counter. "You're one of them strangers, a reporter I'm guessing? Don't look much like a detective."

"Reporter," Leonard admitted. "So … you have time to answer any questions?"

The girl looked around and raised her eyebrow. "No, I'm too busy."

"Sure looks like it," Leonard laughed. "It'll be quick, I promise. I'm Leonard, by the way."

"Nice to meet you, Leonard." She extended a hand.

"Jennifer."

"Nice meeting you too." her hand was soft and a little clammy. "So what exactly is everyone hearing about the Banks boy?"

"Well, the story has it he was found along the side of County Road 21 this past Friday morning. One of the second shift workers at the County Plant was driving home after work and saw him lying by the road. Boy was just resting there, tanning in the sun for anyone to see."

"Yes, that's what I've been told by your Sheriff. The boy just *turned up*. Apparently, he came from nowhere." Leonard sighed. "No one has a clue where he escaped from or how he got here."

"That's what they're saying." Jennifer leaned in closer. "Did Farnswell happen to tell you about who found him?"

"No, he said the guy wanted to remain anonymous."

Jennifer shook her head and bit her lip like she was holding off from revealing a secret. "I know who found him."

"You do?"

"Yea. In fact, he's the reason I'm here right now."

"Why's that?"

"I usually have today off, but I'm filling in for him. After finding the boy, he requested a few days to clear his head. I don't really blame him. I'd have probably done the same, so I don't mind covering."

Leonard sparked with curiosity. "What's his name?" he asked, "And where could I find him?"

Jennifer receded to her original stance, smiling and looking Leonard up and down. "Where are you from?" she asked, avoiding Leonard's barrage of questions.

"St. Louis."

"Long way from the city. Do you like it down here?"

"It's not bad."

"Oh, shut the hell up." Jennifer sneered. "I know you don't like it here."

Leonard laughed, feeling his cheeks turn hot with the embarrassment of being caught in a lie. "You're right. It's a far cry from home."

"What do you say," Jennifer hesitated, her own cheeks turning a shade of pink, "you come out with me tonight? Let me show you around."

A strange feeling shot through Leonard's stomach.

She continued, "If you do, maybe I'll tell you about the man who found the boy."

"Aah." Leonard smiled. "An ultimatum."

"Don't call it that."

"Well, what should I call it?"

"I don't know. Anything else."

Leonard wiped the shaving cream residue from his cheeks. In the stained mirror, his reflection stared back at him. His brown eyes looked as they always did. His hair was cut close to his scalp like it always was. He wore a collared, short-sleeve shirt, riddled with pictures of pelicans. This was it; this was the best he could look.

He picked up his wallet, his keys, and his phone, and he texted:

Be there in 45, see you soon

Seventeen.

Around the same time Leonard was driving towards the most popular
bar in Clyde County, Manfred John Phillips III was waiting in his black
Lexus, stalking the entrance to the South City Home. He never did
holler for Brianna's help, but after his time with his father, Manfred
decided that he'd wait for her. The caretaker wronged Manfred by
saying that his actions were *disgusting*. Therefore, she had wronged the
Lord, and her behavior had to be accounted for.

He waited in his car until 8:23 p.m. This was when Manfred
watched Brianna walk out of the front entrance, still wearing her pink
scrubs. She made her way to a black Corolla and crawled into the
driver's seat. Manfred watched from a distance, idling his vehicle in the
back of the parking lot. He waited there until the Corolla's lights
turned on and the vehicle pulled away from the home.

Following Brianna was easy. Manfred kept a distance of about
three cars' lengths between his Lexus and her Corolla. As late as the
hour was, and as tired as the girl had to have been having just worked
a full shift, Manfred knew that she wouldn't suspect a thing. Why
would she?

The two cars moved about the maze of south St. Louis
County's streets for close to twenty minutes, before Brianna pulled
into a rinky-dink apartment complex. Manfred continued driving past
the Corolla, watching as it parked. He made sure to hide around the
corner of the neighboring apartment building. Once he himself was

parked, Manfred crawled from his seat and crept through the darkness to the corner of the building. He peered around the edge, eyes searching for the flamingo-colored scrubs.

After a brief moment, Manfred found the pink mess walking along the opposite side of the lot. She was headed for the stairs, external to the building, leading to the second level of apartments. From his position on the corner of the adjacent complex, Manfred could see Brianna quite clearly. She walked so leisurely, disgustingly careless, to unit 2E. A key was positioned on the same ring as her Corolla keys, which she used to enter the apartment.

Good, Manfred thought, because now he knew where the sinner lived.

Manfred snuck back to his Lexus, fueled by anticipation. Unfortunately, the excitement of dealing with the girl would have to wait. For the time being, he had other matters to deal with. There would need to be a replacement for Number Three. Otherwise, the prophecy could not move forward.

Eighteen

The Boondock Bar and Grill, or The Boonies' as the locals called it, was everything Leonard expected it to be. Enveloped in a mass of clamoring voices, flannel shirts, and stomping boots, he stood at the bar, hanging his hand over the countertop, in an effort to retrieve the bartender's attention. The other twenty or so outstretched hands didn't help speed up the process. He waited in a huddle of thirsty customers for quite some time before the sole bartender, a woman in her fifties, greeted him with a numb voice.

"What can I getcha?"

Leonard raised his voice to best the noises made by his bar mates and the belting twang of live country music. "Two Buds."

The bartender retrieved the lagers, each poured to the brim of a frosty pint glass. She slid them in front of Leonard, who handed her a credit card.

"Keep her open?" the woman asked.

"Sure."

He grabbed the sweating glasses, and moved away from the bar, headed towards the standing table where Jennifer waited. Leonard's date stood elegantly in a skinny black dress that came to a halt above her knees. Like a painting hung in the Missouri Louvre, Leonard was lost in examination. He was blindly walking towards her, thinking about how odd of an experience he was having in this little town, when the broad shoulder of a Boonies' regular slammed into him, spilling beer onto Leonard's shoes.

"Watch where you're goin', chief," said the man in an accent as thick as tree sap.

Leonard eyed him. He was big. From his Stetson brim to his square toes, every part of him seemed to have been engineered in a lab. Leonard decided it best to say nothing. He silently turned and continued walking towards Jennifer, who looked appalled.

"What was all that about?"

"Nothing," Leonard responded, handing Jennifer one of the semi-full beers. "He probably just couldn't see me. It's pretty dark in here."

They laughed and drank. Leonard looked around at the lake of flannel and ten-gallon hats. A band of three members played on the center stage. One held a banjo, one an acoustic guitar, and one sat on a wooden box, beating it like a drum. A crowd danced in front of the stage, twirling in circles and slamming their feet onto the hollow floor. Several times, Leonard caught people staring at him and Jennifer. They were probably lost in the elegance of his date. *Yea*, he thought, *that had to be it.*

"Do you take every stranger you meet here?" he asked Jennifer, who was scanning the crowd, just the same.

Jennifer broke her gaze and looked at Leonard. "Yes, you're like my fifth one this week."

"Oh God. It's only Monday!"

"What can I say? We get a lot of visitors coming through our tourist trap of a town."

"I guess I should've stayed at my hotel. I didn't realize how insignificant I am." Leonard laughed. "Really though, why invite me out?"

"I don't know," Jennifer shrugged. "Boredom. There's not much to do around here, if you haven't noticed."

"Wow, the honesty stings. I think this is the first time I've ever been asked out because of boredom."

Jennifer laughed. "Oh stop your whining. If you lived here, you'd understand! And anyway, it's not like you would've accepted, had I not lingered that carrot of information in front of you earlier."

"Well," Leonard drank from his beer, "maybe you're right."

"See," Jennifer grinned, "we're both a little fucked up. But anyway, how do you like Clyde County now that you've seen its main attraction?"

"Love it. Cheap beer certainly erases the frustration of being lied to by cops, looked at by everyone, constantly sweating through my shirt, and the shoulder checks from John Wayne."

"Oh, it can't be so bad." Jennifer joked. She couldn't have been so clueless. "You're with me at least."

"Yea," Leonard sipped his beer, "because of boredom and necessity."

The two smiled and downed the rest of their glasses. They then finished two more a piece, often receiving careful looks from strangers. Neither Leonard nor Jennifer cared about the glances. They drank, drank some more, and chatted. They talked about everything, except the Banks boy or the man who found him. They talked until their mouths ran dry and their legs began to grow restless. This was when Jennifer pulled Leonard to the dance floor.

Nineteen

It was nearing one in the morning. The Boonies' was growing empty, but Leonard and Jennifer remained. They had moved to the bar top, where the same tender kept their glasses full. Jennifer's long hair, which fell over her shoulders and down her back, was damp with sweat, as they'd been line dancing, or attempting to do so, for the past hour. Her eyes were a deep shade of blue, appearing almost black in the poorly lit bar. They contrasted with her semi-pale complexion and blanched lips, which Leonard considered kissing. The only thing that held him back was his dedication to his work.

"Jennifer," he said, after waiting for the perfect lull in their conversation.

"Leonard," she replied in a drunken giggle.

"Can you tell me about the man who found Robert?"

Her smile evaporated, shoulders slumping with the weight of the question. Leonard had to go and ruin the time they were having. "What do you want to know?"

Leonard shrugged. "I don't know. I don't really feel like spoiling the night. Why don't you just tell me his name and where I can find him?"

"Well, it's Monday night, so that means he'd normally be working the feed store tomorrow morning. But he's taking this week off, so it's hard to say exactly."

"Okay," said Leonard. His eyes met with Jennifer's. They were like magnets, oceans of navy blue, tides strong enough to pull Leonard in and send him tumbling under. He felt frozen in place, fighting the pull of her gaze.

Jennifer continued, "His name is Oliver Brady. He's middle-aged with redd*ish* hair. Grumpy looking, but nice as can be. Though I must warn you, he's a bit *off*. Has been since his wife died a long while ago. People around town think him to have a couple screws missing, but he's a good man. I know he lives in Plainsview. About thirty or so minutes from here, depending on how you handle the winding roads. I also know his favorite bar is the only bar in Plainsview, if you'd believe it."

"God, tell me it's not like this one."

"It's not." Jennifer giggled again. "It's smaller. A bit of a dive. Might only find a handful of folks in there on a good night. It's called the Plainsview Pub. Very creative, I know."

"Go figure," Leonard said.

He made sure to repeat *Plainsview Pub* and *Oliver Brady, grumpy redhead,* in his mind several times. It was a simple name and a simple description, but he was drunk. He didn't want to forget in the morning.

"Now can we talk about something else?" Jennifer pleaded.

The two continued to talk under the neon lights of the bar until they were forced out. Leonard wasn't even sure what time it was when he stepped into the parking lot. The pale light of the moon cast off the field opposite the bar, making the stalks appear like skeletons, swaying with the gentle wind.

"Scary," he said aloud, speaking to no one in particular. His inebriated brain was no longer capable of controlling his impulses to say, or not say, the first thing that came to his mind. His outburst made Jennifer laugh.

"So," she interrupted his transfixion, "you plan on driving back to your motel?"

"Hotel," he said, dangling his keys in the air.

"Yea, yea, *hotel*, sorry." Jennifer glared. "Why don't you just come with me? I'm, like, five minutes away. Your hotel is way too far. If an accident doesn't get you, a cop will."

Leonard didn't protest her offer. In fact, he was hoping for this outcome before the night even started.

Twenty

Coffee steamed. Manfred blew on the rim of the cup, watching the sun rise through the great pane of his living room window. The drink was made black, the only way that coffee was supposed to be had. He held the coffee in one hand, and the day's paper in the other. On the front page was a headline that described Number Three, or Robert Banks.

A scoff escaped Manfred's lips when he read about the detestable nature of his acts. He couldn't believe the way people talked about him, especially having never met him. They called him a monster in the paper, and on the news, they said he was a villain, a kidnapper! What they didn't know was that Manfred was a missionary, a descendent of God, who was preparing to save the world. And they were muddying his name all over every source available! He wouldn't even dare search the world wide web.

What made Manfred most angry was that nowhere in any of the reports, did they show his sculpture, his shrine to the Lord he had worked so hard on. There were no pictures of the boy – the sinner, who was not powerful enough to withstand God's tribulations – strung upon the tree. There was no talk of God at all. No one photographed the crucified child, the little Judas. Not one fucking source shared a visual or even a description. It was all just bean fields, and corn fields, and interviews with hicks.

Coffee spewed from Manfred's curled lips as he tossed the paper across the room. The pages separated and fluttered to the ground, making the hardwood look like a chessboard. He was furious. The reports of his *crime* were ruining a perfectly decent morning.

After a moment, Manfred took in a breath and exhaled slowly. He decided that he wasn't going to let his entire day be ruined. There was work to be done, and he didn't want his duties to be spoiled by the masses. He knew that the vast majority of civilization would never understand what he was doing. They couldn't understand the prophecy until it was fulfilled. Only Manfred – and a few others, as he had recently decided – had the power to truly speak to the Lord. Only those select few would ever understand the true meaning behind what he was doing.

Manfred moved to the coffee pot and poured another cup. Steam bellowed from the rim, rising in plumes like he was holding a tiny smoke stack. He sipped, blowing on the liquid just before, and considered what he was going to do next.

A serious problem had arisen throughout the last few days. When Three died, so did the process of fulfilling the prophecy. An obstacle formed in Manfred's path. He needed four children, that was what the Lord commanded, but now he only had three. Obtaining another wouldn't be a problem if it were just a baby he needed, but Manfred needed all of the children to be close in age. They all needed to be within a year of each other. Manfred did not know why, nor did he care. He simply understood that the age was important to the One who commanded him. So Manfred would need to acquire a child near the age of thirteen.

This task would certainly be more difficult than nabbing a baby. In the previous cases, Manfred only had to sneak into the homes after dark and slip the children into a backpack or a duffel bag. Each time, he was in and out in seconds, before the parents could ever detect his presence. That's how it was for the Banks boy. Manfred crept in through an unlocked window on the lower level of the home, slunk up the stairs and into the boy's room, and moments later, he was out of the house, using the same route, only with a baby in tow. Poor Francine and Keith never suspected a thing.

Jesus, the imbeciles. If only they had known what Manfred had known, or at least thought he'd known, about their special little child. If so, they might have secured their home, and the boy's room a little better. It didn't matter anyway; the boy ended up being a complete waste of time.

The next task would certainly not be so easy as obtaining Robert Banks. An older child would cause a number of problems. For starters, they could fight back. Manfred was fit and trim, but he wanted to avoid a fight. Second, the child would scream. It wouldn't be like taking a sleeping baby, whose head still bobbled and whose lips still drooled. A thirteen-year-old would shout and scream for help. Likely, the child would have a cell phone. They would dial 9-1-1 in an instant if Manfred didn't catch them by surprise. Third, the child would have many more friends and family who had grown to love them. This would rouse a desire to investigate and search, and

Manfred wouldn't blame them for doing so because they wouldn't know the abduction was meant to serve a much higher cause.

Another sip of coffee. Manfred decided he wouldn't fret over the logistics until the time came; until he was given a vision from God. There was nothing he couldn't figure out. He was confident in that because he had a higher power on his side. For now, he would focus on the three children he had. And at this moment, it was time for the morning feed, as well as the morning lesson.

Twenty-one

Jennifer was turned away from Leonard. She lay sleeping, hair falling over the pillow in a corona of cinnamon-silk. Leonard's head throbbed. There was a pounding between his eyes, like the inside of his skull was a kick drum. His body needed water. At the very thought, Leonard felt the skin shrivel around his bones, like a used kitchen sponge.

He scanned the room, particularly the two nightstands on either side of the bed. There were no glasses in sight. How irresponsible of both of them. Leonard grabbed the bridge of his nose and pinched as hard as he could. He wanted to puke. Goddammit, he was stupid. How could he have let himself get so drunk?

A single shaft of warm sunlight shone through a crack in the window blind. It split the room in half, illuminating the particles of bedroom dust which existed in their own little solar system. Leonard extended his free hand, interfering with the revolving planets of microbial dirt, or cells, or whatever it was that was floating in the space above the bed.

He reached for his phone. It was nearing nine in the morning, and he had already missed a call from one of his bosses. He also had a missed call from Mom, but that wasn't as important. She was probably just wondering how the South was treating him. Leonard cleared the notifications. He would call his boss after he obtained some water, some caffeine, and a hearty breakfast. He needed some of the fried delicacies that the south was known for.

Leonard opened up his contacts and found Van Daniels' number.

Deputy Daniels. Leonard Beard again. I tried calling a few times yesterday. Please call when you read this. I would like to speak with you about Robert Banks. Thank you for your time.

Leonard pulled his legs from the sheets, hanging them off the bed. His toes dangled just above the hardwood floor. He felt a little childish in that moment, for a number of reasons.

"Good morning," a soft mumble of morning speech called from behind.

Leonard turned to see the navy blue of Jennifer's eyes. They were still deep and dark, even under the ray of morning light. He could feel the gravity in the room growing stronger as she looked at him.

"Morning," he answered roughly, feeling last night's alcohol roll over in his stomach. "I think I need to get going."

Jennifer sat up and rubbed her head, the covers falling from her shoulders to her lap, exposing the soft curves of her body.

"Leaving already?" she said sharply.

"No, no, it's not like that. I have—"

"I'm just kidding." She softened. "Go on, get the hell out of here."

Leonard smiled in return. They had only known each other for about seventeen hours, but she made him feel warm and made him laugh. Maybe it was her eyes, or the way her lips felt, or the way she spoke with the sweet accent of a foreign land, one that Leonard was just beginning to explore.

"I'll text you before tonight," Leonard said. "I'd like to see you again."

Twenty-two

Van never saw the text Leonard sent. He never received the calls either. After the conversation in the examining room, when Sheriff Farnswell said they'd be lying about the Banks boy, Van Daniels had felt sick. Really, he'd felt off since he first saw the child, but the conversation just made everything worse, like the other officers squirted lighter fluid into the flames of his illness.

He called in sick the next day and said that he'd call again when he was feeling better. It had been four days with no contact now. Normally, something like that wouldn't be allowed, but Van was sure Farnswell understood, due to the circumstances. He figured Farnswell was even happy about the matter. If Van wasn't around, it would be harder for people to question him, which would make it more difficult for the news about the *religious bullshit* to get out.

After he called in to report his absence, Van tossed his phone onto his couch, where it fell between two cushions and would stay for days to come. He then began to drink. The alcohol helped numb the pain of the internal conflict he was facing. The substance also helped the deputy stray his mind from images of the boy.

After he left the scene that grim Friday morning, Van hadn't been able to stop seeing the boy's face. Everywhere Van cast his eyes, he saw images of the child. He saw his bleeding head and outstretched arms on his living room wall, in the field behind his house, on the television screen. The cold, white eyes popped up behind Van every time he looked in the mirror. The days were long and haunting, but nothing was as bad as when Van tried to sleep.

The deputy's dreams were lucid, horrifying. Every time he drifted away, he'd find himself running through dark woods or cropland, sometimes even cluttered warehouses. Always, no matter where the deputy was, the white-eyed boy would be there. Robert would never speak. He'd only walk, constantly moving forward towards Van.

The reason for the dreams, or what they meant, was impossible to determine, but Van was now terrified of falling asleep. He didn't want to close his eyes for even a moment, even just to blink. That was like the cousin of sleep. Every time the deputy shut his lids, the boy would appear. It was like the image of Robert's bleeding face had been burned onto the hard drive of Van's brain. The boy was now just a loading screen, the default browser for Van's mind, whose head had been rewired the second after he stumbled upon the crime scene.

The boy was a demon. Van was sure of it. There was something wrong with him. It was those Goddamn eyes, or it might have been the skinny shell of a body, housing bones that wanted nothing more than to expand through the child's skin. His body was so malformed that, after leaving the examination room, Van began to wonder if the boy had been crucified for a reason. Maybe someone else knew the child was hell's spawn and thought the world would be better if it were rid of him.

Van shivered in his rocking chair, which had recently been stained yellow from beer or sweat or piss. The television played the morning game shows, none of which Van paid attention to. He only used the TV for noise, for a distraction. The deputy was trying his hardest to stay awake but was failing to do so. The previous night proved a weak opponent, allowing Van to maneuver through the hours of darkness with ease. A few Adderall and a bottle of gin helped with that, but now he was facing daylight's defenses, accompanied by the come-down from the drugs. Sitting in his chair, he began to realize he was fighting a battle where the outcome was inevitable.

The skin beneath the deputy's eyes felt like anvils. He took his fingers and pulled upon the bags, all the while looking at himself in the mirror which stood along the wall to his side. He stretched the skin to its limits, watching as his chubby face contorted into uglier renditions of itself.

Goddamn, he was tired. And scared. And a number of other feelings.

A smack to his own face would bring him around.

Van felt the palm of his right hand meet with his cheek, hard. He winced but didn't feel any more awake than he had before the smack. He wasn't sure what else to do, other than find more pills.

Van scrambled from his chair and into the bathroom. He yanked open the medicine cabinet above the toilet, being sure not to let his eyes meet the mirror above the sink. His hand bypassed the varying white and orange bottles, finding the one which read *Adderall*. Van pulled open the tab.

None left.

"Fucking Christ!" Van cried aloud. He threw the pill bottle against the shower wall, hearing the ping of the hollow vessel against the tile. He needed to be in the kitchen. Gin would help, if nothing else; it might suffocate his conscience.

Van turned to face the doorway which led to his kitchen. His eyes bypassed the mirror above the sink again, but once they reached the doorway, he found the milky eyes of Robert Banks.

"Jesus!" Van shouted and stumbled backwards. He found his heels slamming into the lip of the shower tub. He was falling now, reaching for curtains, yanking them down as he went through them and slammed hard into the shower tile. The back of Van's head met with the corner of the shelf, which was built to hold bars of soap or the occasional shower beer. The deputy cried out in pain as his stout body filled the space of the tub. The curtain had fallen to drape over his body, blanketing him like he was taking a warm summer afternoon nap.

Van, his vision drifting in and out, stared at the doorway. The boy stood in the opening, still for a moment. His only movement was a slight cock of his head to the side.

"Please," Van tried to shout, but his voice was just a soft croak. It felt like he had gravel in his throat. "Please," he said again, louder this time.

The boy began to walk towards Van. His skinny, angled body moved in jittery twitches as he crossed the short distance across the bathroom.

"Stop," Van pleaded, his voice failing once more. "Please, God, just stop."

The boy found the edge of the shower tub and pulled himself to the lip, now standing directly above the Clyde County deputy.

"There is no God," the boy said in the soft, innocent voice of an adolescent. "I know that now."

Van cried as the boy reached out his boney hand. When the rough fingertips met with the skin under Van's neck, the deputy's vision faded to black. It wasn't a violent exchange. Van felt no pain, beyond that which burned through the wound across the back of his head.

"Come now," the boy said, leading Van into darkness.

Twenty-three

It was a windy morning. Strong gusts hammered against Leonard's car as he traversed the winding roads of County Road 21. He sailed past the Clyde County Power Plant, past the fields which Oliver Brady found so beautiful, eventually stopping about a mile past the bend in the road where the white oak stood. This was the spot where Sheriff Farnswell claimed the boy was found. He pulled the car off to the shoulder, listening to the soft crunch of the gravel easement beneath his tires until they touched the edge of the field.

The sun and the wind said their good mornings as Leonard stepped from the driver's seat. The reporter winced behind a pair of sunglasses. His head was still facing the tormenting tremors of the hangover. A Pedialyte, two cups of coffee, and a soggy breakfast hash from one of the only two diners in Saint Clara hadn't quite cured his disease. It was a painful illness, but one of Leonard's own doing, so he had to persevere. He couldn't call his boss and tell her that he had to put his research on hold because of a headache. She'd know what that meant, so Leonard would do his best to dig up any dirt he could, even if that meant actually digging up the dirt at the scene where the boy was found.

Leonard looked around. There were obvious signs of previous traffic, squad cars and detectives most likely, and other reporters. Cigarette butts were scattered along the easement, as were the faint impressions of tire tracks. The edge of the bean field was depressed slightly in some areas, result of car tires and foot traffic.

The sight of the cigarette butts caused Leonard to stir. He reached for his back pocket and pulled out the blue and gold pack of Camels, fishing for a cigarette. He had a lighter this time, luckily, because the slow burn helped his head a little. Leonard savored the experience. He usually only allowed himself one a day.

The fact that there were cigarette butts, along with other litter, didn't bode well for the Clyde County police, or any detectives that had come by the scene. It was Tuesday morning. Five days had now passed since the initial discovery. Leonard had thought the appearance of Robert Banks was a big deal, but apparently the authorities didn't. They hadn't even thought to take care of the crime scene. Before arriving on-site, Leonard figured there might still be caution flagging strung up, or some sort of barrier to deter unauthorized personal, even after the five days, but there was none. He also figured there might still be detectives or forensics specialists snooping around here-and-there for clues, but there appeared to be none in town. Really, Leonard didn't know exactly what he expected, being so new to this, but it certainly wasn't an empty shoulder littered with debris.

After a moment, Leonard decided that he was in small-town Missouri, after all. The police probably didn't get much experience with actual investigative work, judging by Napoli and Saint Clara. Leonard hadn't been to Plainsview yet, but he assumed it was much of the same – roughly seven hundred people, living in worn down, outdated buildings. There had to be a reason why the whole county was policed by only twelve deputies and an ignorant sheriff – lack of crime was probably it.

Leonard wondered, as he walked the scene, pulling slowly on a cigarette, was this really not that big of a case? Was it so simple and obvious that the detectives already wrote it off, just like the Clyde County PD? Maybe that's why his agency sent him down here. Maybe they wanted to get rid of him for a few days, set him up for failure. Perhaps there wasn't any kind of *real* investigative report to be completed at all.

The reporter tossed his cigarette to the rocks and pressed it out with his shoe. He looked up and eyed the panorama of the flat, rich earth that surrounded him. It was consistent, a vast sea of fields with different crops growing in each square section, split by an occasional windbreak of carefully planted trees. Waves toppled through the stalks as the heavy wind blew. In the distance, about a mile north, Leonard spotted a magnificent looking tree, standing like a tower against the big sky.

He didn't know much about trees, but judging by how far away the thing was and how tall it seemed to stand, Leonard could tell it was old. The base looked large, even from this distance, and the limbs countless, stretching out like hands towards heaven. Leonard took in the pleasant view for a moment, before pulling out his phone to snap a few photos of the scene. His lock screen showed two missed calls from Jennifer.

Miss me already, he thought as he dialed her number. It rang twice before her voice came through.

"Leonard," she said with a swiftness, "Van's dead. I figured you hadn't heard yet."

"What?"

"Deputy Daniels, who you were supposed to interview yesterday. He's dead. They found him this morning."

Leonard, a bit taken off guard, said, "I know who he is, I'm just confused. Dead how?"

"Not sure, but you might want to get to Plainsview a little earlier than you expected. He lives about five miles south of the main strip. I imagine you'll see the cop cars out front. There isn't anything but fields past that way, so it should be easy to find."

Leonard suddenly had the craving for another cigarette. "How did you figure out so fast?"

"It's a small town, Leonard."

That it is.

"Okay," he said, "thanks for letting me know."

They ended the call, and Leonard then punched the coordinates for Plainsview into his phone's GPS. He ran back to his car and sped off, tires spitting gravel and cigarette butts into the edge of the bean field.

There were now eleven deputies on Clyde County's staff.

Twenty-four

Deputy Williams was the one to find Van. Sheriff Farnswell ordered her out to his Plainsview home, hoping she could talk Van into getting over his *sickness* and coming back to work. All the other deputies were growing tired of carrying his extra load, if only for a couple of days.

The route to Van's home in Plainsview was like all the other drives in Clyde County: long and winding. Williams pulled into the driveway at about 9:45 in the morning, made her way up the short hill, and parked her cruiser behind Van's dirty pickup. It was obvious that Van was in. He only had the one vehicle and no spouse or friends who would want to drive him someplace. The nearest establishment would have been about a four-mile walk, so Williams was surprised when she rang the doorbell three times and received no answer from her colleague.

After a few tries at the door, she called his cell phone, but it went straight to voicemail. This roused some suspicion in Williams, who began to pace around the house. Although Van was probably passed out on the couch, Williams felt an instinct to place the palm of her hand on the revolver holstered on her hip. Something about the air felt heavy, wrong in some way.

The ground beneath Williams's boots was soft. She felt her soles sink into the earth as she walked. This would not be great terrain if something were to go wrong, she thought. There wasn't much traction to run for cover or to run after a perp, though she didn't think it would come to that. That's what she was telling herself at least, to ease the tense feeling in her gut.

Once around back, Williams peered through the open windows, examining an empty kitchen. Her view was limited, but she was able to see piles of empty beer cans, liquor bottles, and pizza boxes. She knocked again, back door this time, but just like before, no answer.

"Van?" she called out. "You in there or what?"

No reply.

She knocked on the back door twice more, but no one came. Growing anxious, Williams tried the handle. The door swung open, as she had suspected it would. People didn't often lock their doors in the County. They didn't need to.

The odor of beer yeast and man-sweat saturated the air as Williams stepped inside. Her face twisted in disgust as she tried to block out the scent, green eyes darting back and forth, observing an unnerving number of empty bottles and cans. There were also fly-ridden mounds of trash, mainly from food, in every corner of the home. Van's uniform was lying in a heap on the floor in front of his couch, a weathered antique, deformed with lumps.

"Van, it's me, Deputy Williams," she called again, palm still on the heel of her .357.

Again, no reply.

Williams moved through the living room with caution. Her eyes were searching for either a heavyset deputy or an unknown intruder. At this point, she wasn't sure what she'd find.

Lurking past the living room and into the hallway, Williams moved at a crawl. She could see a light bleeding out from the first doorway in the carpeted corridor. What she saw when she peered inside made her shriek and stumble backwards into the wall. Instinctively, she drew her weapon, pointing it blindly towards the bloody shower tile. Lying below the muzzle of her gun was the stiff body of her colleague, face pale with death.

"Fuck!" Williams shouted, just then realizing her arm was extended, holding her revolver, ready to put a hole in something. Shaking, she tucked the gun back into its holster. Under her breath escaped another, "Fuck. What is this?"

The dead deputy's body filled the tub, as did a pool of congealed blood. It had formed a dried stream towards the drain. The blood on the wall behind him was in splattered droplets around one smeared streak which began at the ceramic lip of a soap shelf and tailed off near the tub like a brushstroke. Van's fat legs spilled over the edge, the shower curtain, stained with grime and God knew what else, lay over his chest like a blanket.

It was clear what had happened. Van was on a bender, probably riddled with guilt or shame or any other number of emotions. He went too far off his rocker, slipped in the bathroom, and cracked his skull. The blow to the head had to have been precise in order to take the man's life from him, but it seemed obvious to Williams that that was what happened.

She felt herself breathing heavily, heart still pounding with adrenaline. She wrapped her hand around her collar and tugged outward a few times, hoping to gather herself. She looked at Van. His face wore a mask of horror, the skin around his cheeks and under his eyes immortalized in a frozen bust of fear. He must not have wanted to die. Maybe he was afraid of the afterlife, or possibly he was fearful to discover if there even was one. Williams guessed the look was because of the latter.

Twenty-five

By the time Leonard arrived at Van's house, a row of squad cars was already formed out front. Leonard counted six vehicles and assumed it must have been every car from the depot, seeing as there were only a handful of officers on staff, and they probably split shifts. None of the colored lights were on, apparently there being no need. Jennifer's info must've been good, which unfortunately meant Deputy Van was dead. Leonard would never get his interview with the officer who first found Robert.

He parked at the bottom of the driveway, not wanting to block the line of police cars. The driveway was long, but the officers commandeered most of the pavement. Leonard suspected he'd be unwelcome to begin with, and didn't want to step on any toes by blocking the path. He had no problem walking up the hill, at least so he thought, before he stepped into the assaulting sun.

The sky was cloudless, and the wind still abused the Earth, blowing hot air, like microwaves, through the fields and the trees. The blue stretched on forever, touching the horizon in a 360-degree panorama. The sun looked immense and lonely, and also indifferent. The burning mass of hydrogen and helium did not care about Van's death, same as Robert Banks's. Even in this time of tragedy, the fiery bastard pulled itself over Clyde County and made sure its presence was felt. Ninety-five-degree heat and God-awful humidity did not take time off to mourn.

The scene in front of the house wasn't what Leonard expected. He thought there'd be caution tape rolled out, or some sort of barricade with a deputy standing guard. Instead, all of the officers were inside, with the exception of one, the crew-cut who Leonard had nodded to at the station. Leonard nodded today, just the same. The man looked at him but offered no response.

Crew-cut was smoking a cigarette, though nearly finished, and wearing the pressed, brown uniform that was standard issue for the County. His eyes were dark and cold, fixed on Leonard as he approached the house. Standing about six-three, he towered over the reporter and was much broader. It seemed that everyone was broader down here, working farms and feasting on a diet of corn their whole lives.

"What are you doing here, boy?" the officer kindly greeted.

"Just doing my civil duty." Leonard smiled.

"Really now?"

This officer didn't speak in a drawl. Unlike the rest of Clyde County, his voice was crisp and clean, similar to his haircut. "And what duty is that?"

"To investigate. And to report."

Crew-cut scoffed and tossed his cigarette between Leonard's shoes. The reporter couldn't tell what the officer's issue was. He looked at Crew-cut's uniform, finding his name tag, which read, *Juergensen*. Juergensen either hated reporters or people of Leonard's complexion. That was probably an explanation for why he had eyed Leonard so intensely at the police department, and again now.

"Do you have a badge there, guy?" The giant stepped forward, looking down on Leonard, who continued to smile. "Because if not, then you're not going to be investigating anything." Juergensen spit to the side. Leonard could smell the residual stink of tobacco on his breath. Oddly, it made him crave another cigarette. "Go on and report what you want though."

An exhausted sigh escaped Leonard's mouth. He pulled a cigarette out of his pocket and lit it in Juergensen's face, looking the officer in the eyes, hating himself for breaking his one-a-day rule. "It's funny. I actually had a meeting scheduled with Van. I was just coming to see him. What's going on in there? Why are you all here?" Leonard interrogated, looking over Juergensen's shoulder, into the doorway. Through the small frame of view, Leonard spotted movement. There were other officers, standing in their brown uniforms, some in street clothes, seemingly chatting. The green-eyed woman who sat with Juergensen at the department appeared to be among the officers. She looked as fierce as she had when Leonard first caught a glimpse of her.

Juergensen stepped in front of Leonard, blocking his view through the door. "What are you peeking in there for? There isn't anything to see."

The smile stuck to Leonard's face. He drew from his cigarette and blew the smoke from the corner of his mouth, being sure to respect the officer's lungs and eyes. Neither said a word, each keeping their ground, staring at, and through, the other. Beads of sweat formed assembly on each man's forehead.

"What are you smiling so much for?" asked Juergensen after some time.

Leonard dropped his cigarette between his own shoes. The butt made friends with the one that Juergensen previously tossed down. "I just like being here."

"Here?"

"Yes, here," Leonard said, "Talking with you. So you going to let me past or what? I have a meeting. I can show you the texts. Got the number from Sheriff Farnswell's receptionist just the other day."

Juergensen looked back towards the house, seemingly considering his next move. Leonard was going to get into that house, one way or another. The cops obviously didn't know how to do their jobs, so he would have to cover for them. Otherwise, they'd butcher the investigation, then lie about it to reporters and detectives.

"You know what?" asked Juergensen, but before another word was spoken, a third voice cut in.

"Whatcha doin', standin' outside in this heat for?" Sheriff Farnswell called out.

Leonard watched his counterpart shift as the large man, even bigger than Juergensen, came strolling from the front door. The wide brim of the sheriff's hat covered his eyes and helped shelter his skin from the sun.

"Well, I hate to say it Lenny." Sheriff Farnswell smiled, something between genuine and mockery. "But I don't think you're going to get your interview."

"It's Leonard."

"Sure," replied Farnswell. "I see you've befriended one of our fine deputies."

"I sure have."

"Is that right, Joe?"

Juergensen, first name, Joe. "Sure."

All three men stood in silence for a moment, looking at each other. Leonard was certain both officers detested his presence. Cops usually didn't like reporters snooping around. He assumed *these cops* especially didn't like people like *him* snooping around.

"You mind if I look around inside?" Leonard asked the sheriff.

"Absolutely."

"Great, I apprecia—"

"After we're through. And the house is clean and clear. And you get permission from Van's next of kin."

Leonard hesitated. He looked at the sheriff. The officers had the same effect as the Missouri heat: they made Leonard want to smoke more than usual. He'd already broke habit once and couldn't allow himself to do so again. Leonard pushed the desire to the back of his mind.

"How did he die, Sheriff?"

Both men's eyes widened a bit. Joe glared, while Farnswell reached for the brim of his hat, pulling it off and cupping it underneath his armpit. The man's hair was still held in a perfect combover.

"That's official police business."

"Is it?" Leonard hummed. He was beginning to realize that if he was going to get in the house, it wouldn't be right then. He'd have to wait for the police to clear out.

"It is." Joe glared.

"Well," Leonard offered his usual smile, "I guess ..." He waited, looking past the officers one last time. "I guess I'll get out of your hair then."

Twenty-six

It was already past noon by the time Leonard left Van's and drove the four miles back to Plainsview. He wanted to try and find Oliver Brady, but that would involve staking out the town's only watering hole for a possible seven or eight hours. The idea didn't strike Leonard as appealing, still being under the assault of last night's beers.

Plainsview was even smaller than Napoli, and more run down. He couldn't officially say the same about Saint Clara, having only spent one drunken evening there, but by first impressions alone, Leonard figured Plainsview was the worst of the three. He slugged down the road, idling by the few houses and even fewer businesses. There seemed to only be about three shops that were open. There was a two-pump gas station that doubled as a convenience store. The outside walls and the lot were dirty, littered with trash and concrete-cracking weeds. From the look of it, as the sun poured in through the large glass windows, the inside possessed a similar wear. A large sign was handwritten on the window: *Cold Beer and Live Bait.* Leonard passed by, hoping he would never need to go in there.

The only other two business Leonard saw were a Dollar General, which every small town in America seemed to have – Leonard was certain that it was a government mandate to construct them – and the pub which he sought. The bar looked like it might have once been someone's house. It was small and cheaply built, just like everything else. The siding was the lightest shade of blue Leonard had ever seen, though splattered near the base with black grime, and peeling away in strips near the back of the building. Like the gas station, the grass around the lot was tall and weed-bearing. The only way that an outsider of the town could tell it was a bar was by the blue paper sign that stretched the length of one of the windows and read, *Busch*.

Leonard circled the lot, which housed three other vehicles, all pickups. After parking, he sat in the air-conditioned interior, wondering what he was going to do to pass the time. He could either go into the pub and wait it out with his laptop, ask some questions, possibly find Oliver; or he could drive back to County Road 21. He still wanted to look around there, though he was almost certain he wouldn't find anything. A third option was to go back to Saint Clara, for no other reason than to see Jennifer.

A head-throbbing moment passed before Leonard found himself in the heat again, headed towards the chipped door that only a handful of others had ever seen. Inside of the pub, Leonard found what he expected – a small, poorly lit room, housing only a few seats and even fewer occupants. Three men sat at the bar while two others shot pool in a swirl of smoke. They all turned their heads and peered at Leonard through the dim lights when he walked in. Leonard half-expected the Merle record to scratch and go silent as the door creaked closed behind him. After a brief moment, the two men started up their game again while the other three turned back towards the bartender, a portly woman who probably owned the place and spent every waking minute of her life there.

Leonard, laptop case tucked under his arm, walked towards the bar. He observed the space some more, noticing a dartboard hanging on the wall. It looked like it didn't get as much attention as the pool table, whose baize was tattered and stained. There were tacky signs all over, boasting the red and white trademark of the King of Beers. Most portrayed women wearing next to nothing and drinking frothy lagers. This wasn't Leonard's usual type of place, but at least it had AC.

He found a seat at the bar, a corner chair, so he could clearly see the faces of the other occupants, all of whom were grizzly, rough-looking men. Leonard could see hardness in their faces, even through the plumes of smoke and poor lighting. They spoke to each other, Leonard suspected about their families and their land. Talks of tilling and combines and high school football filled the air, taking up whatever space the smoke didn't.

"What can I get for ya?" the bartender asked, sounding irritated. Leonard assumed it was not because of his presence, but with life. Her eyes were sullen, exhausted. She looked like she'd lived a thousand years.

Leonard considered what to order. It was a little early for him to start drinking, and an inkling of the morning's hangover still owned property in his head. No desire to drink a beer existed in Leonard, but he needed information and the men might be more willing to share it if he had a drink in his hand.

After a moment, Leonard said, "Just a beer, please."

The bartender looked at him, expressionless. "This ain't the damn television, kid. You gotta tell me what kinda beer you want."

Embarrassed, Leonard coiled away. His headache flared, but just as quickly, retreated. He had never ordered like that before and wondered to himself, *Why did I just say that?* Gaining his footing again, Leonard kept picturing the paper sign out front – the blue one, that rolled the length of the window. He kept hearing the hissing call of, *Buuuuuuuuuuusch,* like that of a locomotive pulling away from station. This helped lead him to a decision.

The bartender set a giant mug in front of Leonard. He placed a palm on the body, feeling the cold sweat of the glass against his skin. The sensation was comforting.

"Two-fifty," she said.

Leonard placed a five on the table.

"Change?"

"No, ma'am."

He looked across the bar. One of the men, the one in the middle, hadn't stopped staring at Leonard since he sat down. The other two were talking to each other, their voices passing through the starer like he wasn't even there. Leonard made eye contact, smiled, and offered a nod. He was beginning to grow irritated with the constant glances but didn't want the locals to see it. The stranger refused to nod back. He just kept his steely gaze. Leonard, wanting to avoid conflict, retracted his eyes towards the beer, noticing the glass's condensation had already soaked through a cardboard coaster in front of him.

"What brings you in here?" the starer questioned.

Leonard looked up, meeting eyes with the stranger once more. His hair was thinning, evaporating from the top of his head and cycling down to the beard, which hung to the center of his chest. He was burly, the size of a black bear, and his voice was a growl.

"I'm just doing some research," Leonard responded, looking back to the contents of his mug. Bubbles raced through the glass, the finish line being the head of foam around the brim.

"*Research?*" another man interjected, the one furthest from Leonard.

"Research on what?" asked the balding one, cruelly, as though he suspected Leonard had come to take his guns.

"The missing boy who was recently found here," Leonard answered. When he did so, out of his peripheral, he noticed one of the pool players perk up and look in his direction. Just as quickly, the player went back to his game.

"What you think?" the interjector began. "You gon' find out who kidnapped him or something?"

"That would be nice," replied Leonard, "because it seems like the police won't."

Leonard could tell this statement infuriated the balding man, likely all three of them, though only the one who sat in the center let his emotions be read. His bear-like lips curled into a snarl and his eyebrows furrowed. "So you think you're gon' do a better job than the police?" Bald-bear asked.

"No." Leonard drank from his mug, thinking of what to say. The taste of beer made his stomach somersault. He desperately wanted to avoid an altercation, especially one where he was severely outnumbered. If he got in a fight in this bar, he might just disappear. And the Clyde County PD might just let it happen.

"Not a better job. A different one."

"A different one," said Bald-bear. "So, I guess—"

"Won't you leave him be, Earl?" the bartender led in, hand stuffed into an empty mug, wiping it down with a towel.

Earl shot a pleading look at the bartender. He looked like a dog begging for a dinner scrap, and Leonard must've looked like seasoned beef.

"Alright, alright." Earl eventually caved and sulked back into his chair, holding his palms up in a form of retreat. "I'll ease up, Kim. I'll ease up."

Leonard wanted to thank the bartender, Kim, for saving him from a berating. A generous tip would be left if he had another beer. Looking around, Leonard figured she didn't receive many of those.

The men started up again, to each other, running through their daily grinds. How many times did they share the exact same stories? The men probably knew every word to every tale. Leonard listened and had another sip from his beer, and then another, even though it stirred up memories of last night within his organs. He knew if he kept drinking, the pain would pass, and his body would settle down.

Across the bar, the pool players seemed to be nearing the end of their match. Leonard needed to talk to one of them – the peeping man from before. The man was middle-aged, with a scraggly head of light brown, possibly red hair. It was too dark to tell exactly. His face was clean-shaven but rough, exhausted, just like Kim and every other inhabitant of Clyde County. Leonard examined him, drinking from his two-handed mug. The man perfectly matched Jennifer's drunken description of Oliver Brady.

"Afternoon." He approached and introduced himself. "Leonard Beard, reporter from St. Louis. I'm sorry to interrupt your game, but do you mind if I ask you just a couple of questions? It will only take a few moments."

"Reporter?" one of the players responded and pulled his cue into both hands. "Can't you see we're trying to have a game here?"

He was a short man, standing about five inches below Leonard's chin, and portly. His hands looked dirty, as did his clothes. Leonard suspected he was a mechanic or some other occupation that worked with engines. Maybe he fixed farm machinery or freight trains. His stature and the jacket of grime made him look a little like a rat.

"It will only take a moment. Please. It has to do with a boy, Robert Banks. You've heard of him, yeah?"

The man, who Leonard could now see definitely had red hair, looked up. His eyes were curious and soft, contrasting with the roughness of his face like flowers growing through a jagged cliff, but they indicated nothing. Leonard couldn't tell if he actually possessed any knowledge on the subject of Robert Banks. His expression was impossible to read.

"Look, Mr Beard," The red-head started, his voice calm, "haven't you heard? One of our deputies passed away this morning. We're just trying to drink up and relax. No one is really in the mood for answering questions about some dead boy."

"Yea, show us and show Van some respect," said the rat, voice imitating an out-of-tune banjo.

Leonard, his wrist beginning to feel the weight of his mug, rested the beer on a nearby table. He held out his hands as if to say, *I'm sorry.* He set his laptop down as well, signaling to the men that he wasn't planning on leaving them alone just yet.

"I'm looking for Oliver Brady. I heard from a girl he works with that he knows something about the boy." Leonard looked directly at the red-head. The two pool players looked at each other.

"It's important that I interview this man. Other children's lives might be at stake, and I'm sorry, but the police don't seem to be doing making any progress in the case."

The rat snarled and made for his drink. He walked with a sort of waddle, hobbling from side to side like a diapered toddler.

The red-head stayed put, chalking his pool cue and looking between Leonard, the rat, and the green velvet. He was a stone, his soft eyes and stone face giving away nothing.

"Please," begged Leonard, "if you know where I can find him, tell me."

The red-head placed the chalk on the table and pulled out a pack of Reds, stuffing one between his lips. He held the pack towards Leonard, who denied the offer. His limit for the day had already been breached, and anyway, he didn't care for Reds.

"Don't offer that boy no cigarette," the rat screeched. "He's a disrespectful ni—"

"Shut the fuck up a moment, will you, Dale?" scathed the red-head. Leonard knew exactly where the rat's sentence had been headed.

"You're from St. Louis?"

"Yes."

"How you like it down here?"

"It's not so bad."

"That's a lie." The red-head burst out laughing. "This whole county is a shit hole. You been outside? You seen around town?"

"Sure, but I've seen worse."

Smoke went into the man's lungs and came out through his nose.

"Then I know for a fact you don't fucking like it here." He sighed. "No one does. But it's home, I guess."

There was a pause. Silence fell through the pub as the juke went from one song to the next. The sound of clinking glasses near the bar was all that could be heard.

"Look, I'm Oliver, and I'm sorry about my friend here – and probably about a lot of the other townsfolk too."

"Nothing I'm not used to."

"Still." Oliver held the cigarette in his mouth and hung over the table, driving a solid into the corner pocket. He then cleared his remaining two solids, and casually pointed at a side pocket, before delivering the eight-ball home. "Tab's yours, Dale."

Dale groaned and looked at Leonard. There was an unnecessary hate burning in the rat's eyes.

"Let's go talk," Oliver said. The exasperation in his face made him look as though the weight of the world was fully his own to bear.

Twenty-seven

The two men sat on the bed of Oliver's pickup truck, along a bend in County Road 21, beneath the shade of a white oak. Leonard examined the limbs in disbelief, wondering exactly why the police had lied to both him and the detectives.

"I just don't get it," Leonard said. He held a can of beer he'd been nursing for the length of the conversation. Oliver conveniently kept a cooler in his cab.

"Don't get what?" asked Oliver.

"Why would they lie? What do they gain from covering up where the boy was found?"

"It's not about where they found him," Oliver said with a shrug. "It's about how they found him. That's what they're hiding."

"What do you mean?"

"You see, I didn't just find the boy lying on the ground here, beneath this tree." Oliver looked away, seemingly searching for something. "He wasn't just *lying* anywhere, although that's what Farnswell and the deputies have been saying. What did they tell you? That he turned up on the side of the road down there?"

Oliver pointed about a mile down the road, where Leonard earlier investigated – the edge of the bean field riddled with tire tracks and cigarette butts. Leonard nodded.

"He was right here." Oliver pointed up at the tree. "Looking like Christ."

117

"What do you mean, *like Christ?*"

"He was fucking hanging there. Crucified." Oliver rubbed his forehead, which was sweating, even in the shelter of the shade. He drank his beer, crushed the can, and tossed it blindly behind his shoulder, where it landed in a pile of empties.

"He was hanging right there. Strung up by the wrists. One tied to that limb," Oliver pointed, "and one to that limb. Wearing a crown of thorns, like he was sent here to save us from our sins."

Leonard's eyes grew wide, as did a pit in his stomach. What Oliver was saying couldn't be true, could it? Jennifer had warned that he was a bit *off,* but this story was too odd and too specific for someone to just imagine. And why lie? What would he gain from doing that?

"That boy. I haven't been able to stop thinking about him since that day." Oliver's soft eyes looked weak in his hard face, like a damaged levee about to burst. "I see him sometimes. I see him at night when I'm watching TV with Becca, or when I'm brushing my teeth. I saw him the next evening, after finding him, while I was walking my route at the power plant. He was just standing there on the opposite side of the fence, staring at me with those giant white eyes. Fuck. It was unnerving. That's why I've been taking off work. I can't stop seeing the damn kid."

Oliver took in a deep breath. Leonard just sat there, not knowing what to do, what to say. All he could do was listen. Maybe some shred of truth, something at all useful, would bleed through Oliver's words.

"You're the first person I've really talked to about this. I can't tell my daughter. She thinks I found him beside the road. I can't tell her what I really saw or why I've been taking off. I don't want to haunt her like I've been haunted. I don't want her to see the boy. Though I don't think she would. She'd probably just think I'm crazy, like everyone else does."

Oliver let loose a few sad laughs. Leonard, still confused, smiled an awkward smile. How could he possibly respond to this? Oliver certainly did seem crazy. Leonard, conflicted, began to wonder if he had even found the boy at all. Maybe he was just claiming he did to get into the paper or something, in search for his fifteen minutes of fame. If it wasn't for the look in his eyes, Leonard would have abandoned Oliver already. There was something about the way Oliver looked at the tree and then back at Leonard that made the whole story, crazy as it was, seem like it had a slight possibility of being real.

"I think that's why Van died," Oliver blurted out while he fished through the ice in the cooler for another beer. "I don't think he fell. Well, maybe he did, but it wasn't an accident. It was that fucking child. That boy. I think Van saw him too. Or maybe I'm just hoping that he saw him. Maybe I just don't want to be the only one. Maybe I just don't want to sound crazy – to go crazy. I don't know."

"I don't think you're crazy, Oliver," Leonard comforted, not knowing if he believed his own words, but it was what Oliver needed to hear. Leonard rolled with the story, thinking, *What's the worst that can happen from listening, from playing along?* "What I think is crazy, is why the police would cover up the fact they found the boy hanging here. Why would they lie about that? Why would you go along with it? Detectives had to have questioned you?"

"Because it's sacrilegious. Obviously. Farnswell doesn't want everyone in America to know little boys are being sacrificed in Clyde County, or anywhere for that matter. He doesn't want anti-religious protests and Godless speeches being preached all over the country. So …" He drank, as did Leonard. "So he covered it up. Say he tells people the true story, then the news is more prominent, maybe even global. There are pictures of a child hanging from a tree, with a crown of thorns on his head, plastered everywhere. The anchors are talking about it for months. There are multiple sides to the issue, arguing back and forth, until another child turns up on a tree, or some other exciting story emerges. But let's say Farnswell lies, and he says the boy was just found on the side of the road. Then there's a lot less of a frenzy. There's just a short few days, maybe a week or two of the media circus, and then on to the next scoop. It's gone before we know it. Not exciting. No sacrilege or blasphemy to be shared with the world. Everything is nice and calm, just how Clyde County likes it. Until someone like you comes along. And as for me, I didn't want to stir the pot up any more than it already was. I didn't think it really mattered what I said. And to be honest, Farnswell's plan to keep things quiet sounded alright at first. The kid was found. What would it matter *how* he was found? But I've been feeling mighty guilty the last few days. Speaking with you has been the first time I've been able to get some air since finding him up there."

Leonard sat aghast. He was still sweating, but a wave of cold tremors erupted across his body. The story was outlandish, but also, for some fucking reason, believable.

"I know the whole thing is kind of out there. But Leonard, I am a lot of things, and a liar is not one of them." Oliver's head drooped towards the Earth. "There's no point in lying. Especially when everyone thinks you're crazy already. I ain't lied since the day my wife died. I just say whatever I'm thinking, and people think I'm insane for it. Maybe they're the insane ones."

"Maybe you're on to something. Maybe they are," Leonard responded. "So everything you're telling me is true?"

"Every damn word."

The two just sat there a moment, observing the tree. The sun was pulling the shadows of the oak's limbs across the truck and the surrounding fields. The entire moment felt surreal. Leonard wondered if he was in a dream. Maybe his brain had made up the last two days. That seemed more plausible than reality.

"Did you capture the scene, with your phone camera or anything?" asked Leonard.

Oliver shook his head. "No. I didn't want that shit anywhere near my phone. But I'm pretty sure Van did."

Frustration was all Leonard felt with this statement. A photo would have proved every word. How could Oliver not take one? He was letting evidence slip away with that mishap. Now the only other person who could prove the story true was dead. Leonard was certain that Farnswell and his tribe of deputies would have found Van's phone at his house earlier and destroyed anything that could have spoiled their plot. Now Leonard would have to investigate and try and find out for himself if Oliver's story had any backbone to it.

A car zipped around the bend behind the men. Leonard watched it dart towards the distant stacks of concrete, and a thought formed in his head.

"You work security at the power plant, up the road there?"

"That's correct."

"Are there any cameras? I'm sure there are some, right?"

Oliver nodded.

"Are any of them pointed towards this road? Can you perhaps see any traffic on any of them?"

Oliver's soft eyes widened.

Twenty-eight

Oliver felt weird being inside the security office during the day. He felt even weirder sharing the space with a reporter who he had met only a few hours ago. Still, he and his new friend scrolled through the main gate's camera footage, allowing the daytime guard a short break.

The tape showed a blurry image of about twenty feet of County Road 21, just enough to catch vehicles as they zoomed through the darkness. The majority of the image was nothing but still, static pavement. Most nights, there wasn't much traffic along the road, and while watching the footage, the two men realized that during the night of the crucifixion, there was almost none. They forwarded through the entire night's worth of footage several times over, making note of every vehicle that passed. There was a total of seven over the course of twelve hours. After watching, Oliver realized just how small his county actually was.

On the list, they ranked the vehicles – the top of the list being those makes and models which Oliver wasn't familiar with and those that looked like they might be carrying tools, enough to string up a boy. There was a brown Silverado with a steel rack suspended over the bed, a black Camaro with tinted windows, that although it likely wasn't carrying a dead boy, looked out of place. A gray minivan with an extension ladder on top was another of the suspicious vehicles and it passed by around three in the morning, separated by a window of nearly two hours between it and the next vehicle. It was circled on their notepad, along with a second truck, a brand-new black Sierra that appeared to be loaded with loose tools and a stepladder.

Oliver shuddered as he watched the tape and looked at the notepad. Any one of the listed vehicles could have transported a murderer. Then again, every one of them might have been innocent. It was impossible to tell, and that tore Oliver apart.

"Wild, isn't it? If only we could go back in time and stand in that spot on the road. I'd like to ask every one of those drivers what they were doing. Why were they driving down a small county road at that time of night?"

"Yea," Leonard answered. "I would too. But they'd probably just tell us to fuck off."

"True," Oliver laughed, "but it's painful to watch. To think a kidnapper was so close to me that night, stringing up that boy, and I could have possibly stopped them. If only I had been on my route at the precise time, I might have even seen the driver. But I don't remember seeing anything but some raccoons."

"Raccoons?" Leonard asked but started again before Oliver could answer. "Anyway, at least we have some sort of a clue now. They're tiny. Almost nothing, really, but at least it's something. All of these drivers are more than likely innocent. Who's to say the kidnapper even came by this route?"

"No one. But there's only two routes to that tree. North and south on 21."

Leonard shrugged. "This is at least more than the police have, I guess. Maybe one of these vehicles will be spotted the next time a child turns up on a tree."

"Let's hope it doesn't come to that."

The thought that Robert Banks wouldn't be the only child to die haunted Oliver. It wrecked his mind, thinking about more children at the mercy of a madman.

"So, what are you going to do now?" Oliver asked.

"I don't have a clue."

Outside the office, the sun began to set. Daylight was fading into night, which would finally bring some cooler weather, though not much cooler.

Leonard broke a short silence, "I have something I need to check out. Can I get your cell?"

"Sure."

"Let me know if anything comes up. Anything at all. Even if you're just seeing the boy again."

"Will do."

"I believe you," Leonard said, which made Oliver feel odd. It was nice to be believed, but annoying that he had to be reassured in that belief. Oliver tried to remember what it felt like to be normal, to not feel crazy.

"Thank you."

"I'm going to find out just what the fuck is happening."

"I hope you do Leonard. I hope you do.

Twenty-nine

Leonard napped in his car, sleeping off the beers he drank with Oliver and the remainder of the evening's light. It was nearly two in the morning when he woke and made his way south of Plainsview to a pullout on the road, about two hundred yards from Van's house.

The moon was just a sliver, but the stars, unhindered by light pollution, sparkled over the fields, a thousand tiny flashlights in the sky. Leonard's shoes sunk into the soft ground as he made his way through the head-high wheat adjacent to Van's. He was breathing heavily, though only walking, in part because of the adrenaline he felt by breaking the law. In about five or ten minutes' time, he would be breaking and entering – a crime that might have been punishable by death with the officers in Clyde County, so Leonard had to move cautiously. He didn't feel like dying just yet.

He moved to the edge of the field, crouching in the undergrowth to observe the backside of Van's home. There was no movement and no light inside the house, just a calm darkness. Leonard moved to where he could see the driveway and the front door. No signs of life there either. This was good. Leonard didn't suspect anyone would be in at this time of night, and it seemed he was right. Van's family might have come down earlier, but they certainly weren't going to stay in the house where their loved one had just died.

Leonard moved around back again, finding his way to the rear door. His eyes darted, and his head shifted tirelessly, searching for witnesses of his trespass, but he saw none.

The back door was locked, leaving Leonard to search for a key. He overturned some rocks and lifted the doormat but found nothing. He tried the top of the frame and some of the window sills, but they were no good either. Leonard picked up one of the stones, and after a second look for witnesses, he used it to smash a hole in the glass over the door. He made for the lock on the other side. After fumbling with the latch, he opened the door and was greeted by a long creak. A stench of rotten food and alcohol lingered in the air when he stepped inside, fallout from Van's implosion. Leonard gagged and pinched his nose, feeling vile just from breathing in the toxicity.

The kitchen where he stood was a complete mess. In the starlight, Leonard could see piles of dishes, still possessing remnants of meals, and beer bottles everywhere. There was an indistinguishable stain on the floor where the kitchen's tile met the dining room's carpet. On the dining table stood stacks of pizza boxes and dirty glasses. Leonard wondered how long they'd been there. A day, a week, a month?

Past the dining room, in the living area, were more starlit stains and heaps of garbage. Leonard stepped cautiously over the mess, wondering all along just how someone could live in a place so filthy. He looked around, examining the space, remembering how earlier it had been full of Clyde County police officers. Why hadn't they cleaned the place up a bit? It was the least they could have done for Van's family – if he had any.

Leonard kept walking past the living room, having spotted nothing of interest. He looked down the corridor of the house's lone hallway. A door was open, and a dim light bled from it, seeping out onto the carpet about five feet ahead of Leonard. He hadn't spotted the light before. The room must have no exterior windows.

Leonard crept forward, feeling eerie. Something twisted in his gut, telling him to move with caution. The silence of the night and the stillness of the home was frightening. Just twenty-four hours ago, there was a man living here, walking the halls, throwing his clothes and his trash everywhere but the bins, watching television and eating microwave dinners. Van cursed and he stank and he filled his gut with cheap beer, right here, in the same room Leonard was sneaking through. But now – now the place was an empty vessel, housing only the memory of an owner.

The light in the room grew brighter as Leonard inched closer. The knot in his stomach cinched tighter with every step. For the first time in the reporter's life, he wished he had a gun. He also wished he had a cigarette, although he'd been wishing that too often over the last few days.

Though nervous, Leonard kept moving forward. His mind said, *Retreat! Get out of this place*, but his legs didn't listen. He needed to see the room. It might have answers. It might help him find the kidnapper.

Leonard stood at the crest of the doorway, the light inside pouring into the hall in a trapezoid of blue. On the other side of the door, all seemed silent and still, just like the rest of the house. Leonard waited a moment, shoulder up to the wall. Even though he knew nothing was inside, fear gripped him. It was a strange feeling, like the skin around his bones was trying to crawl away, back towards his escape hatch.

Finally finding the courage, Leonard breached the corner, only to see an empty bathroom. A first glance alerted him that there was nothing special about the room, except that, unlike the rest of the house, it was sparkling clean. A moment passed, and Leonard started to realize this must have been where Van had died. It had to be. There was no way this room, where Van shat and pissed, would be so clean if the living room looked the way it did. The officers, or someone who worked with the officers, must have cleaned up the mess left from his death.

After settling his nerves, Leonard noticed the shower curtain was missing entirely, as was the rod. On the wall, there was a ceramic shelf that had been chipped on the corner. The wall to the side of the shelf possessed a patch of tile that looked cleaner than the rest, the grout between squares as white as the day they were first installed. Leonard was no detective, but it seemed obvious, judging by the scene before him. Van had fallen through the curtain and into the shelf. He probably hit the back of his head, a vulnerable spot, where if struck precisely, even a small blow could end someone's life.

What an unremarkable way to die – in a bathroom, helpless and alone.

Leonard pulled his phone from his pocket and took some photos. He walked through the room, examining everything he could. He knelt by the tub and inspected the tiles and the shelf. He pawed through the medicine cabinet, finding an array of pill bottles, most of which were nearing empty. It was clear that Deputy Van had some problems long before finding a boy on a tree. This wasn't just a few days' worth of binging and trashing.

After a while of searching and finding very little, Leonard began to grow weary, defeated. He had hoped he'd find something more. Before breaking in, he figured that somehow the deputy's death was connected to Robert Banks, that maybe Oliver's theory was correct. All of that seemed like a stretch now.

He inspected the bathroom a moment longer before considering it'd be best if he left the house. The wrenching in his stomach had never really gone and was beginning to become unbearable. His body kept urging him to leave but his mind was telling him to stay, to find something. Leonard, dejected, finally decided to give up and listen to his gut. He turned to face the dark hallway, looking once more to make passage through the obstacles of trash and clothing.

The trapezoid of light was to Leonard's back as he reversed his trail, creeping back through the living room towards the kitchen. He passed a mirror on the wall, seeing himself in the starlight. His face looked unlike his own. It was more creased than usual, stricken with stress and exhaustion. He kept moving, passing the mirror and turning his unfamiliar face towards the dining room table and its mountain of trash. He stepped forward, walking a little less cautiously than before, making way to the back door. He couldn't wait to be out of the stench.

Feet finding the tile, Leonard looked down at the unknown stain on the floor of the kitchen again. *What made you?* he thought. When he looked towards the door handle that would lead him out to the starlit fields, Leonard discovered that he wasn't alone in the house.

"Wha … What the—?" Leonard gasped before losing the ability to speak. His throat felt like someone's hand had seized it.

At the edge of the kitchen, near the sink, stood the slender body of a dead boy. Robert Banks wore a crown of thorns, piercing through his long hair into his dead flesh. His head glinted where the dried streaks of crimson reflected the natural lights of the night. The child looked at Leonard, mouth hanging open, as though the jaw was unhinged from its skull.

They were locked in a staring contest until the boy began towards him, moving at a crawl like he was strolling through the park on a Sunday afternoon. Without thought, Leonard leaped towards the door, ripping it open, immediately hearing the catcalls of crickets and the wind. He screamed across the lawn, feet slipping through the soft earth as he stumbled into the field behind Van's house. His legs felt weak as he sprinted through the wheat, feeling the light lashings of the stalks against his cheeks. At full sprint, Leonard felt like he was doing no more than a jog, like he was floating, possessing no power over his own body. Fear pulled his beating heart against his sternum. He huffed and he heaved, not wanting to look back, not wanting to see the boy's face, not wanting to see those eyes.

Leonard didn't stop until he was at the pullout. Once standing at the door of the car, he shot his hand into his pocket, thumbing for his keys. This was the first time he turned back. Across the starlit plain, Leonard could see nothing, no one, except the crops which slow-danced beneath the night sky. He was alone on the road. There was no boy in pursuit. There was no one at all.

Leonard had imagined the whole thing. He had to have. That was the only explanation.

Heart still beating with adrenaline, mind still racing, he stepped into his car. His lungs were on fire from the pursuit that didn't happen. Leonard hadn't run like that since his high school track meets.

For what seemed like an hour, he sat in his car, letting his body recollect. He looked at the field once more. In the distance, Leonard watched the unmoving silhouette of Van's house. It appeared just as quiet, just as still, as it had before when he was pacing its halls – alone.

Thirty

It was morning again. Leonard tossed in his hotel bed, unable to sleep after returning from Van's. The thought of being followed through the fields by a dead child kept him turning, watching the shadows chase the walls of his hotel room. He wasn't sure if seeing Robert really even happened. Maybe his mind conjured the images as a result of talking with Oliver. That was the only thing that made any sense. It wasn't possible Robert's ghost was actually in the house with Leonard last night.

Hoping to stray his mind, he checked his phone, seeing notifications from CBS Sports saying something about an offseason trade that went bad; from Janine, his boss; and from Jennifer. The swipe of a thumb cleared the notifications. Leonard had no desire to begin the day's web of communications just yet. He needed to decompress first. A few cups of coffee and a hotel breakfast would fix that, but he needed to hurry. Breakfast would be breaking down in about twenty minutes.

Wearing the same clothes from the night before, mud-stained and coated with the stench of dried sweat, Leonard traipsed into the breakfast hall. Haggard and exhausted, he looked around, examining the room and its occupants. There were only a few others dining so late in the morning. At the end of the room sat an elderly couple with wiry grey heads, eating waffles the size of their plates. The only other diners came from a family of six. Leonard watched the parents shovel

133

powdered eggs into their gullets, paying zero attention to their miscreants, who clamored around the breakfast room with complete disregard for all other life. The children shouted while they pocketed jams and butters from the toast rack, occasionally tossing them at each other. Leonard frowned, considering the concept of birthing any more than two children an act of neglect. It would be next to impossible to properly nurture every child, which was probably why these children acted like insects.

Leonard's belly grumbled. After a night of twisting itself into knots, the empty capsule was starved. On white fold-out tables were metal containers standing over heating pods, full of unnaturally yellow eggs and wet sausage links. Leonard's body groaned, shriveling away like a snail on salt. He had no desire to put anything from these containers into his stomach.

Standing a moment, looking in terror at the heaps of nutrient-less grub, he decided he'd have to settle for a waffle and a cup of yogurt. This, combined with hotel coffee, would surely do the magic of freshening his weary body.

Leonard sat as far away from the family as possible. He ate in what silence he could find, watching the Channel Two NEWS. A lady in a colorful dress talked about the weather, though there wasn't much to say. Leonard, having no experience in meteorology, could probably have done her job quite adequately at this time of the year. *Hot and sunny.* That's all he'd ever have to say.

He waited for a photo of Van Daniels to flash across the screen, but it never did. The untimely death of a Clyde County deputy must not have been enough to make the morning news. Perhaps, if someone leaked that Van's death was connected to Robert Banks, a boy whose death was connected to a frantic, religion-crazed murderer, then the late officer's face might have made the screen. That wouldn't happen, not unless Leonard could provide some truth to the matter.

A soggy, syrup-drenched bite of waffle hit Leonard's tongue. Goddamn, it tasted good, if artificial. In a few hours, the fluffy quick bread would soak up the past few days' worth of beer. This was a good thing. Leonard normally didn't drink so much, but he was in the habit of breaking habits since coming south. There wasn't much else to do.

Leonard continued to eat and drink his coffee until the paper cup ran dry. In desperate need of more hot caffeine, he made for the machine. He was already thinking about his next sip when one of the four rodent-children scooted back in her chair and bumped into his legs. Leonard glared, but the child said nothing.

"Goddamn," Leonard snapped, too exhausted to control himself, "can you keep an eye on your kids?"

The mother hung her jaw in an exaggerated gasp. She looked at Leonard, then to her husband, then back at Leonard. The father, who wore a ball cap with a fishing hook on the brim, murmured something to his daughter and then cursed Leonard under his breath.

Drained to the bone and already fed up with the south, Leonard kept walking to the coffee machine.

Thirty-one

"And that's pretty much it. We've done it. We've reached the end of the crusades! Any questions on today's lesson?"

The boring man with a voice like sandpaper smiled at the head of the class, looking like a rail in his oversized clothes. Not a single hand was raised. Clearly, none of the students wanted to learn more about someone else's history. They were antsy for the bell to ring so they could get the hell out of Andrews' boring class, and even better, out of school. It was seventh period, which meant that the day would be over in about three minutes. The eighth-graders were buzzing, ready to run to the buses, or run home if they lived close enough, like Janiya Peters did. There wasn't a soul in the building who wanted to ask questions about the freaking crusades.

"Okay then," said Mr Andrews. "Well, the bell's about to ring, so thanks for another good hour. I hope you were all taking notes. The PowerPoint will be up on MyDrive tonight. Next class, we will have a review day. Our test will be on Friday, so make sure you—"

The school bell rang through the classroom, startling Mr Andrews. The noise was succeeded by zipping bags and scooting chairs, accompanied by the chatter of students, who weren't talking about the crusades, or tests, or anything at all related to school.

"Have a nice day, everyone," Mr Andrews muttered, watching as the students piled through the door like zombies, nearly trampling each other as they exited.

Janiya was one of the last to leave the classroom. She didn't care about blitzing with the mob towards the buses. She didn't need to rush to find a back seat with the cool kids because she walked home. The thirteen-year-old strolled past the already idle Mr Andrews into the hall, past the droves of her classmates, to her locker. She tossed everything that wasn't needed for the night's homework into it, slammed the tin door shut, and made way for the school's main doors. She said *hello* to her favorite teacher, Mr Shepard, along the way.

The torment of the city sun was in full effect when she stepped outside. The school building, looming like a gothic church behind Janiya, failed to provide any shade. All that it, along with the surrounding fortresses of brick, did was keep the wind at bay.

"Janiya, wait up!" a voice called from the crowd of teenagers who were filing outside behind Janiya.

Now halfway down the great concrete staircase that led to the street, Janiya turned to see her best friend, Jacky. She wove in between students, shuffling her feet and gripping the straps of her trademark backpack – known for being big enough to carry six or seven students' supplies. It looked like a parachute on Jacky's shoulders.

"Well, hurry up then, slow poke," Janiya called back as she stopped to wait for her friend.

They didn't always walk home together, only a few times a week when Jacky went to her father's house. Her stays with him were usually on a schedule, so today was off tendency, which caught Janiya by surprise.

"I didn't know you were staying at Pop's tonight," Janiya said to her smiling friend, who was showing off a mouthful of aligning hardware. Each of them melted underneath a cloudless sky, trying to drown out the clatter of bus engines and car horns and the perpetual bustle of the city.

"Mom's going on a date tonight. So, I'm with Pop," Jacky said, indifferent about which house she'd be staying in. "Which meeeeans … we get to walk together one extra day."

"Girl, I ain't trying to walk with you. I don't even like you none," Janiya joked.

Jacky responded by socking her in the shoulder.

They walked the sidewalk, passing by trees whose roots were confined to tiny squares of cut pavement, laughing. Neither had a clue that this would be the last time they would ever walk home together.

Thirty-two

Enclosed in the tattered walls of the two-bedroom apartment were Janiya's four-year-old twin brothers and her two younger sisters. It was about eight o'clock now, which meant that Janiya was in charge for about one more hour before Mom would finally come walking through the door.

Janiya was used to raising her siblings while Mom worked. She had been doing so for as long as she could remember. Her mom worked multiple jobs, which left the chore of picking up the slack around the house to fall to the oldest child, which just happened to be Janiya. She never minded – in fact, she enjoyed the task. Running the house gave her a sense of pride. She liked to imagine she did a better job than her mom, though that would be a lie.

Playing with the twins and keeping them busy was Janiya's favorite task. She thought her brothers were the cutest little babies in the world, though now they had breached into the toddler-sphere. It didn't matter what their age or size was, Janiya would always see the twins as babies. She was nine when they were born. At first, Janiya would get them confused, being as they were identical, but now she could tell James from Jamel as easily as she could determine the differences between the Crusades and Spanish-America War. She enjoyed learning how to understand her brothers and each of their intricacies. It was a skill that not many others possessed, including Mom sometimes, when she was tired or drinking.

James was just a bit taller than Jamel, maybe by the width of a hair, but Janiya could see it with the naked eye. Both of them were always giggling, as toddlers tended to do, but often arguing as well. Jamel liked to call things *mine,* which didn't sit over well with his twin brother. James seemed to be more outgoing, while Jamel was often internal, though each would smile and babble to strangers at the park or at church on Sunday. These were the things that Janiya noticed about her brothers, that others often missed. People just looked at the twins and expected they'd be the same person, with the same temperaments, same personalities, since they were made of mostly the same genes, but that couldn't be further from the truth. This sort of mindset irritated Janiya because she knew just how special each of her brothers was.

The young babysitter also enjoyed the presence of her two sisters, Jasmine and Jade. These two were the ripe ages of eight and ten. Each was a task of their own when it came to babysitting. Janiya often helped Jasmine with her math homework, or Jade with English, putting her own studies aside until late at night, sometimes until early the next morning. She didn't mind. Something made her feel good about helping her sisters succeed, even when they struggled to grasp concepts. Seeing the light in their eyes when they finally figured it out was one of the best feelings.

There wasn't much fighting in the Peters' apartment. An occasional bickering contest arose between the two younger sisters, or from twin against twin, but this would usually sputter out as quickly as it started. It seemed that all of the children understood their situation and wanted to help Janiya help them. None of the children wanted to see their big sister fail, and they enjoyed it when she watched them. Mom had always threatened that if the kiddos acted up, then Janiya would be replaced by someone bigger and older, who wouldn't be as nice. The youngest siblings bought it and usually tried to stay on their best behavior, but Janiya wouldn't make purchase. She knew there was a reason she was always watching the kids at only thirteen years old. It was because that was the only option. There was no way they could afford to pay an outsourced babysitter.

Tonight, all of the kids were in the living room, where they spent most nights. Janiya sat at the kitchen table, scribbling through her Intro to Algebra homework. She looked at her problems and used the FOIL method to solve them. It was easy, as math had always been for her. Janiya could never understand the complaints of so many of her classmates. Everybody seemed to be failing math or whining about how they hated math, dating as far back as the third grade. Janiya didn't get it. All you had to do was try, in any subject, and you'd pass. That was her mindset. Just try. It wasn't that hard.

On the living room carpet sat the twins and Jade, each resting their backs against the couch, watching whatever cartoon was on television. Janiya didn't bother to learn what they were pouring into their brains. She never watched TV. She never had the time.

Jasmine sat at the same table, working through her homework alongside her big sister, only at a slower, more frustrated pace. Janiya paid attention to both the worksheets in view – hers and her sister's. Whenever she would see Jade start to heat up, Janiya would say something like, "You gotta flip the second fraction when you're dividing." Or she'd point to a mistake that her sister had made in her formulas and ask, "What are you forgetting?"

Janiya felt like a little teacher. She wondered if her sisters thought she was as boring as Mr Andrews. Probably not. He would be hard to beat. He spoke at snail's pace and looked like one too, with his bug eyes and bald head.

As the girls were doing their homework, a pot of spaghetti and meat sauce cooked on the stove, now at a simmer. Janiya had started it about an hour ago, as Mom had instructed through means of a post-it note on the fridge. It would be ready to eat as soon as Mom came through the door. All of the kids were waiting in anticipation for this moment. Mom coming home was the highlight of the evening. She was a superwoman, even to Janiya.

The night dragged on as the girls attempted to finish all of their schoolwork before Mom's arrival. The yellow lights of the city poured into the apartment through open windows, stretched wide because the Peters couldn't afford to keep the AC constantly blasting. It was a windy night, but the gusts didn't help to cool off the sweaty children. It was a hot wind, blowing nothing but hot air into the home. Janiya could feel her legs sticking to the wood of her chair. She feared that when she stood, the chair would follow right along with her, forever a fixture to her body.

The image in Janiya's head was interrupted by the rattling of a door handle at the opposite end of the living room. Seconds after, Mom tumbled in, holding her purse and her things from work. The superhero's hands were full, and her eyes were tired. She looked like she had spent the evening fighting crime, and now she was back in her street clothes, so to conceal her hero's identity from the family.

"Momma!" the twins called out in unison. The two hobbled from their spots on the floor, running across the carpet to give Mom a hug. Janiya watched as they slammed into the woman's legs, each wrapping their arms around a separate thigh.

"Hey, boys," Mom greeted. She continued to walk, now dragging the full weight of the twins. She looked exhausted but still managed to smile. "And hey, girls." Mom looked at Janiya and asked, "Has everyone been good?"

Janiya nodded, truthfully. They really had been great.

"Good."

"Boys, you better get off of her!" Janiya called out. The twins released their grip and went tumbling over each other, back to their spots in front of the television. They had to watch as much TV as they could, while they could, because in just a few minutes, Mom was going to come and turn it off. She didn't like anything on during dinner.

"Hey Jade," Janiya called to her sister, who was sitting comfortably on the carpet, "now that Momma's home, go ahead and watch these three for a moment."

"Why? What are you gonna do?" Jade replied.

"I gotta go get something real quick. Only gonna take a second. I'll be back before Mom's out the shower."

Thirty-three

The 7-Eleven was only about two blocks away. Janiya had run there, hoping to be back home before Mom was ready to eat. When she returned from work, she usually spent about twenty minutes in her room, decompressing. Janiya knew she only had about ten minutes left to get what she needed and return home.

In her hands were six Hostess pies, of all different flavors. Janiya had been saving up every penny she could for the past few weeks, waiting to make this purchase. Tomorrow would be Mom's birthday, but Janiya wanted to celebrate with everyone tonight, for tomorrow, Mom would endure another long day. This surprise would help take her mind off the grind of working fourteen hours through her birthday.

"Seven-seventy-five," said the clerk from behind the Plexiglas barricade separating him from the rest of society. Janiya tossed her money – eight dollars, mostly in quarters – under the exchange slot. It took him some time to calculate the change. Janiya tapped her foot impatiently.

"Need a bag or anything?" the clerk finally asked.

"Yes, please."

Janiya stuffed her pies into a plastic bag that had *7-Eleven* written across it in big green and yellow letters. She tossed what change she received back from the clerk into her pocket. Every nickel and dime would eventually count towards something.

The two blocks leading her back home were dark – very dark. As Janiya jogged away from the silver glow of the 7-Eleven lights, she found herself retreating into a tunnel of darkness between two large buildings and a vacant dog park, where the city lights never reached. The surrounding scenery might have frightened a different girl, but Janiya had traversed this path on many occasions.

She moved hastily, hoping to surprise her mom with the pies, rather than with her absence. To her side was the chain-link fence of the dog park, worn and rusty, unable to perform its job of keeping animals on the patches of brown grass as half of the fence had collapsed on itself. It was now mainly used for housing the tents of transients. Even tonight, Janiya spotted some. Two silhouetted figures, appearing like scarecrows, followed her with their eyes as she headed home.

To her opposite side was a warehouse building that hadn't been in operation for years. The last time a laborer was paid to work the machinery inside, Reagan was probably president. Graffiti covered the outside walls, and presumably the inside too. There was broken glass strewn about the sidewalk from when the windows, most of which now boarded, had been busted out by teenagers.

Janiya was considering the history of the hollow building, examining the tags, when she slammed into something. The object was firm, sending Janiya to the glass-covered concrete, forcing the wind from her lungs. She gasped, crying out as she dropped the bag and skidded her palms on the dark pavement in attempt to catch herself. She looked up, investigating the source of her collision.

Her eyes found a figure, standing like a demon in the darkness. Janiya, horrified, pulled away as the figure began to lurch forward, palms extending towards her hair. Its hand yanked one of her braids, and the other clamped tightly to her shoulder. She winced and screamed, knowing no one was going to hear her, besides those she had seen in the tents; but worse than that, no one was going to give a damn if they did hear. Screaming and shouting didn't cause alarm in this part of the city.

The figure was a man. Janiya could tell from the scent of his cologne and the way he grunted when he tussled with her. His grip was fierce, hands soft but as strong as vice grips. The warmth of his breath against her neck made her skin recede. He was gruesome, and Janiya was mortified.

She continued to scream, though muffled by a palm covering her mouth. She had never been so scared. She kicked and clawed and tried to bite, but in what seemed no longer than a second, Janiya found herself thrown into the back of a minivan like she was nothing more than a bag of golf clubs. The abductor then slung a hand into her jaw, forcing her to cry out, vision sparking with pain. The next thing she felt was a rag stuffed into her mouth.

The hatch slammed shut, closing her off from the world. Janiya cried and gagged for air as she looked through the broad window, down the block, where the darkness of the sidewalk faded to light as it met the yellow windows of her apartment building. The thirteen-year-old's vision then went black, as she was struck again, this time on the side of the head.

Thirty-four

The coffee at Jennifer's house was better than the Holiday Inn's. A porcelain cup sat on the table before Leonard, steaming between him and the cinnamon-haired girl. He had told her everything that had happened the day prior – about Oliver's story and what happened at Van's. He didn't know if he could trust her with the knowledge that he broke into the dead officer's home, but he had to get it off his chest to someone besides Janine. The updates he gave his employer were brief and vague. Janine had no idea what Clyde County was like. The stories that Leonard was feeding her might as well have been in braille. There was just no way his boss, who had never been south of Arnold, could picture what Leonard had witnessed in his two long days in the county – but Jennifer could.

She sat cross-legged on a wooden kitchen chair, wearing a loose-fitting pair of shorts and a large tank top, one of the grey straps falling down her shoulder. Underneath the morning's rays, Jennifer looked otherworldly. Leonard wondered how her skin might feel against his sober fingers. The memories of the last time they were together were a blur. He regretted letting himself get so drunk.

"What are you going to do now?" asked Jennifer as she sipped her coffee, pulling Leonard away from his thoughts.

"I don't know." Leonard shrugged. "I really don't know what else I can do. I can't report anything yet. I have no evidence that any of the cops actually lied to me. I've got my notes from the interviews with Farnswell and Collins, as well as Oliver, but nothing's concrete. All I really have is hearsay. I can go write a report that says, *the boy wasn't actually found on the side of the road, but was instead strung up on a tree in some religious display*, but no one is going to believe me. All my knowledge is based solely off of the story of a man who the entire town believes to be crazy."

Jennifer set her cup down. "Well, did Oliver photograph the boy when he was there?"

"No." Leonard shook his head. "He said he was too shocked. He texted his daughter and called the cops, and that was it. Didn't want the boy on his phone, and I don't really blame him. He said Van got a photo, but that does me no good now. Farnswell most likely destroyed his phone as soon as he found it."

"Well …" Jennifer went silent, searching for her next words. She didn't know how to help Leonard, and he didn't know how to help himself. "What do you plan on doing next?"

Leonard sat a moment, considering his next steps. Then a thought came to him. "I guess my only option is to get back down to the station and speak with the sheriff again. I need to persuade him to tell me the truth. I need to tell him what I know, or what I think I know at least. Maybe he'll cave. Maybe I'll tell him I won't put it in my report that he and Collins lied to me – though that would certainly be a lie."

Leonard knew he had to proceed with some sort of caution. Jennifer was nice, much nicer than everyone else in Clyde County had been, but that didn't mean she wasn't loyal to her townsfolk to some degree. If he went off bad-mouthing the police department any further, he might cross a line. Leonard hadn't known her long enough to know how she truly felt about her county-neighbors. He considered how he might like to find out, get to know her more, but it wouldn't be right then. There was too much work to be done.

"Yea, I think I'll go down to the station."

"Then what?" asked Jennifer, genuinely curious. Leonard could see the concern bleeding through her eyes. He wondered if she was concerned about him, or just interested in the case being solved. Leonard didn't have a chance to respond before she asked another question. "What if they don't crack; if they don't give you anything? What are you going to do? There's not a whole lot more you can do down here, is there? There's only so many corn fields and dive bars you can run through."

"Woah, that's a lot to respond to. Are you looking for a job? Because you ask better questions than I do!" Leonard laughed. "I guess I don't think I'll stay here if all of my leads die out. I think I'll go back up to the city, at least for a couple of days. I'll need to report to my editor and start putting some of this mess into writing. Though I'm not quite certain what direction I want to take this story when it comes to a report. There really isn't a clear direction yet. I need more. I need to start finding answers."

Leonard took a drink of his coffee, felt the warm liquid pour down his throat, and then placed the empty cup on the table. "I have a feeling that there's a lot more to be uncovered," he said, the idea shaking him. He didn't want to think about another child dying. He didn't want to think about the white-eyed boy. Leonard hadn't been able to stop envisioning Robert. He wasn't yet seeing the boy in the mirror or in Jennifer's living room, like Oliver had described his visions, but was instead continuously replaying his experience in Van's kitchen. Leonard had recalled the memory a hundred times since. He didn't even know if he had really seen the child, but he was being haunted nonetheless. Leonard was beginning to understand how Oliver felt, if only slightly.

"Thank you for the coffee." Leonard stood from the table.

"It'll be three-fifty." Jennifer mimicked his movement. The thin strap of her tank fell even further when she grabbed both empty cups, exposing more of her body, which was like looking at an O'Keeffe. As she walked away, Leonard had to fight every instinct to make for her waist and kiss her neck like he had the other night. He wanted to stay and waste the morning with her, but he couldn't.

"I'll let you know how everything goes, later on. Are you working the feed store today?"

"Yea, until seven, but I'll close down early if no one is coming around."

"Maybe I'll come around if I've got the time."

"God, you're clingy."

"No, I …"

"I'm just joking." She laughed, scrubbing the two cups, eventually turning to meet his eyes. "I'll see you later, Leonard." Her voice wasn't so much a question as a statement.

Thirty-five.

Snatching Janiya, the new Number Three, was easier than Manfred
had thought it would be. It was actually the most successful abduction
he'd ever had. It was certainly easier than Number Four, whose father
nearly caught him in the act. Shivers rode Manfred's arms as he
remembered lunging into the closet and watching the little girl's door
creak open. The father had gotten up to take a piss, and in the process,
thought he might check on his baby. Such a fool. He didn't even kiss
his daughter or go tuck her in. All that he did was pop his head in and
look around the room, unaware that it'd be the last time he'd ever see
his girl.

Taking Janiya was nothing like that. All Manfred had to do
was wait. God told him to go into the city that night. At first, Manfred
was reluctant but eventually did as commanded. An alleyway between
some old warehouses was where he was led. The sky was so dark it
would have been impossible to see him or his van tucked away
between the alley's dumpsters. Janiya, who's name Manfred learned
from the television, certainly didn't see him. She jogged right past to
the 7-Eleven, and Manfred knew on her way home, she'd jog right
back, only into his arms rather than into her apartment. And that's
exactly what happened.

Manfred smiled, sitting on his back deck in a rocking chair,
half-erect from all the excitement. He looked across his plot, which
stood just south of the city. His eyes wandered over the trees and

across the gentle hills, to the barn which housed his children. It was tucked away beneath some Missouri pines at the end of a well-worn path. A little pond sat on one side, just big enough to comfortably toss a rod into, though Manfred never did. It also housed an unused gazebo that Manfred often considered tearing down. The thought of people taking lunch there and jumping into the pond from its railing drove him sick. He didn't like the idea that someone else used to live in his home.

Manfred pulled away to new thoughts. Janiya should be awake in her cage. She'd be confused and scared. Probably, she'd try to escape, though that was impossible. The cages weren't incredibly sturdy, but the cellar beneath the barn, where the cages were placed, was a fortress. There would be no getting out, no matter how hard Janiya tried. There were no windows and only one door, which stood atop a set of stairs. The steel door was chained and locked on the outside. For extra security there were stacks of hay piled on top, to conceal it from the outside world and act as weight. The children would need the power of God to escape, but Manfred understood that only he possessed that gift – for the time being at least.

III

"We live, as we dream – alone…."

– Joseph Conrad, *Heart of Darkness*

Thirty-six

Janiya opened her eyes but saw nothing. Darkness encompassed her. She was cold. She was afraid. And worse than either, she was alone.

She sat up, feeling her hair skim the top of what seemed to be a metal cage. Her eyes were only now beginning to adjust to the darkness, doing as best they could to see through total blackness. She didn't yet understand her reality. Her mind traveled through broken increments of the previous night's memory.

Last night – what had she been doing? She was walking home. No. She was jogging. She was running through the dark stretch between the convenience mart and her apartment building, between the warehouses and the park, where the streetlights never touched. She remembered the tents and the scarecrow-like eyes of their owners. She was looking at the big building, carrying a bag full of pies, a gift for her family. A cool wave of shivers rode the length of Janiya's spine, forcing her jaw to unhinge. She ran into a man.

She was taken.

Janiya instinctively brought her hand up to the side of her head. There was a large knot near her temple, and her mouth felt stiff and swollen. Both were sore to the touch – very sore – but there was no blood. If there had once been, it was wiped clean by the one who took her.

The one who took her.

158

The thought echoed through her mind. She had really been taken. Kidnapped.

Panic began to fill her scrunched up body. Janiya tucked her knees into her chest and buried her face between them. She wanted to hide, to escape the room and the cage, which didn't seem to allow her to even stand upright.

She had to be dreaming. It didn't seem real – no, it wasn't real. She wasn't actually taken. She was just asleep. She never went out to get the pies. What actually happened was that she fell asleep at the dinner table. Mom would be a little upset, but that was better than being taken.

Janiya closed her eyes, hoping she would open them and be back in her home. She wanted to wake up to the smell of spaghetti and the noise of four chattering siblings and their superhero of a mom. That's all she wanted. To wake up. To be away from where she was. Away from the darkness.

Why was it so dark?

Noises began to erupt around Janiya's cage. The sound of metal. Rustling sounds, like the shuffle of feet. Were there others?

"Who's there?" Janiya called out, her voice sounding tiny. She felt as though she were standing two feet beside herself, watching her trembling body, which wasn't quite her body, trying to speak with a voice that wasn't quite her voice. Nothing felt real.

The sounds of grunts and moans greeted her, like those of yawning dogs. But Janiya could tell by the tone that these sounds weren't coming from man's best friend. They were coming from people – from children. Jesus, she felt sick.

Janiya's eyes were still adjusting. They had never experienced such darkness. The shapes of three cages began to take form around the room, as did the silhouettes of three other inhabitants, all of whom appeared to be brittle looking children, white as the moon and stunted from living in cages. There was also shelving, which housed paint tins and the outline of other hardware supplies. To her left was a hallway that disappeared into the unknown. Where did that lead? How big was this place? Where, and what, was this place?

"Please," again she called out, beginning to cry, "who's there?"

Once more, she was greeted with the moans. There was a rattling on the other cages. Was this how the children communicated? Through groaning and cage-rattling? It couldn't be. Surely, they knew some words. Surely, they knew how to say their names at least. One of the others would be able to explain where exactly they were or why they were there.

Janiya began to grow frantic. Her body felt hot, and her head began to spin. She thought she might pass out. After a moment's consideration, she decided that passing out would be a nice surprise. Doing so would at least take her away from reality.

"Number Three?" a voice finally called in a revelatory tone. The sound of the other child, another girl, somehow made the situation all the more horrifying. It brought to Janiya a sense of reality, that this was actually happening. She had been taken.

"What?" Janiya responded.

"Number Three," said a boy this time.

Janiya's voice was a tremor. "What are you talking about?"

"You will learn, Number Three. As Papa said you would."

"You are part of the prophecy now."

"Papa said you would come."

Janiya retreated to the back of her cage. Her back slammed against steel wires. The impact would leave a bruise, but she didn't even notice. She was scared, and her adrenaline was surging, body humming as she hyperventilated. Anxiety swelled, while her vision swayed.

Where was she?

Where was she?

Where ... was ... she?

"Papa said you would come," the others repeated, together, like a haunted chorus. Their voices seemed soulless as they sung Janiya into the darkness of dreams.

Thirty-seven

The sleep that followed was not pleasant. Janiya was in a lucid state of dreaming. Her body, though in a state of unconsciousness, was lurching about on the damp concrete. The cage rattled when she struck it with her arms. In her dream, she was running. She was running towards the lighted section of street before her apartment building. The one who took her was right behind her, his slimy fingertips making attempts to snatch a piece of her clothing or a flailing limb. Eventually, he did.

Janiya whipped her head up into the cage when she startled awake. She let loose a whimper. Her voice again felt small. She was sweating, even though the room's temperature was cold. She was flaming with illness. The walls of her stomach had been stretched out and twisted into knots, causing her entire body to ache.

The darkness of the room was overwhelming. It was the kind of darkness that enhanced the other senses. Janiya, as she lay wondering what the hell was happening, could hear exceptionally well. She could hear the others as they rolled around in their own cages. They seemed to be asleep now, and Janiya was certain she could hear the sound of their breathing – she was even convinced she could hear their little hearts thumping, but it might have just been her own, echoing through her body and into the space of the room. The worst sound was a perpetual dripping of water, splashing off of the concrete between her and the other girl's cage. It was a cheap metronome, keeping Janiya's heart rate in rhythm.

Drip. Drop.

Drip. Drop.

The lungs which, on a normal day, would unconsciously cycle air through Janiya's body, didn't seem to be working. She was at a loss for breath. Her chest was tight, and she realized that her teeth were grinding together. This had always been her release from nerves, but right then, she was more than nervous. She was deathly afraid.

Drip. Drop.

Breathe.

Janiya took a large breath and crawled forward, to the front of her cage. As she progressed through the distance of about four feet, she realized that the cage was beveled, so that the front had a higher ceiling than the back. At the forefront, she could stand, barely, but barely was enough. The weight of her body felt strange. Janiya had never taken the ability to stand on her own feet for granted, until now.

The muscles in her legs trembled and retracted a moment before gaining their usual strength. Her body still ached, but standing helped in that regard. She didn't remember any trauma to her frame, only to the side of her head. She figured she must have been thrown around and dragged down to the cellar. That might explain why every inch of her structure felt damaged.

"Are you awake, Number Three?" a voice called quietly, so as not to disturb the others. This time the words belonged to a boy. Again, *Number Three*.

"I take it you're talking to me?" Janiya answered.

"Yes."

"My name's Janiya. I am not Number Three."

"Janiya?" The boy repeated. "I have never heard that name."

"Well, it's my name."

"It's your name?"

"Yes, it's my name."

There was silence for a moment. The boy seemed to be taking in the idea of having a name that wasn't a number. Janiya watched his still silhouette from the comfort of her cage. He stood at the edge of his own, each of his hands wrapped through slots in his cell. He was so white that his fingers acted like glow sticks.

"My name is Number Two, but mostly I am just called Two."

Janiya wondered how long this boy had been down here. He had forgotten his name or had chosen to forget it. There was a horrifyingly calm pitch of clarity in his voice, like that of a prophet sharing a Sunday message.

"How many are there?" Janiya asked, afraid of the answer.

"There are now four. There was always supposed to be four, but recently, the Number Three before you was taken to the light. You have replaced him. You should feel blessed, as now you are part of the prophecy."

"Blessed?" Janiya snapped, slamming her palms against the cage. "I should feel blessed?"

The boy sighed. "You will learn."

"I am far from fucking blessed. I am scared and cold, and I don't want to be here. God, I don't want to be here." Janiya felt like vomiting. Her body was shaking uncontrollably.

"What do you mean, *here*?" the boy asked, as though he knew nothing of the real world. How long had he been trapped in this place?

"In this cellar, or wherever we are. In this darkness. I don't want to be in this dark cellar. I want to be home."

"Home?"

"Yes, home. You know? With carpet and couches and TVs and music." Janiya began to cry, her words becoming choked by sobs. "And family. James and Jamel, Jade, Jas ..." She could no longer speak. Her throat swelled, and her lungs grew rigid, no longer sacs of oxygen, but of wet cement.

"No, I don't know. I don't know much of any of those things. Only what Papa has told me," the boy stated as Janiya fought off what felt like a heart attack. "I don't know couch or carpet or TV, but I know of the light. I see it from the portal. That is where you came from, from beyond the portal. Can you bend the light like Papa?"

Janiya stayed at the front of her cell but sat down. She was afraid if she stood any longer, she'd faint again. The prospect of suffering a head injury by collapsing onto the concrete didn't appeal to her.

"What the hell are you talking about, *bend light?*"

"Like Papa."

"Stop. I don't know what you're talking about. Who is Papa? Is he the one who took us? The one who kidnapped us?"

Like a neon light, the word *kidnapped* flashed in front of Janiya's eyes. She had really been abducted. It still didn't seem real. It still *wasn't* real. She was sure of this. She was just hallucinating.

"Papa is the one from the other side of the portal. He is a powerful being, a direct descendent of God. And he teaches us everything that God shares with him. He teaches us the prophecy and about how we will fulfill it. He is a wise teacher. He's helped us learn to speak, and learn to pray, and learn to see through the darkness."

This boy spoke as though *the man from the portal* was God himself. Everything her companion said was surely untrue. Two was brainwashed. There was no Papa, and no fucking portal – whatever that meant – and no bending of light. There was only a sick bastard who kidnapped five children, maybe more. Janiya wondered what all the kidnapper's teachings included. Were they just verbal, or physical too? Her skin crawled at the thought of him touching the children.

"What is the portal?" Janiya asked. She was confused by how the boy spoke and was forced to choose between the thousands of questions she wanted to ask. She decided that if Two *was* brainwashed, and if he *did* believe what he was saying was true, then this question would be a simple one to answer.

"The portal, atop the stairs."

Janiya thought she could see the boy pointing. She rotated her neck to see a dark stairway in the corner.

"Papa comes from there when he teaches lessons. He comes from the other world. A world beyond this one. He says there is light there, and colors, and all sorts of amazing things. He says we will go there one day. That we will be able to make the connections between worlds. But we are not ready yet. He brought you from there just recently. You were sleeping when you arrived. I asked who you were, and he said that you were a gift. That you would be our guide."

What the fuck?

"That's not a portal. That's a door. There is no other world. That man, *Papa,*" Janiya's throat filled with bile at the sound of the word coming from her mouth, "is not a messenger from God. God wouldn't teach a man to kidnap kids!" Janiya was no longer speaking quietly. Her voice felt like her own again as she shouted. Her words rattled off the walls with the ferocity of giants. There was silence for a moment, and then a hiss from another cage.

"You shut your mouth, Three," another boy commanded. "You do not speak about Papa, or God, with such ignorance."

"Please, One," interjected Two. "She will learn. She is new. Do not be so bitter."

Janiya grabbed her cage. This entire moment seemed surreal. It felt more like a dream than her dreams did. She shook the metal with all the force her adolescent body could provide, but it didn't budge much, making only a soft, jingling noise.

"There is nothing I need to learn," she barked. "I know more about life than any of you. How long have you even been down here? Have you forgotten what it's like to be outside of these walls?"

"We have been down here our entire lives," another voice whispered. It was the girl, presumably Number Four, if chronological order held true in the cellar.

"Your ..." Janiya froze. "Your entire lives?"

"Yes," the girl responded. Her voice, like the other children's, was prophetic. They really did believe they were a part of something larger, something supernatural – of a prophecy from God. None of them seemed bothered by the fact that they were in cages. That was probably, Janiya now shockingly realized, because that was all that they knew. The children had never tasted freedom. They'd never played tag with their friends, eaten ice cream on a hot day, or played hooky from school with their besty. These children knew nothing but darkness.

Janiya squirmed. Knowing the others had been there for the entirety of their lives meant they were completely dependent on their captor. They weren't brainwashed to be this way; they were raised to be. He really was their papa – a fucked up version of one, who kept his children in cages and told them it was because *God wanted it this way*. She wondered how she could convince them that life extended beyond the cellar. It would be nearly impossible. They wouldn't believe her words. It would be like trying to explain algebra to one of the twins.

"How often does Papa come down here?" Janiya asked.

"As often as he does."

"What? What kind of an answer is that?"

Baffled at first, and equally frustrated, Janiya began to realize that the children likely had no concept of time. They probably had never even seen a clock or held a cell phone. They might have never even seen the sun rise.

Thirty-eight

"You callin' me a liar, boy?" said Farnswell, pounding his fist against his desk, causing every photograph and wall ornament to rattle as though the New Madrid had just shifted. "You think I would lie to you and fellow officers of the law? Fuck off with that!"

Leonard was nearly shaking in his seat, not from fear but from surprise at the outburst. Several strands of gelled hair fell over Farnswell's sweating forehead, making him appear less professional and more like the fraud he was.

"No sheriff, I'm just telling you what Mr Brady shared with me. I wanted to get your side of the story is all."

"There ain't no *my side of the fuckin' story*. There's only the story. And the story is that we found the boy right where we said we found him. Got that? We ain't got no reason to lie to you or to anyone else, but especially you."

The sheriff's voice was hard and full of spite. Leonard knew his maliciousness wasn't just because of the investigation. It was coupled with the fact that Leonard didn't look like him, or like Juergensen. This was an ancient spitefulness, one that had been bred into the man, becoming an inexcusable and ignorant thread of Farnswell's DNA.

"What does that mean, *especially me*?" asked Leonard, prying to see how far the officer would push.

The sheriff said nothing.

"Come on, Sheriff. Tell me what you mean."

"You know what I mean. A nosey little reporter who hasn't even had a column in the local paper yet. There's a reason you're down here – because you ain't done nothin' yet to prove your worth. Why else would they send you to report on such a simple case? You ain't solvin' no mysteries, boy. Robert Banks was missing, and then he turned up again. Plain and simple. Now let the authorities do our damn jobs and stay the fuck out of our hair."

Leonard let a silence pass through the room and watched the golden fields stand at attention beyond Farnswell's window.

"I know you're lying to me."

The sheriff's eyes narrowed. The eyebrows above them were thin, bending towards the bridge of his nose. He looked drawn, like a character in a cartoon, one about dirty cops. "I told you before boy, and the story ain't changed. I ain't told you no lies. Now, if you'll accuse me one more time, there's goin' to be some recourse."

"*Recourse*. That's quite a big word for you, Sheriff. So what is this recourse going to be? You planning on shooting me? Taking me out back and beating me? Stringing me up to a tree by my wrists?" Leonard let that last one linger a bit. "What's it going to be?"

An uncomfortable silence passed before Farnswell said, "Well for starters, I could have you charged for breaking into Van's house last night."

Leonard kept silent, staring at Farnswell.

"Yea, that's right. You've got nothing to say about that do you?" the sheriff continued.

"I don't know what you're talking about. I was at my hotel last night."

Farnswell glared. "Well how come I got a call from one of my officers this mornin' saying that there's a shiny new hole in one of Van's windows? And you know what else? The back door was unlocked, and I know for a fact we locked it yesterday before leavin'. So this leads me to believe someone helped themselves in. And I wonder just who that *someone* was. I don't know, a hunch tells me it was the nosey reporter who was poking his head around just hours before."

Leonard's feet began to sweat. He felt nervous and knew he couldn't allow the sheriff to notice. "I would be wondering the same thing."

"Would you?"

"Of course. *Wondering* is all the authorities seem to be good for around here. It's really a shame you'll never find out who broke in, seeing that no one around here understands how to investigate."

The fingers on Farnswell's hands began to curl into his palms, and his veins pulled through the skin around his neck. He looked like a not-so-incredible version of the Hulk, trapped in the moment before turning into the abominable version of himself – the one which he usually kept hidden.

"Boy ..."

"What?"

They shared eye contact for a moment.

"How's about you just get the fuck out of my office, that's what. The story ain't changin'. What happened is what happened. You can go ask any one of my officers. It ain't no different from what I told you. I don't give a damn if some batshit crazy, *oh-God-I-miss-my-wife* town drunk told you otherwise. So why don't you just stick with our story, and there won't be no problems?"

Leonard stood. His face was cool and masked, smiling as always, hiding the anxiety and rage consuming him. "Okay then Sheriff, but you can count on this: if you're lying, I'll find out. I'm going to uncover exactly what is going on in this backwards town of yours. So you just sit and think about that, and have a nice day."

Leonard pushed his chair to its home under Farnswell's desk. He remained as calm and collected as possible, though really, he wanted nothing more than to drive his knuckles into the sheriff's jaw. If he did, he'd certainly receive a heavier blow in return, but his single punch might be worth it. At least he'd know that tomorrow the sheriff would still be thinking about him.

"Out." The sheriff pointed towards the door, speaking to Leonard as he might to a house-soiling mutt. "And you *best believe* I'll find out if you're the one who broke into Van's."

Leonard offered no words. Boiling, he turned and walked out the door, gently closing it behind him. While hidden on the other side, palm still clutching the rounded handle, he swore he heard the sheriff's voice, almost inaudible, say something along the lines of, "Goddamn nigger."

Thirty-nine

Oliver pulled his old Ranger through the country roads, watching the sky go on forever. His hands slapped the steering wheel as his voice croaked along with the radio. The windows were rolled down, and the wind was blowing the red hair atop his head. He was in his best spirits since discovering Robert. He hadn't seen the child in nearly twelve hours, and it was an incredible relief. Oliver theorized his brain was healing itself of the trauma.

He and Leonard were to meet at the tree, which was something Oliver wasn't particularly happy about, seeing as he was finally getting over his visions, but Leonard needed to see him there, and Oliver was always willing to help out a friend. That's just how he was raised. When he pulled around the bend, Oliver found the reporter already waiting. The young man leaned against his car, puffing on the dying remains of a cigarette. A long strand of ash clung for its life, not wanting to be blown into the fields below the tree. Oliver pulled up directly beside him, hanging his head out the window.

"How's it going there, Leonard?"

"It's going."

Oliver stepped out of the truck. He could tell that his friend was furious about something. Leonard's eyes were burning narrow, and the skin above his forehead was wrinkled.

"Need a beer?"

"Please."

Oliver made for the truck bed, where a red and white Coleman cooler perpetually leaked. The plastic lid opened with a *pop*. Most of the ice inside had melted, but there was still ice-cold water for the Buds to call home. Oliver fished two out and tossed one over to Leonard. The can toppled end over end through the air before landing in Leonard's palms. The crack of each can opening was to Oliver what a seventh hour's bell was to high school seniors on their last day in May.

"What happened down at Jay's?" Oliver eventually asked, knowing it couldn't have been good.

Leonard looked up, presenting a wry smile. "What do you think?"

"Called you an asshole or a liar or something? Called me crazy?"

"That's the short of it."

"Yea, he tends to be a bit stiff sometimes."

"Sometimes?"

"Well, to folks that ain't from around town."

"Folks like me, you mean?"

"Don't be too hard on him. He don't know any better. It's just the way he was brought up. Not everyone in Clyde County is like me, but I'm sure you've more than discovered that by now."

Leonard's beer met his lips, and Oliver decided he'd have a sip as well. "Yea, I'd say I've learned, but I'm not sure *being brought up that way* is a valid excuse for being a racist asshole."

"No, I would agree with you there." Oliver shook his head, disappointed in his townsfolk. "So, what you thinking now? What's next on the agenda?"

"I don't know just yet. That's not what I wanted to meet you for."

"What then?" Oliver again brought his can to his lips. Each drop was as delicious as the last.

"I just wanted to let you know that I believe you. I'm not going to lie, I wasn't so sure about your story at first. I hate to admit it, but it sounded unbelievable. The whole thing, just unreal. I'm sorry that I didn't take your word for it, but ... you know."

"Accepted." Oliver nodded. "Now, go on."

"I went to Van's last night, not long after speaking with you. And I saw him."

"Saw who?"

Oliver asked the question but already knew what the answer was going to be. The look in Leonard's eyes gave the secret away. Although the idea that someone else had seen the boy was a bit haunting, Oliver was glad it had happened. It meant he wasn't crazy after all. It meant that he wasn't the only one seeing things. There was something about a shared misery that was comforting.

"The boy," Leonard answered, unease filling his words. "Robert. I saw him in Van's house. He was in his kitchen, just standing there, staring at me with a set of white eyes. They were empty, like staring into the sea. I just couldn't stop. How could they, those two eyes, have such gravity?"

"I don't know, but I get what you mean. Those eyes are basically all I see anymore."

"That's how I know that everything you said is real. After I saw that boy, I wasn't sure at first if I just imagined it – hallucinated him, you know? But I know I didn't. I know because it felt so fucking real. So I know your story is real. Every word of it."

Each emptied their beer. Oliver tossed another in Leonard's direction. There were two more cracks, which carried a more wistful tone this time.

"That means there's still someone out there, at large," Leonard said, turning his tab to the side.

"Might even have more kiddos locked up."

"That's the worst of it."

Oliver looked at his arms. They had become overrun with goose flesh. Even in the heat, the cool sensation of fear, of anxiety for the possible deaths of more children, overwhelmed him. "We have to find this person."

"I know." Leonard sighed, and the August air between them turned silent. All that stirred was a warm gust of wind. Oliver watched the branches of the hundred-year-old oak tremble under the force of the gust. The leaves and the limbs looked somber, lamenting the fact that a boy had died on them. Like Oliver and Leonard, it wanted to see the course of justice play out.

A hum – no, a buzz – erupted away from Oliver, breaking up the silence of the evening. It originated in Leonard's pocket.

Oliver watched as Leonard pulled a phone out. The reporter's eyes widened as he stared at the screen, which was hidden from Oliver, who could only see the soft, blue illumination of the device. Curiosity began to rattle Oliver's bones. What was Leonard seeing? Who texted? Who—?

"Jennifer," said Leonard in a hurried tone. "A girl is missing."

Forty.

Channel Five news played on Jennifer's TV. Too energized to sit, Leonard stood behind her couch and watched, waiting. It had played for an hour without mentioning the girl Jennifer had texted him about. He was starting to wonder if they would ever show her again when a tall reporter with a slim, pointy face finally appeared on a city street.

She was standing in the middle of a St. Louis neighborhood Leonard had never been to, wearing a nice dress and holding a microphone that read *STKN*. Behind her was the backdrop of a large red-brick building, which looked like it had been vacated for centuries. The picture of a young black girl, apparently about the same age as Robert Banks, hung steadily in the top right corner of the screen. The reporter looked into the camera and offered a brief excerpt, detailing the girl who had gone missing.

"Janiya Peters lived in this neighborhood for years," the woman started, voice coded with the robotic clarity that all television anchors seemed to have. "She was only thirteen, the oldest of five siblings, and a hardworking student at school. Last night, she was said to have gone missing around this area, just outside of her apartment building. The warehouse that you can see behind me …"

Leonard watched as the camera panned over her shoulder and rotated through the scenery. Shattered glass and litter covered the streets surrounding the building. The camera continued to pan, moving across the street to a dog park that had seen better years. The grass inside was patchy, every existing blade a dying shade of brown. There were tents, two of them, and the fence around the perimeter was in pieces, eaten by rust and weather.

"... and this dog park here, are what lie between Janiya's apartment and the 7-Eleven where she was last seen," the reporter continued. "It is believed she was on her way home from the convenience mart last night, taking this sidewalk behind me, when she disappeared. If you have any information on the missing child, please contact the local authorities or the number you see across the screen. Back to you, Gale."

The on-location reporter disappeared from the screen.

"That's it?" Leonard questioned, angry with disbelief. "That's all she got, a two-minute piece? What the hell even was that? They didn't show any interviews, nothing. Was she really even seen at the 7-Eleven? Who knows, because they didn't even—"

Jennifer placed her hand on Leonard's shoulder. She must have snuck from the couch without him noticing. He was too transfixed by the television and his internal combustion to realize there was a world outside of the screen.

"Calm down," she said. "They showed more earlier, but not much more. Maybe you can go on their website and track down the story. That way, you can see the full report."

Leonard scowled, not at Jennifer but at the cheap reporting of the local news. He guessed they didn't want to show the girl's face for very long during primetime hours. Too many viewers might grow displeased with what they were watching. They'd rather hear stories about celebrity lip injections and singing shows.

"I guess missing children just aren't worth more than a minute of the viewer's time." Leonard's head was beginning to ache around the temples. "Maybe if she was from Clayton, there'd be a bigger story. There'd be plenty of interviews and footage of search parties wandering the streets."

Jennifer's hand, still on his shoulder, squeezed into the muscle, gently massaging it. Her touch was calming. "It's okay," she said.

It wasn't, but Leonard didn't feel like ranting anymore. "I know this is connected with Banks. I know it. I can feel it," he said. "It has to be."

It probably wasn't connected at all. This little girl, who happened to be around the same age as Banks, probably just ran away from home. Leonard's mind processed this but quickly washed it away. It pained him to realize that he wanted the abductions to be connected. Absurdly, he needed this girl to be in the same hands that Robert Banks had been in. It would mean his investigation wasn't over. It would mean he could still figure out who was taking children and making shrines out of their bodies. The idea that the girl might be in a murderer's hands was disturbing, but her abduction could help Leonard save any other children.

"I'm going back to St. Louis. I have to do the research the police and STKN obviously want to avoid. I have to find out if Janiya is connected to Banks somehow."

There was a twinge of sadness in the blue eyes which met Leonard's when he turned to gather his things.

Forty-one

Francine and Keith Banks were generous hosts. They welcomed Leonard's initial phone call, and about an hour later, they welcomed him into their home. It was a late hour for a random visit, but Leonard intended on making it quick.

About ten minutes into his drive back to the city, he decided it would be smart to make the detour to Rolla before finishing in St. Louis. This extended the trip by several hours, but Leonard had to hear from the boy's parents. He now sat at the center of their dining room table. Keith and Francine sat at opposite ends. Leonard noticed the distance between them – not just physical, but mental. Their eyes looked remote like they were only living together because neither wanted to start over. They were either bonded together or severed in two by the tragedy of their missing child.

"Would you like any wine? I have red and white," Francine asked, lifting her own glass as a gesture. Her breath was strong, already perfumed with the sweet smell of a rich red.

"No, thank you. Still have a bit of a drive ahead of me."

"Okay then, water, ginger ale, anything else?"

"No, I'm alright, really."

Keith cut in. "So why are you here, so late in the evening, and several days after our boy was found?"

Leonard looked at Robert's father. Keith's eyes were timid, sheltered behind a thin pair of glasses, lenses short and square. He appeared to be both looking through, and over them, all at the same time.

"I really just wanted to hear your sides of the story."

Keith asked, "What about our sides?"

"For starters, what did the police tell you?"

"Well," Francine answered, "I first got the call from the sheriff – polite gentleman, but sounded a little rough around the edges by the tone of his voice. Anyway, he's the one who told us Robert was found. Said our boy turned up on the side of the road. Just turned up, can you believe that? They examined his body, the coroner or whatever they're called did. Then Robert's body was …" She choked a little. "Sent back here. Back home."

Leonard nodded and realized he was nervously tapping his fingers on the table. He stopped. "Did you notice any odd scaring or injuries on Robert when you saw his remains?"

"Well," Francine said, and paused to think.

Keith replied, "He had some cuts, minor, all over his body. He was malnourished and thin as a rail. When we cut his hair to have a wake, we did find some cuts and scrapes around his head, but nothing crazy. We figured he'd struck a branch during his escape or something. There was nothing too odd. But his eyes." Keith shuddered and stopped, looking away towards the floor.

"It was like he was blinded, Leonard," Francine stepped in, washing her words and her memories away with a heavy swig of wine.

The hair on Leonard's neck and arms stood up. He knew about the eyes, but he couldn't let them know that he knew. "That's odd. Did he show any signs of having vision issues as a baby? Blindness, anything like that?"

The word *baby* seemed to throw each of the parents overboard. Their eyes welled up. Keith was the first to calm down. He began to speak in a shaky voice, but settled enough to get the words out. "The doctor never mentioned anything about it. For all we and the doctors knew, he was in perfect health. Those things are hard to tell in a baby, though. They stare at anything and smile. Or cry. Or—" He stopped.

"It's alright," said Leonard.

Thick streams of tears began to flow from Francine's eyes. Leonard decided he'd change the subject.

"Did you ever …?" Leonard hesitated. "This is going to sound weird."

"Go on with it. It can't be too weird if it's about our boy," said Keith. His timid eyes had turned to stone. He didn't appear to be mad, or even sad now, just walled.

"Did you ever see Robert?"

"What do you mean?"

"Like, see him around the house? Playing in the yard outside? While you were at work, in the park – anything like that?"

Keith, who didn't appear to have been drinking before Leonard's arrival, made way for the liquor bar. He poured himself a scotch with a heavy hand, and looked at Leonard as though to offer him some. The reporter shook his head.

"Sure, I've seen him," Keith said as he drank all of the scotch in one pull. He poured another and sat back at the table. This one he would nurse. "I saw him almost every day of my life for about six or seven years."

"So did I," wailed Francine, her voice weak and broken.

"Can either of you explain at all?"

Keith sighed. "Well, I would always go into his room. We left it exactly like it was when he went missing, you know? Anyway, I would open the door and look in. Sometimes I'd see him sitting there, his little body lying in the crib, or standing at the rails, looking like a precious little convict. Or sometimes I'd see him in the living room when I was watching TV, or when I drove by the park. I'd always imagine him grown up, playing soccer or baseball or whatever sport he'd want to play. I don't know, because he wasn't allowed to make that choice."

Francine was a wreck now. Keith probably was too, but appeared more preserved, like a sea captain watching his ship take on water. He sat, a man who could withstand anything, until the boat would inevitably become completely submerged. Leonard had a feeling that one misstep, one poorly asked question, could capsize the man's vessel.

"Have you seen him recently? Since he was found? Not in the physical world, but like … like how you were just explaining?"

Keith shook his head. "No, I haven't seen him at all of late. Over the past two or three years, my visions have been less and less frequent, like the memory was dying or something. I felt like I might finally get over the loss until he came back. God, it was hard to see his face again, battered and bruised, a ghost in a casket."

"I cannot imagine."

"No, you cannot." A sip of scotch, accompanied by a sip of wine from Francine. "And I hope that you never have to."

Francine said, calmer now, "What made you ask if we've seen him recently?"

Leonard considered his response. He didn't want to tell them that he had seen Robert himself, or that their child was haunting Oliver. "No real reason," Leonard decided was the best response, but when the words escaped his mouth, he realized it was a stupid thing to say. "I was just curious."

"Curious, why?"

"Because I think this case isn't over. I think that Robert is connected to something bigger than just a lone abduction a few years ago."

"Nine years."

"Yes, nine." Leonard suspected the nine years for this couple must've felt like an eternity. "Anyway, I think there are more children, like Robert, under the captivity of whoever it was that abducted your son. And I intend to find out where they are."

"Please," Francine begged, "please do so. Find them so no one else has to see their boy or girl like we saw our Robert."

"He was hardly even our boy anymore," Keith said, his voice an anvil. "He was changed. There was something about him that just felt off. He was a shell. The soul was gone. I don't think Robert's true self had been in that body for years."

"Oh, stop it, Keith," spat Francine.

The couple looked at each other. Their eyes were glass. The tears on Francine's cheeks had dried and turned a waxy rose color.

"I didn't intend to cause a rift," Leonard said softly. "I just wanted you to know the situation. The cops and the detectives don't seem to give a damn about finding who took your son, but I do. I'm going to figure this out. I can promise you that."

Forty-two

Leading to the barn was a well-traveled trail of beige dirt, scattered with a lay of twigs and small rocks. Manfred left these alone but saw to it to remove a fallen branch if he ever passed one. He particularly liked the rustic look of the small debris. Something about its presence was comforting.

Dust began to coat the traveler's loafers, the speckles contrasting with the black gleam of his shoes. Manfred wasn't much for wearing boots or switching shoes just to walk the short distance to the barn, so he almost always donned his usual attire of button-downs, slacks, and loafers. He didn't mind if his expensive clothes got a little dirty. A two hundred-dollar pair of pants could experience the same wear as a five-dollar pair. It never made a difference to Manfred, who actually liked dressing nice for his visits. He thought it made him resemble a pastor, and it gave him a stronger sense of power. When the children looked at him, wearing nothing but the finest, they respected him more. They knew he possessed a gift that they could only ever hope to obtain – which would occur in time, but only if the children bought into the messages Manfred preached.

Through the door of the barn was a wide, mostly empty room of hay bales and tools which could be used on the surrounding acres. It was a boring looking place, nothing to raise an eyebrow at. Manfred designed the interior this way for a reason. If anyone ever came snooping around, they'd find nothing out of the ordinary. It wouldn't take long for a trespasser to grow sick with boredom. Even if teens snuck in to drink or smoke or fool around, they'd never find his children. The door was buried under eight stacks of hay which completely covered the chained door, each stack weighing about thirty or forty pounds. No one would ever go moving them just for fun. Manfred didn't like doing it but justified the action by telling himself that it was a workout.

After completing his exercise today, and unlocking the cellar door, Manfred found himself standing atop the stairs of his kingdom. He stared down into the black abyss, seeing the longing stares of eight white eyes. The soles of his shoes stayed planted above the first step. He never moved too quickly when making his visits. Like all men of power, of status, Manfred enjoyed the prospects of a good show. His entrance was a ceremony of sorts. He imagined himself an angel, descending from a place the children would not see until the prophecy was in effect.

The four must have worshipped these moments. They must have looked forward to them, waiting at the edges of their cages, unable to rest, like kids on Christmas. Manfred was everything to them, the very breath in their lungs, and he knew it. He brought them food and drink, light, and the sacred words of God. Without Manfred, they would be nothing. They would be like every other lost soul, traversing through life like blind serpents.

Manfred stepped down into the cellar. The light from the barn shone over his shoulder, casting his shadow upon the dark floor. A dimmer switch hung on a post at the bottom of the stairs, hidden from sight of the children. Manfred slowly rode the switch upwards, which caused a faint light to fade into existence, barely eliminating the previous pitch black. The light couldn't be too bright, as it would hurt the children's eyes. Using his foresight when constructing the cellar, Manfred placed sheets of dark cloth over the bulb strip on the ceiling.

"Papa," the voices of the children called out. The sound was a worshiping call, a hymn exalting Manfred. He always loved hearing it, but would never show the children. He needed to remain consistently calm and serene, giving way to no emotional connection. This was the only way to share the word of God. He was not a zealot or a sweaty lunatic in a cheap suit, like the morning television pastors. No, Manfred was much more than that. He was a true descendent, who could converse with the Lord, and carry out what was demanded of him. Sometimes God would even speak through him during his visits to the four, like Manfred was a vessel from which a divine river of words flowed out.

When the dim light was glowing against the faces of the four, Manfred called out, in a gentle voice, "Hello, my children."

He was greeted with more recitations of his favorite call, "Papa."

"Papa."

"I have missed you, Papa."

He was also greeted with the rattling of a cage, joined by repeated curses and insults. The slights erupted from Number Three's residence. Manfred looked at the girl, formerly known as Janiya Peters, and offered a stern glare, succeeded by a gaze of forgiveness. He wanted her to know that what she was doing, her little outburst, was unacceptable but understandable under the current circumstances. It had to be hard for her, being taken from her family and her way of life, but it was to serve a higher purpose. It was vital that it happened, and in time she would learn. After hearing what Manfred had to say, Janiya would accept her role as Number Three. By learning the prophecy and understanding her role in preserving the world, she would cease her outbursts and begin to worship, as the others did. She would call him *Papa* as the others did. She would learn to see through the darkness, in both the physical world and the one unseen, as the others did.

"Number Three," Manfred said in a calm voice, interrupting the continuous stream of insults. "It is not polite to curse and call names."

"Fuck you!" Three slammed her fists against the cage. Her voice was a shriek, piercing the ears of all those in the cellar. "You kidnapped me, you sick fuck! You kidnapped all of us. Who …? What …?" Her pitch was growing higher and higher, and her words began to come out in broken stutters. "Why? Why did you kidnap me? What the hell is this place?"

She began to cry heavy tears. Their splashes off the ground rivaled those made by the habitual drip between the cages. Manfred watched, keeping cool, as Number Three wiped at her face with the back of her forearm. She sucked back her sobs and continued to scream and curse. Manfred felt a little twinge of arousal as she spat fire, but he couldn't allow her to continue.

"You are going to fucking bur—"

"Silence!" Manfred demanded, his words echoing off of the cellar walls. The metal of the cages shook, and the paint tins nearly fell from their shelves. "You will not speak to me like that, child."

Manfred stepped to the ravenous girl's cage and slammed his palms against it. Startled, Number Three fell backwards, skipping her head off the back of the cage and landing hard on the concrete. She yelped with pain and pawed at her skull. There didn't appear to be any blood, which was a good sign. Manfred had only just gotten her and didn't desire the task of finding another teen so soon, though if this new Three did pass away, that just meant she wasn't strong enough – that she wasn't a true angel of the prophecy. It would mean she was just like the original Number Three, who was weak and had the devil in him. That was the reason for his death. God took the boy from Manfred so he could continue with his work, uninfluenced by the soils of Satan. After coming to realize the evils that filled the Banks boy, Manfred dedicated the child's weak body in a shrine to God. He hoped he wouldn't have to do the same with this writhing girl, but would if it was required.

"You're disgusting," Number Three started again, having regained her strength from the fall. "I hope you know how fucking disgusting you are."

"I said, *silence.*"

Manfred pulled a key from his pocket, unlocked the cage, and ripped open the door. His blood flowed through his body, stimulated with authority. He grabbed the girl by her hair and yanked her from the cage to the center of the cellar. The others watched silently as Number Three kicked and screamed more insults. Manfred placed his hand on the back of her neck and pinched, shoving her face towards the other cages.

"Do you see this face? Do you hear these words?" Manfred said, ever gently, like he was putting a baby to sleep. "This is the face and the words of one who has not yet heard the true message of God. Look upon this wretchedness and know that this is what you will become if you don't heed my words and listen to what the Lord commands. Is this what any of you want to become?"

"No, Papa," the children spoke as one.

"She is a sinner, Papa."

"She does not yet know?"

"She will learn."

"Yes," Manfred proclaimed, still pinching Number Three's neck and rotating her face between cages. She was silent now. The only noise coming from her sinful lips was a whimpering. "Indeed, she will. But why? Why must she learn?"

"Because," Number One started, "the prophecy states that there will be four. Four angels of god, each selected by you, our earthly Father and disciple of the Lord. We will one day rule the four corners of the Earth – each commanding the winds, the skies, the oceans, and the land was once dominated by sinners. More importantly, we will command the world that we cannot yet see. We will look through the darkness, uncovering the demons that lurk in it. We will expose them, and they will know the true wrath of God. No longer will they be able to tempt and corrupt the world's people. They will tremble and break before us. Before the four. Before your children."

Like a proud father experiencing his boy's college graduation or hitting his first home run, Manfred beamed. He was elated to hear the words spill from One's lips in such a passionate manner. The boy truly grasped the reality of the prophecy. He was a student of Manfred's messages and would one day lead the four and bring light to the world, with Three by his side — but there was first more darkness to overcome.

"Very good, Number One. My, you have come so far." Manfred smiled at the other two. "How far you all have come! My sweet children."

"What in the actual fuck is wrong with you all?" Number Three cried.

"Quiet, you!" Manfred whispered in Three's ear and pinched, making her wince. "There will not be a message today. You can blame this on Number Three. There will also be no meals, no cleansing, and no restroom, not until she learns to be quiet and respect me and the One who speaks through me. I suspect you three will see to her behavior in my absence. Teach her how we act here, and do not listen to any of her sinning rants or the devilish tales she might try to stray you with. Every word that comes from her mouth will be blasphemy until she learns the way of the four."

"We will teach her, Papa," the children announced in their chorus.

Manfred looked at them and smiled. His eyes met Number Two's and fixated on them. The boy was a good subject. He never acted out or talked back, and he always listened intently to Manfred's messages, but he'd been developing a habit lately, one Manfred needed to nip in the bud. The boy lately seemed fixated on Number Four. Two was always watching her. Manfred noticed a few weeks ago and had been monitoring it while preaching, and through the camera system hidden in the ceiling's fixtures. Any time Two was awake, he was looking at Four's cage. The child's gaze never wavered.

"You."

"Yes, Papa?"

Manfred, wearing an omniscient yet gentle expression on his face, looked at the child. He wasn't quick to respond, allowing the silence to hang over the boy's head like a weight. He wanted Two's mind to scurry in an attempt to figure out why he was being singled out.

"Papa?"

"I know your thoughts, my boy," was all that Manfred said before turning away.

He tossed Number Three back into her cage and locked her up. She squealed as she bounced off the concrete floor. "I expect this one to behave better by my next visit. Understood?"

"Yes, Papa."

Forty-three

Janiya sat in her cage, hungry, scared, and sore. There were three children alongside her, but she'd never felt more alone in her life. She wondered if this was what it felt like to be lost at sea, surrounded by dark, raging waves, losing hope of rescue. She didn't know what to hope for, because she didn't even know where she was.

God, she was scared.

Nothing made any sense. Why had she been taken? Janiya Peters was nobody, just a regular girl, a sister, a daughter. Her family wasn't wealthy and held no status. So why was she taken?

Janiya shuddered with anxious chills. The complete randomness could only mean the man, *Papa,* really believed he was fulfilling some sort of divine prophecy. That was the only reasoning Janiya could give to make sense of what was happening. Papa took her because he really thought she was needed to serve some higher purpose, which was probably why the children clung to the man's every word because they believed right along with him.

Alone in her cage, Janiya began to cry. The voices of the others spoke out to her. Two boys and one girl, all crazed with a sense of fulfillment. Since their papa left, all that the others had talked about was the prophecy and God, who Janiya now knew didn't exist. Every word that left their mouths turned Janiya green. She couldn't comprehend how they could believe in some foolish prophecy.

"How long have you all been down here?" Janiya asked, interrupting the preaching children.

"What do you mean?" asked the girl, Number Four.

"How long have you been in this cellar? This prison? Whatever it is."

"We have always been here," Four said, nonchalant. She had no fear of the darkness that enveloped them. It was her home. "I told you before."

"You don't remember anything before this place?"

"No." Four answered.

"None of you? What about you guys? You don't remember anything?"

"This is the only place," said Number One sharply. He seemed the strongest of the children – the pack leader. "And through that portal is a world of darkness."

"That's not even close to being true," Janiya answered. She did not like this boy and felt guilty for it. He had no responsibility for his behavior. He was brainwashed, raised to believe he was an angel of destiny.

Number One replied, "You do not understand."

"No, you don't. I'm not from here, and neither are any of you. I lived a normal life with my family, with my mother. Do any of you remember your own mothers?"

"We don't have mothers. Only Papa and God. We are his children, which is why we belong to this place. We only know here, because there only *is here*. You may think you know the truth, but you will soon learn that *here* is where you belong. This is the only, one true place of being until it is our time to resurrect the light of the world."

The boy spoke like a prophet, sounding nearly as frightening as their abductor. One spoke about the world almost like a scientist, as if there were multiple levels of reality. Earlier he had mentioned a world that couldn't be seen, and now he was talking about *the one true place of being,* as though Janiya, in her life before the cellar, had been in some false dimension. Janiya didn't know much about multiple realities, or the supernatural, besides what she saw on cartoons and read in books. What she did know was that it was all bullshit. There was only one world, and everyone only had one life.

"You came from beyond the portal." The other boy, Number Two inserted himself in the conversation. Janiya was glad to hear his voice. He spoke with more curiosity. The conviction that fueled Number One was weaker in this boy but was still evident. Janiya wondered what it would take to convince him to start pulling away from the beliefs that had been boring into his head since he was an infant.

"Yes, but it's not a portal. It's just a door. I'm guessing Papa told you it was a portal? To, like, another universe or something?"

"He says it leads to the world we will one day control."

"I don't know about that, but it does lead to the world I grew up in and that all of you *should* have grown up in."

There was a brief silence. Janiya could hear One grunting from his cage. He didn't like her speaking and she knew it, but for some reason, he was allowing her to continue. Maybe he saw it as a teaching moment and was waiting for the proper time to interject and share his wealth of knowledge.

"What is it like?" Number Two asked, his voice rich with interest.

"It's not dark. It's full of trees, beautiful brown trees with big green leaves, and when the weather turns cold, they go orange and red. And there's tall buildings and airplanes and mile-long trains, and dogs and other people. Most people are good and smile at you, but some are kind of assholes. I come from a family full of the good ones. We used to smile a lot. And no one lives in cages or sleeps on concrete unless they do something bad. Then they go to jail."

"Jail?"

"It's a big building full of cages that bad men and women go to. That way, they can't do bad things to any of the good people anymore, but sometimes even good people end up there."

"So it's kind of like ... we're in jail?"

"Kind of." Janiya shrugged, but the gesture was imperceptible in the darkness.

"Do you think that you did something bad?"

"No, of course not."

"What about us?" This time it was Number Four who asked the question. "Did we do something bad?"

Janiya started to fill up with tears. She tried to stop them from coming, but couldn't. Envisioning the children, even Number One, locked up in these cages for some twelve years or so, broke Janiya. What a horrible waste of life. Even if they ever saw the real world, they couldn't possibly be normal. They couldn't adjust to a normal society. Their entire reality was cages and darkness.

"Of course not. None of you did anything wrong. The only person that should be in a cage is your papa."

"That's *our* papa," One boomed. "None of us could ever do any wrong because we are the chosen Four. Whether you decide to believe or not is up to you, but I won't let you speak about our father in such a way."

"Really?" Janiya said, thinking about how she wanted to approach her next remark. She didn't want to drive too large of a wedge between her and Number One, even if he was a prick. She would need him – she would need all of them – if she were to ever escape from the cellar. The decision was made that she wouldn't say anything else to provoke the boy.

"Yes, really," One snapped. "You don't know what you're talking about, but you will soon learn. You will one day be a part of something far bigger than those fantasies in your head."

The tears that Janiya had dammed behind her eyes began to fall. Her life wasn't a fantasy. To the others, it might have seemed that way, but Janiya knew the truth. She lived a good life, though it was sometimes hard, and she was a good person. She didn't deserve to be in a cage. No child did.

"No," Janiya said in a broken voice. "You don't understand, but you will one day. I promise you. We are getting out of these cages. I'm going to see my family again, and you're going to be reunited with yours. That's the only prophecy there is."

"Do you really think we have a family?" asked Number Two.

"Somewhere."

"I wonder what they look like?" Four said.

Number One responded, harshly, "They look like nothing because they don't exist. Stop listening to her. She's trying to fill your head with lies, just like Papa warned she would. We five are a family, and that is all we need."

Again there was silence. It was obvious that neither Two nor Four wanted to challenge Number One. The weaker ones might have been curious, but they still believed they were in cages for a reason. Janiya could tell it in their voices. When they asked questions and spoke about the world beyond the cellar, beyond the *portal,* it was out of interest in the fantasy. Janiya's stories, to them, were nothing more than fiction.

"You will see," Janiya said.

The room went silent again. Number Two and Number Four began dreaming about worlds they had never known. Number One lay down in his cage and began to meditate and pray. Janiya sat there, thinking about her family and rubbing her bruised head and neck. Her skin was sensitive, but it felt good to massage the pain away. In the back of her mind lingered the thought that she would never see her family again. In a whisper, she told herself this wasn't true. She couldn't believe it. She had to believe she would escape. The day that she stopped believing would be the day she became a part of the Four.

Forty-four

The 7-Eleven, the vacant warehouse building, and the decaying dog park surrounded Leonard, who stood on a cracked sidewalk, smelling the faint scent of sewage as it wafted through the air. The sound of a busy city met his ears. People crowded the sidewalks and the lot of the convenience mart, all sweating through their clothes. A passerby asked to bum a smoke, and in the distance, a man was having a conversation with no one at all. Light reflected off of the windows and the gray sidewalks, piercing Leonard's already stinging eyes.

This was the city that Leonard loved. This was his home, and it felt good to be back.

The convenience store clerk who Leonard had just interviewed offered no help. The camera footage from the night Janiya Peters went missing only showed her walking off towards the warehouse and the dog park. The field of view was limited, and the cameras only surveyed the length of the small parking lot. The footage and the night clerk were the last official sightings of the missing girl. Apparently, the police had tried to question everyone on the scene the night that Janiya went missing, but found no help from the interviewees. All anyone said was that she was headed back towards her apartment.

Leonard now inspected the path she was said to have taken. To one side was the park and to the other was the immense building, that while empty and tagged with spray paint, lorded over the street, the ghost of a grander past. It cast its shadow over the two-lanes and into the park. Leonard welcomed the shade. It didn't do much to block the heat, but at least kept his skin sheltered.

The dog park, in a heap of ruin, was very small, clearly not designed to let dogs run wild, chasing Frisbees or tennis balls. The area was just big enough to let a canine off the leash for a bit to keep its waste off the streets. It was obvious that even that hadn't happened in quite some time. The park, Leonard assumed, had housed the tents of the less fortunate for the last five or six years.

There were two tents that Leonard could see, parked beside a shopping cart full of stuffed trash bags and a lean-to. They appeared to be the same tents that Leonard spotted during the STKN report the night after Janiya disappeared. He approached, stepping over the debris of a fallen fence and some plastic waste that would never see another home. He moved past the patches of brown grass and dirt, sure to avoid broken bottles and other trash, but couldn't avoid the fragmented pieces of the chain-link fence, which sprung when he stepped on and over them.

Between the two tents sat a man and a woman. They looked downtrodden, wearing sullen faces, dirty with grime and wrinkles, wounds from the sun and the stresses of living. Their ages were undeterminable. Leonard suspected they could have been anywhere from thirty to sixty.

"Excuse me," Leonard said, seeming to startle the two companions. They each offered a slight jump and shot a look towards the reporter, eyes weary from life's exhaustions.

"What are you doing here?" the man asked. His voice was coarse, as though dirt and fragments of street debris had been accumulating in his throat over the years. His black skin was pocked and dirty, as were his tattered clothes, which used to be a white tank and a brown pair of shorts, now grayed with age. He wore sandals, patched together with duct tape. A gray beard, ratty and long, covered his cheeks and sat below the most tired pair of eyes Leonard had ever seen.

"I just wanted to speak with you," Leonard finally responded.

"Speak with us?" The woman spoke this time. "Now what business you got, speaking with us?"

The woman was white, or used to be some version of white. Her skin glistened with sweat, even in the shade of the warehouse and the makeshift lean-to they had constructed out of discarded cardboard boxes. She was equally dirty and tired. Her hair was long and carried the texture of copper wire.

"How long have you been here?"

"Depends on what you mean by *here*. You talking 'bout this dog park, this city, or this planet?" the man answered.

"This park." Leonard smiled. Something about the man seemed incredibly honest. It might have been his eyes, or his beard, or even the sound of his voice, which poured from his throat like a hot spring, reminding Leonard of his grandfather.

"About two weeks," the man responded.

"You got a cigarette?" asked the woman, before Leonard could question further.

"Sure," said Leonard, pulling a crushed pack from his back pocket. He removed three, lit his own, then helped the man and the woman light theirs. Each drew on their cigarette like it would be their last.

Leonard asked, "You spend your nights here then?"

The woman replied, "Of course, son. Where else you think we're going to be, the Hamptons?"

Leonard laughed. "So you were here two nights ago then? Have you heard about a missing girl? She was young, only thirteen. Went missing two nights ago and was said to be in this location when it happened."

The man and the woman looked at each other while Leonard's voice dissolved in the city's bustle of sounds. They each chased the cherry of their cigarette, a pillar of ash forming on the ends of each.

"We know something about that girl," said the man.

"Really?"

The woman answered this time, "Son, we saw the whole thing."

Leonard's eyes shot open. "Are you serious?"

"Wouldn't lie to you. What reason have we got to do such a thing?"

"None, I suppose." Leonard was reeling to hear their story now. "So what happened exactly?"

The man began, "Well, we were right here, doing the same ole' thing we always doing. Just living. We see this girl walking, kind of jogging, right on that sidewalk there." He pointed over towards the looming red brick. "She was holding a bag, from 7-Eleven's my guess, and looking around, not really paying no attention much. But we was paying attention. That's all we can do, you know? You live the way me and Cat do, ain't nothing more to pass the time than people watching, especially when it gets dark. So we were watching, like we always do. We watched that little girl jog on down the street, then we saw her stop jogging. Out of nowhere come this man, and she goes right into his chest."

A man, thought Leonard.

"Next thing we know, he's dragging the little girl away down the alley. She's kicking, screaming, cussing, all that, but it don't matter none. He had her stuffed in the back of his van before me and Cat here could even get to the fence line."

A van. Could it have been gray? Did it have a ladder on top?

Cat began, "Ain't never seen nothing like that before, Mr ... uh ..."

"Beard, but call me Leonard."

"We've probably seen a hundred fights, and people yelling, shouting, robbing, sometimes even shooting, but ain't never seen no little girl get taken like that, Leonard."

The man scratched his head. He truly looked remorseful, like he could have done something but didn't. Really, he couldn't have done a thing, other than call for help. A man in his condition, even with Cat's aid, would have been easily overpowered.

"You said he tossed her in a van. What kind of van was it? Can you describe it?"

"Well, it was pretty new, a recent year's model I'd guess," Cat said.

"Gray, maybe even silver, and the windows were pretty dark."

"I'm not sure how else we could describe it. It was just a van."

"Had four tires and some doors."

"No, that's good, that's good." Leonard nodded. "Was there, by chance, a ladder on top? Like an extension ladder you might see at a construction site?"

"Nope," answered the man. "No ladder. Just a van, a man, and the poor little girl."

"Anything else about that night you remember?"

Each shook their heads. Their cigarettes were burnt through, all the way down to the filter. Leonard offered them the rest of the pack, as well as his lighter. They gratefully accepted.

Cat said again, "Nothing. We told you exactly what happened."

"It was quick, happened in a flash."

"What did the man look like? Could you see his face? The color of his skin? Anything helps."

"Couldn't see a thing. Not in that darkness."

"Ain't no light reaches that side of the street, Leonard. It was all just shadows basically. The only thing that was clear was the van, once its lights came on. Shame, we can't help you no more."

Leonard cursed the poorly lit streets. "That's alright. What you've told me helps a lot. Have you told anyone else? Police or reporters?"

"No reporters or local police," the man said. "We spoke to a detective though."

Cat intruded, "Some white man. Looked like any other man in a suit, but had a nasty little face, like someone had smushed it down when he was a child. He made sure none of the local PD talked to us."

"Odd," Leonard scrunched his own face. "What did you tell him? Did you mention the van?"

"Sure did." answered Cat.

Leonard retreated into his thoughts of the news reels he'd seen since the abduction. There had yet to be a mention of any a kidnapping or a van departing the scene. They had just been saying that Janiya was missing. Either the detective was deliberately curtailing the story or the reporters were being negligent. Whatever it was, something seemed off.

"Do you remember the detective's name?"

"Called himself Baumgartner."

"No other rank or anything? First name?"

"No. Just Detective Baumgartner."

Leonard began to feel like he was sticking to ground, melting from the heat and pressure of his surroundings. *Detective Baumgartner.* The name echoed through Leonard's skull. Why the hell was this story not on the television? Janiya's face had been plastered on the screen every couple of hours, but just like there hadn't been any reports about Robert's crucifixion, there had been nothing about a man stealing Janiya. As far as the nation was concerned, Janiya was simply *missing*. There hadn't yet been any mention of a gray van. Nothing about an abduction. There was nothing. Holes and gaps were everywhere and Leonard seemed to be the only one attempting to fill them.

"Did you talk to anyone else? Anyone besides Baumgartner?"

"We did tell two little girls," the man said and coughed a phlegm-thick cough. Some of the projectiles got caught in the bristles of his beard, forcing the back of his forearm to act as a towel.

"Two little girls?" Leonard asked.

"Yea, they said they was Janiya's sisters. That's the name of the missing girl, right? Janiya?"

"Yea, that's right."

"Well, we told them, and we said they need to go tell they mother."

Leonard looked up at the apartment building that sat quiet and still on the corner beyond the warehouse building. "The girls who came to you, they live in that building there, yea?"

"Yea, they come from in there," shared Cat. "We seen 'em here-and-there, even before they came asking about their sister. Like we said, we watch everybody. There ain't many people around this area we don't know. And there ain't many that don't know us."

"Well, what about the van then? You ever seen that before?"

"The van, no," answered the man. "Ain't never seen no van like that around this block. Now if it were more beat up, then that might be a different story. Ole Miss Vanessa down on Fifth drives one similar, but it's beat to hell."

An unknown man, driving an unknown van, which just so happened to match the color of one that Leonard and Oliver spotted on the power plant's camera footage.

"Well, thank you for your time," Leonard said, noticing that the shadows of the red building were running away from the tents. The sun was once again beating down on his skin. He had to get into some air conditioning. The apartment building would be a good place to hide away, and Janiya's family might offer him something that they hadn't shared with the police. The chance was slim, but one he had to fish for. Either way, it would be good to speak with the family and let them know that if Janiya's abduction was related to Robert Banks's, Leonard was going to find her. That was a fact that he'd never been more certain of in his life.

Forty-five

"Come on now. You have to be more patient than that. Stop acting like this is your first time," Oliver said as Becca reeled in her line.

The father-daughter duo stood at the edge of a small pond, one Oliver was certain had never been fished by anyone but he and Becca. The water was murky and still, pooled up in a gulley near the train tracks that ran south from the train yard. It was so close that, if standing in the right spot, Oliver could see the tops of the freights roll past as they carried their haul from one Midwest state to another. The pond wasn't stocked and rarely supplied a catch, but it offered a tranquility that brought Oliver back again and again. There was a peace in watching the pond water drift in ripples with the wind, in observing the wheat around the rim bow, and in listening to the occasional interruption of a train. Oliver enjoyed being the only soul present, save his daughter, who often accompanied him.

"You and I both know that it doesn't matter what I do, I'm not going to catch anything." Becca frowned and cast her line again. Oliver watched the tiny splash made by Becca's lure as it sunk into the opposite end of the pond.

"Nice cast."

"Well, you know, I'm kind of a pro by now."

They stood, watching the sun reflect off the dark water. The silence was serene. Becca tugged on her line, hoping her worm would appeal to one of the few fish swimming the depths. Oliver pulled his gaze to his daughter, whose hair sparkled in the dying light. Her cheeks – pale, round, and speckled with freckles – gleamed just like her mother's used to. The sight of her there, Converse sinking in the mud of the pond's shoreline, nearly crippled Oliver.

"You look a lot like your mom right now."

Becca turned and looked at her dad, eyes glistening. She kept her hands on the fishing rod and continued to gently tug the line. Eventually, she peered back over the pond. A soft wind crept in and bent the growth that protruded from the water.

"What was your favorite thing about her?" Becca asked, her voice drenched in the grief of memory.

"Everything," Oliver responded.

"That's a cheap answer."

"I mean it." Oliver laughed, eyes beginning to feel heavy. "Every Goddamn thing, I loved. I remember she used to hold you when you were little, and caress your three little wisps of red hair, and tell me how big you were going to grow, and how your life was going to turn out. She used to call you Becca-Bear, sometimes Becca-Boo. She'd giggle every time you responded to either of those. I remember …" Oliver reeled in his line, letting the sound of his voice fuse with the nature around him. "I remember everything about your mother, but what I remember most is how much she loved you, loved being your mom. That's probably what I loved most."

Becca began to sniffle and distracted herself by reeling in her line. Once the lure popped out of the water, it revealed a chunk of plant gunk had wrapped itself around the hook. The glassy-eyed girl peeled the mess off her line and tossed it aside. She wiped her hand on her pants, set another worm, and cast the line again, choking back sobs. Oliver wrapped his arm around her and pulled her head into his shoulder.

"I love you, Becca-Bear."

"I love you too, Dad."

The harmony of the moment had Oliver considering his recent life choices. He wondered if it would be too late to change some things. Maybe he could drink less, and smoke less, and try and go back to school for a trade or something. He always liked welding, though he'd never received any formal training. Maybe he could do that. This moment made him realize he needed to do whatever it took to ensure the best possible life for his daughter. He didn't want to be the cause of his own death. The thought of Becca parentless made Oliver want to sink into the pond.

"You know, you're not crazy for talking about Mom so much," Becca said.

"Thanks, Becca."

Oliver needed to hear her, his daughter, say that. It didn't matter what anyone else thought, but Becca's opinion was everything. No one else in their little county understood what it was like to watch their loved one wither away with disease. If they did, they'd know Oliver wasn't crazy, he was just pained.

A buzz erupted in Oliver's pocket, pulling him from the peace of his moment. Becca left his shoulder as he removed his phone to see that Leonard was calling.

"Hello?"

"Oliver, it's Leonard."

"I know. What's going on up there? You finding anything?"

"The girl who went missing the other day – she was abducted. And guess what kind of vehicle was spotted leaving the scene."

"Oh, I don't—"

"A gray minivan."

Oliver nearly dropped his rod into the mud. A gray minivan was one of the few cars on the list he and Leonard had made while watching the security footage from the plant. It wasn't an incredibly rare car – in fact, it was just the opposite – but it was suspicious enough. In the pit of his stomach, something was saying that the boy and the girl were connected, and the van was the same van they saw on the footage. Oliver figured Leonard's gut was saying the same thing.

"You sure there's no other cameras down there? Perhaps one that might have caught a license plate or anything?"

"Come on, Leonard. You've seen the place. Unless someone was standing beside the road that night, filming with a night vision lens, that plate didn't get captured."

There was a huffing on the other end of the line. Oliver looked at his daughter, who was staring up at him and tugging on her reel, face twisted with concern.

Leonard spoke, "Well, I'm still trying to figure some things out here. I'm about to go speak with Janiya's family. Going to see if I can figure anything out that might help me find her. I just have this feeling, you know? Like, I can just tell. I know that these two abductions are linked."

"I do too. I felt it as soon as you mentioned that minivan."

"Well, I'll keep you informed, and you keep me informed. Let me know if anything turns up down there. Maybe ask around town, try and see if anyone happened to spot that minivan. Longshot, I know, but it's worth asking about."

"Will do, Leonard. You take her easy now."

"Yea, see you later, Oliver."

The phone call was brief but cumbersome. Oliver felt himself drifting further into the shoreline's mud. He wanted to ask how Leonard found out about the van and how he knew Janiya was abducted, seeing that the news was only saying she was missing. His mind was plagued with a lot of questions, but he didn't want to disrupt his moment with Becca. There would be time to call Leonard back. It's not like Oliver Brady was going to be the one to solve the mystery anyway. He was no one in a nowhere town. How had he even gotten himself wrapped up in a kidnapping scandal?

"You alright, Dad? I heard what y'all were saying."

"I'm fine," Oliver said, looking at his daughter, and he meant it. He was as fine as a man in his state could be, because he was with her.

"Okay, then."

When he looked into Becca's eyes, the eyes of her mother, Oliver saw the universe. For the sake of knowing what it was like to have a child, he really did hope that Leonard could unravel the case. He couldn't imagine what it would be like to be the parent of a missing kid.

"Dad, look!" Becca shouted. Her line had begun to yank away from her, the rod bending towards the water.

"You got a bite!"

Becca pulled up on her line and began to reel in the fish. Oliver watched, taking in the twinkle in his girl's eye and the smile on her face. She reeled and pulled until a little fish, the size of a coin purse, flopped onto the shoreline. In that moment, Oliver was the happiest he'd been since Lela left.

Over Becca's shoulder, the sun reflected off the golden wheat, causing the horizon to look as though it was on fire, capturing Oliver's attention. That was when the boy appeared. For a moment, Robert stood there, looking down on the two of them like a tiny God. His hands were outstretched, just as they were when Oliver first found him. When their eyes met, a flash erupted across Oliver's mind, and suddenly he was elsewhere. He was standing center in the dark walls of a cellar. There were kids in cages surrounding him. Four children.

They were skinny and pale, hollowed-out casings of teenagers, except for one. One was different. One was unlike the others. The girl, who Oliver recognized, lunged towards the door of her cage and started to speak, but he never heard her words. A flash erupted again, and he was back at the edge of the pond.

Shocked, Oliver fell backwards into the mud. Becca cackled like a lunatic as she yanked the fish off her hook. She then held the lake creature up like it was a prize bass. It flopped and pleaded to be placed back in the water.

"You alright, Dad?" Becca laughed as she tossed the fish back to the center of the pond.

"Yea, I'm fine," he said again, his voice less sure than before. A headache split his temples, cutting behind the bridge of his nose. "I'm fine."

Oliver looked back up to the top of the gulley. The boy was gone.

Behind the father and his daughter, a train began to rumble by. The vibrations helped steady Oliver's heart. Becca plopped down in the mud beside him and buried her head into his shoulder. They laughed. He was once again at peace, for the time being at least. He couldn't let the boy spoil this moment.

Forty-six

Manfred stood in front of his bathroom mirror, staring into a set of shameful eyes, having just given way to one of the torments of the human body. Regretfully, he washed his hands and flushed a handful of tissue paper, attempting to find some sort of resolve by telling himself that even he, a descendant of God, had to indulge in the pleasantries of mankind every once in a while.

After the incident with Number Three and the others, he had no choice but to find some relief. It had been a long time since he'd felt so powerful. The old Number Three was basically born to Manfred and adopted the messages early. Banks never contested, just like the others. *How could they? They didn't know any better.* But this new girl, she was causing a rift. This fact was something Manfred was ambivalent about. On one hand, she would likely slow down the process of God's work, but on the other, she would test Manfred's ability to teach and be a true prophet of the Lord. It was a conundrum, but Manfred was ready for the challenge.

Looking into his reflection, Manfred found himself yearning for that sense of power he felt earlier when he was making an example of the girl. Janiya really was everything that was wrong with the world, entitled and rotten to her very core. Manfred would fix that, while he transformed her into Number Three. And after, he would fix all of humankind.

Water and lavender-scented soap washed over his hands. Manfred splashed his recently shaven face with water. It felt cool on his cheeks and raced down to his chin. His black hair looked greasy from sweating into the gel. The simple brush of a hand did the trick of cleaning it up.

"God, forgive me for what I have just done," Manfred said to the ceiling, hands spread out on the marble of the bathroom sink. "I am sorry to have sinned against You. I am doing my best to carry out Your word. Please forgive me, and give me strength in the future. Forever, and ever, amen."

Outside of the bathroom, Manfred prepared his things for his trip to the city. He was going to visit his father, and after that, Brianna. He would see to it that she was cleansed.

Forty-seven.

The inside of the apartment building reeked of wet carpet and mold. The building was tall, but the ceilings were low, the hallways consisting of long stretches of gray carpet and cream-colored doors. Some doors had mats in front of them; others didn't. The only signifying symbols were the numbers, like 2-A and 3-F, that carried on in succession down the lines of doorways. Leonard was on the fifth floor, looking for the door that read 5-K.

The hallways were loud, a result of the thin walls. The incomprehensible sounds of music, televisions, and chatter bellowed down the hall. Leonard listened as he walked. The place reminded him of his childhood home, a memory he wasn't incredibly fond of. It brought on memories of Dad coming home from work, stinking of smoke and whisky. Liquor had always caused him to become a different person – a more violent version of his already tainted self.

Leonard shook his head. He didn't have time to reflect on his past. He needed to find the Peters' residence. One foot fell in front of the other until he was standing in front of what he was told had been Janiya's family's home. Apartment 5-K's door stood still, blank as the rest, possessing no welcome mat or identifiable personal touch.

Leonard knocked firmly three times and waited. After a moment, it swung open, revealing a little girl, no older than nine. She stood short and slim, her hair tossed up into two curly tails. She was cute, and resembled the girl who Leonard wanted to find. It was evident right away the girl who opened the door was one of Janiya's sisters.

"Who are you?" the girl squeaked in a mousy voice.

"My name is Leonard Beard. I was here to see if I could speak to your mom. Is she around?" Leonard looked past the little girl, examining a crowded apartment, crammed thin with three other children. One was an older girl, maybe eleven, and the other two were boys who looked incredibly alike, twins most likely, no older than three or four.

"What you want ta speak ta her for?"

Before Leonard could answer, another voice yelled from across the apartment.

"Jasmine! You better let that man in if he's here about Janiya. Why else a boy that young and dressed like that want to see Momma for?"

The voice came from the other girl. Leonard met her eyes, and she smiled faintly before her face contorted into a frown. Her entire body was slumped with the kind of exhaustion that a girl her age should never have to feel. Leonard suspected she spent a lot of time babysitting the kids, especially now that the oldest was missing. This, combined with the physical toll of dealing with the loss of a sister, was an unforgiving cocktail.

"Well," the little girl, Jasmine began, "Jade says you can come in. Momma's in the back room. I'll go get her."

225

Leonard followed Jasmine into the apartment, where the heads of the children all shot glances his way. The twins only looked a short moment before turning back to their television set. They watched a show that Leonard didn't recognize. The older girl, Jade, followed him with pleading eyes that said, *please find my sister.* She looked away towards the boys and smiled, distracting herself from whatever thoughts were haunting her.

The carpets were the same color as the hallway's and stained in several places. The walls were cream-colored, just like the door, and adorned with portraits of the kids. Leonard looked for Janiya's but couldn't spot one.

"You here about Janiya?" asked a voice from behind Leonard, interrupting his observations. He knew before he even looked that it was the children's mother.

"Yes," Leonard said as he spun around. "I'm Leonard Beard, an investigative journalist with Arches, Inc."

"I'm Janiya's mom, Dani. Them twins there are Jamel and James. You met Jasmine at the door, and that one there is Jade. Not sure she introduced herself to you or not."

"She didn't, but she let me in, kindly enough."

"That's fine of her. So, what questions you got, Leonard? Let's see if you can come up with anything I haven't already been asked. Go on ahead, whenever you're ready."

Dani walked past Leonard. She was tall, about an inch or two taller than he was, and quite trim for having had five kids. Her face was worn, exposing the memory of when she used to be very pretty. She looked tired from working and tired from losing a child. The past few days had to be the cause of a few of the lines on her face.

"I'm not sure I can ask you anything special, anything that no one else has asked," Leonard said as Dani reached into a cupboard. From it, she plucked a plastic cup that had scratches and nicks running its surface. Into it, she poured water from the tap.

"Then what good are you?" Dani asked, irritation flowing through her voice like the water from the tap, thick and cold.

"I'm just here to learn about her as best I can. I'd like to hear from you, from her family, rather than from the reporters, who honestly, don't seem to be doing their jobs."

"Ha." Dani forced a short, sharp laugh. "Police ain't either."

"No, I agree, they aren't." Thoughts of Farnswell and Detective Baumgartner crossed Leonard's mind.

Dani softened up a bit but still looked numb like she was floating through life in a robotic state of functioning. She moved because she was programmed to move. She ate and drank, and went to work, took care of her babies because she was programmed to. She was a powerful woman, Leonard could tell. It couldn't have been easy, functioning after losing a child. He needed to let her know that he was going to find her.

"You here to do their jobs for them then?"

Leonard shrugged. "To be honest, I don't know. I'm not sure I have a clue what I'm doing. I'm just trying to put together a puzzle, a difficult one, that I believe involves more pieces than just your daughter."

"What do you mean?"

"I'll explain, but first, could you describe to me everything you remember about the night Janiya went missing?"

"I can't tell you much. I had just gotten home from work that night, about eight, maybe nine o'clock. Kids were working on homework. Janiya was babysitting, helping them where she could. Boys were watching TV, I remember that, and they came jumping on me soon as I walked through the door. Janiya yelled at them, playfully, telling them to *hop off*. That was the last thing I ever heard her say." Dani wiped her eyes, though Leonard spotted no tears in them. The well must have run dry over the past forty-eight hours. "I went in my room to shower up and get ready for supper after the boys climbed off me. I come out, and she's gone. We waited a bit because the girls said she went out, said Janiya was going to come right back. But she never did. So we went looking. And that's just about all. We couldn't find her. No one can, apparently."

Leonard shook his head and looked at the girls. They were now both sitting at the dining room table, listening to the conversation between the stranger and their mother. The boys were still sunk into the television set.

"She told you two where she was going?" Leonard asked.

Jade spoke first. "She didn't really tell us where she was going, but she didn't have to. She'd only go to one spot after dark around here."

"The 7-Eleven?"

"Yup. She said to me, watch the kids a bit, I'll be right back 'fore Mom's even out the shower. So I knew that's where she was going. I mean, only a few blocks. Shouldn't have taken her more than ten minutes. She goes there all the time."

"She was helping me on my homework right before she went ta the store." Jasmine began to cry, her sobs small and hopeless. "Who's going ta help me with flipping my fractions now?"

Leonard shook his head, unsure how to answer. How could he answer? There were no words in the English language that could help a little girl cope with the loss of her sister.

"I'm going to find her," he assured, though when staring into the eyes of Janiya's sisters, and of their mother, his certainty teetered. They'd be counting on him now. Before, it was just Janine, hoping he'd unravel something to spin a story. Now, he was looking into the eyes of a missing girl's family and telling them he was going to find her. Failure would mean so much more at this point. To the girls at the table, and the boys at the TV, and the exhausted mother beside the sink, it would mean the world.

Leonard looked back to Dani, longing to redirect the conversation. "Did you happen to speak to a Detective Baumgartner?"

"Yes," she said, placing the cup on the counter and crossing her arms.

"What did he say to you? Did he mention anything about an abduction or a man in a gray van?"

Dani sighed. "No, he didn't say nothing about no gray van. That's them's down at the park story. Those crazies told them two the same thing," Dani pointed at her daughters. "This whole thing's a mess. I don't believe nothing come out that man and that woman's mouths. I'll let the real reporters and real authorities do the investigating."

Leonard wanted to curl away. For some reason he felt fond of Cat and the nameless man. Dani didn't share the same sentiment.

"Well I'm going to leave their story on the table," Leonard said and shrugged. "You never know."

"I guess."

"Do you happen to have the detective's contact info?"

"He left me this," Dani replied and walked to her fridge, plucking a small card from it. She showed the information to Leonard who snapped a picture. He would be certain to contact the detective later.

"Thank you," Leonard said, now feeling as confident as a rowboat captain. The waves of the investigation were beginning to rage around him. Until he stepped into this apartment, Leonard was positive that he would be the one to do what the police and the other reporters couldn't. But now, he wasn't so sure. He might have been tossing out his only working oar, sipping his last drop of water, when he looked back to the girls and said, "I'm going to find your sister. I promise you that."

Forty-eight

The television was on, but he wasn't watching. It only helped Leonard avoid the mental entrapment of silence. He wasn't even aware what channel was streaming. His eyes were through the window, watching the swaying silhouettes of sidewalk trees. Behind them were the darkened presences of old homes, constructed with brick and plaster. They were beautiful in the daylight but looked haunted after the sun set.

His mind was racing. Legs kicked up, bare feet resting on the coffee table, Leonard sat, thinking about everything. An untouched glass of gin sat on the table. He had poured it thinking it might help, but the smell made his stomach turn. There was something about drinking, in that moment, that seemed repulsive.

Clyde County, the sheriff, Oliver, the Peters family, and the detective he'd yet to meet all flashed across Leonard's mind. On a loop, he replayed everything that had taken place over the last few days, constructing his own highlight reel of investigative experiences. Every conversation, every sight he took in, every beer he drank with strangers, every painful interview with the police, and the message he had just left on Baumgartner's voicemail rolled across his living room like the channel streaming on the TV.

In the midst of recollection, over and over again, Leonard found his thoughts wandering to Jennifer. Every time his mind drifted towards the notion that he wouldn't find Janiya, or the other children,

Jennifer's face appeared. Leonard could see her deep blue eyes and her dimpled smile. He could smell the scent of her cinnamon hair and feel the softness of her skin, could hear the soothing notes of her voice, asking him questions with her touch of a Southern drawl. He wished she was sitting beside him. If she was, his mind wouldn't have been twisting into knots. He'd have someone beside him saying, *It's alright. You're going to figure it all out.* Instead, he was trapped in the complex web of his own thoughts, infected with anxiety and uncertainty.

Leonard looked at his phone, which sat on the couch beside him, screen facing towards the ceiling, black and calm, reflecting Leonard's face so he could see the top of his forehead. No one had texted or called since he had returned to his apartment. This normally was welcomed, but right now, Leonard hoped that someone, anyone, would reach out. He needed something to break up his thoughts, to jumble his scattered mind and offer a different picture to look at, but nothing came.

Leonard stood and reached for the gin, then walked around his apartment, letting the sounds of his feet against the floor make concert for his ears. Movement was nice. Activity was always good at pulling his mind from stressing, though walking the length of an apartment wasn't much of an activity. Not knowing what else to do, he brought the glass up to his lips, but again, couldn't stomach it. The stench of the poison drove off his desire to numb.

The thought of texting Jennifer, or maybe even calling her, laid assault on Leonard's mind. He wanted to reach out to her and tell her he needed her to come up. They hadn't talked since he left her standing in her home. He should have just kissed her, invited her to come to St. Louis with him, but was too worried doing so might complicate his investigation. What a stupid thought. He should have just done it, just committed. It's not like she was really going to jeopardize anything. For all Leonard knew she might have strengthened it, offered different perspectives, kept him sane if nothing else.

Leonard walked to the couch and snatched up his phone. He searched for her number, planning what he was going to say when she answered, but before he could dial, a flood of green and white texts poured across his screen. They were from Oliver.

He had seen the boy again. He had seen other children too, living in a cold darkness. One of them was the girl Leonard sought – Janiya.

Forty-nine

The South City Helping Hand Home was quiet, as it usually was. It stunk of people who weren't quite at death's door, but were close like they were playing croquet in the front yard. Manfred leaned on a table in Manny's room, observing his father's habit of eating from only one corner of his mouth. It was odd, but so was everything that took place in the home. Manfred wondered if his father had always eaten in such a fashion. He searched his mind, but couldn't recover a memory of his dad doing so. That wasn't to say much; he couldn't recover many memories of dining with the man.

It wasn't a good night for the withering brain inside Manny's skull. The disease eating his mind was steadily making progress in its mission to destroy every memory the organ ever saved. Manfred contemplated how long it would be before his father forgot who his son was entirely, or who *he himself* was, and just delved into vegetation. If he had to place a bet, he'd probably guess within the next year, two at the very most. Manny could hardly even wheel himself to the bathroom without getting lost. He struggled to feed himself, often forgot where he was, and could never remember that Manfred was his son.

This was a painful fact for Manfred to grasp. Seeing his father lose memories of their times together hurt. He had forgotten about Manfred's first day of school, their first time seeing the Cardinals play, watching Shakespeare at the Muny, and their times together in the basement, where Manny first showed Manfred what it meant to be a man of God.

Manfred would never forget. He would keep their memories alive for as long as he could – possibly until his own mind faced the degenerative torments which rotted his father's. He would always remember every lesson Manny taught him, every fine time they had together, as well as the bad ones. The occasional raise of the voice or stray hand would render themselves forever in the back of Manfred's thoughts. It would be a disservice to act like those things never happened.

No matter the circumstances, Manfred had always loved his father, even when fingertips fell to Manfred's cheeks, or below the belt of his trousers. Sure, as a boy, Manfred was uncomfortable, but now, he understood his father's motives. Every action his father committed was done in order to build Manfred into the disciple who would fulfill the prophecy and salvage a dying world. Manfred now appreciated all of the sacrifices. He appreciated every single memory, even if Manny couldn't anymore.

"All done," his father said as he dropped his dinner tray on the bed between them.

"Dad, you almost cleaned your whole tray. Nice job."

Manny looked at Manfred with a pair of distant eyes. They said, *I don't care what you think because I have no idea who you are.*

"I'll get it cleaned up for you," Manfred said as a single tear strolled down his cheek.

Unable to stand the sight of his dying father any longer, he grabbed the dish and told him goodbye. A day wasn't planned for his next visit. He was too overwhelmed with dismay in that moment to do so. It didn't matter anyway. Manny would forget as soon as a time and date escaped his son's mouth.

The parking lot to the home was almost empty upon arrival, so Manfred was able to park near the lobby's main doors. Now, he strutted across the lot to the first row of spots, unfortunately guiding himself to his minivan. He didn't choose to drive the van unless it was required, and his Lexus was in the shop receiving new ball joints, so the van it was.

It wouldn't be too much of a hindrance, he decided, seeing as he was about to visit Brianna. It might even come in handy.

Fifty

"Wake up, Brianna."

Brianna's eyes opened, and she shot upright, causing the thin blanket that covered her body to fall to her lap. Her skin was now exposed, and a needle of chills zipped through her spine and down her arms. Her eyes darted to each corner of the room, but they only saw the familiar darkness that filled her walls every night. She had heard a voice, she was sure of it.

"Angel, did you hear that?" Brianna asked the man sleeping next to her. The caretaker's boyfriend, who had shared a bed with her for the past three years, lay still, sound asleep. He was usually a heavy sleeper, but the voice that called seemed so real, so close, it should have woken him.

"Angel," she said again, louder this time. "Did you hear that?"

The brown body of her boyfriend remained still.

"Angel!" Brianna nearly shouted, her heart beginning to beat faster than normal. When he didn't move again, she gave his body a violent shake. As her palms met with Angel's skin, they were greeted by a warm, sticky substance.

Brianna, horrified, flicked on the bedside lamp. His face, illuminated by the light, revealed a black beard and hairy chest, glistening with fresh blood. The brown skin around his neck was stained red, as was the bedsheet beneath his curled body, acting as a sponge. A jagged slash trenched the length of Angel's neck.

He was dead.

With a hard shove from her fumbling, wet palms, Brianna pushed her boyfriend away. Her body slithered in retreat, frantically kicking off the sheets. She was scared and wanted to scream, but her voice was lost. In the fit of fear that overcame her, Brianna's body grew numb and powerless. No longer able to control her muscles, she fell from the bed to the floor, planting two bloody handprints into the white carpet.

"Brianna."

The near-naked caretaker, cold and trembling with fear, shot a look towards the closet door. From the darkness emerged a man. He wore a skull cap over his head, along with rubber gloves and rubber booties. Though masked by darkness his face looked vaguely familiar.

"You're ..." Brianna found her voice as the glow of the bedside lamp shone upon the intruder's cheeks. "I recognize you. You're from—"

"Be quiet now," the man whispered and stepped over her, a foot on either side of her body. Kneeling, he shoved the blade of a bloody knife towards her face. Brianna winced in fear, instinctively doing as she was told. She was certain now who the murderer was. His father was a resident at her work. Manny or Manfred, or something like that.

"You," the intruder began, his knife still lingering before her face, dropping her boyfriend's blood onto her lips. His full body weight was on her waist now, and his free hand gently made for her throat. Brianna shook as she felt the clasp of his gloved fingers. "You are a cancer. You think you can just barge into people's lives, into their privacy, and say whatever you please?"

"What are you …?"

The gentle hand around Brianna's throat tightened, forcing her vocal cords to collapse.

"I said, I want silence from you." Each word was a whisper. "It is not polite to interrupt."

Brianna's eyes were watering, as was every other part of her body. She sweated with fear. Never before had she felt so helpless. So alone.

"You insulted me. You said that what I had done was *disgusting*. And when you speak ill of me, you are speaking ill about Someone much more powerful, much more divine than myself. Do you believe in God, Brianna?"

God wasn't a part of Brianna's life. She had never gone to church, not since childhood. Her life was science and medicine, with rules and formulas. She never understood how someone could believe in any God, any supernatural, unexplainable being. But right then, as Manfred hung over her, threatening her existence, Brianna began to pray.

"Yes," Brianna quivered. In her head, she was pleading for the Baptist God, who she knew as a child, to come and rescue her.

"That wasn't the right answer," Manfred said softly. "Because if you believe in God, then you understand that she who blasphemes the Lord shall surely be put to death!"

"No. Stop, please!" Brianna shouted, seeing the knife pull back and then slide into her stomach. Any strength that she had was gone. She saw the knife again, then another flare of pain erupted in her belly.

"God, help ... help ... someone ..." Her voice trailed off into nothingness as the blade sunk into her organs, over and over, leaving her thoughts to run through ancient memories.

Brianna did not go to sleep earlier that night with the mindset that it would be the last time her head ever touched a pillow. She didn't eat leftover Chinese food, thinking it would be her last meal. She didn't avoid making love to Angel, thinking that their last time would be their last time.

If she had known this night would be her final one, Brianna would have done so many things differently. She would have never laid down to sleep. She would have made Angel take her to dinner downtown. After, they would have gone for drinks. They would have gotten drunk and come home and fucked – the kind of sex they used to have, when they were newly in love and still passionate about each other. After, sweating, content with the life they'd built with each other, content with the night, they would have turned on a record and watched the moon drift across the sky from their balcony terrace, awaiting their deaths. They wouldn't have made any of the choices that they actually made.

As breath escaped Brianna's lungs in stuttered gasps, her vision began to fail. With every blink of her eyes, the room grew smaller, darker. The man who stabbed her was standing now, wiping his knife on one of Brianna's garments. The whites of his beady eyes shone upon her.

"Why?" Brianna managed. The sound of her failing voice frightened her. She began to twitch in uncontrollable spasms. Her skin grew cold, and she began to cry, not from realizing her death, but realizing her past and how she hadn't even told Angel she loved him before they went to bed a few hours ago. They just ... went to bed.

"Because the world cannot exist with people like you in it. To hell is where you'll go. And my children will take you there."

The sureness in the man's voice was horrifying. Brianna didn't believe in hell, even when she was a churchgoer. The concept always seemed to contradict the message of God, but when her murderer spoke of hell, the place seemed as real as the holes in her stomach. Brianna began to think that maybe she was going to burn for eternity, but the thought faded with her own defiance.

No, she told herself, *I will not burn.*

This man would not kill both her body and her spirit. Brianna would not let him determine where she was to end up in the afterlife.

"No." Brianna's voice was but a whimper. "But you will, if that's a place you believe in."

The man only laughed. Brianna watched as he crept away, leaving her lying there, gasping for air. As the door closed behind him, three new faces emerged – the faces of children.

Brianna wanted to say something, but no longer had the ability to do so. She could only lay still and watch as the children inched towards her. Their bodies were thin and white, clothed in rags, and their eyes were like galaxies.

"Come now. Come with us," one of the children said in a soft voice, placing an icy hand on her bleeding stomach.

And Brianna went.

Fifty-one

The door to the apartment closed behind him. A yellow light from the stairwell blanketed Manfred who walked away cautiously, scanning the area but seeing no one. The entire complex was dead.

Once in the van he removed the booties, gloves, and the skull cap, placing them in a Ziploc bag. The sound of the elastic pulling against his skin made Manfred cringe. He tossed the bag underneath the passenger seat and stuffed the knife into a wooden box that he'd bury later, along with the garments. Turning the key in the ignition and hearing the soft sound of the engine, Manfred let out a long sigh. It wasn't a desperate release, but one of pure exhilaration. His body was surging. His cock swelled against his jeans. Only a few times before had he felt such elation.

The drive home was suffocating. It was an impossible task, sitting idle while the world rushed by. He had so much excited energy flowing through him. As he pulled away from the lights of the city, Manfred realized he wasn't going to be able to make the full trip without stopping. In the distance the yellow signage of a Shell station worked hard to light up the sky, cut in half by the surrounding trees. The lot was nearly empty when Manfred pulled in, which wasn't out of the ordinary. He was about fifteen miles south of the city and it was roughly three in the morning. There was only one worker inside and a pickup truck at the pumps.

Manfred pulled to the front of the station. The sole worker didn't say a thing when Manfred zipped by, headed straight for the bathroom. Normally, this would've insulted Manfred, but he was so focused he hardly took notice. He had to get to a stall immediately. Good for him, the bathroom at this establishment was a single room with a door that locked. A restroom for multiple customers wouldn't have stopped Manfred from doing what he had to do, but he'd obviously rather have the privacy that this one offered. Inside, he dropped his pants, nearly ripping his belt in two.

When he was finished, Manfred stood a moment, breathing heavily and gazing at his reflection in a stained mirror. His face appeared dirty now, ashamed. The excitement was gone and replaced by dread. Quick thoughts of being caught by the police darted through his head. Would they find his DNA? A hair, maybe some of his sweat on Brianna?

No, Manfred told himself. They wouldn't find anything. He was too cautious. There wouldn't be any prints. That's what the booties and the gloves were for, and the skull cap would've kept any hairs from falling on the ground. His face was clean and every morning when he showered, he made sure there wasn't a hair on his body. There's no way he could've left any traces of himself at the apartment.

A smile came back to his face at thinking of the apartment. Seeing the sinners punished by his own hand was like a drug. Visions of the two naked, bloody bodies sparked in his mind. God, it felt good to do the Lord's work.

Manfred washed his hands and splashed his face. When he left, he made sure to tell the worker, "Good morning."

Fifty-two.

Friday morning, a week after Robert was found.

In the kitchen, Leonard fried some sausages and whisked some eggs with milk. A pot of coffee dripped in the corner. The mixture of aromas wafted through the air and met Leonard's nose. It was enough to pull his mind to thoughts outside of the investigation for a moment. The smell reminded him of times at his grandma's, growing up. Every Sunday morning she'd have Leonard's family over for breakfast. Grandma always fixed a feast and had a large pot of coffee brewed, which she'd sip all day, her cup eternally full. She'd always sip it so gingerly, with two hands wrapped cautiously around the cup, and smile at Leonard. Her voice was sweet and slowed by age. She'd ask if Leonard was doing alright in school, and no matter his response, she'd slip a dollar in his pocket and tell him to *keep it up*, always followed by, *and don't tell your Daddy 'bout that dollar.*

Leonard rolled the sausages over in the pan. He didn't want to think about his father. All he could think about was his phone in the other room. Before breakfast started, he'd listened to a voicemail left by Detective Baumgartner, who'd called back very early in the morning. The detective said he'd be free to speak around noon and now Leonard couldn't stop thinking about what questions he was going to ask. There was so much he wanted to know.

Leonard lowered the heat on his stovetop and moved to the living room. He clicked the home button on his phone, watching the

247

screen brighten. It revealed a notification from his local news app, but nothing else. A second take at the notification from STKN sent a spin of dread through Leonard's body. In a frenzy, he scanned the room for the television remote, flipping throw pillows over until he found it.

On the TV, two people hung in frame, a man and a woman. They were smiling in their photos, but the anchor's voice and the thread of text which scrolled below the images were grim. The couple had been murdered in their own home. The on-scene reporter, who stood in front of a generic looking apartment complex, stated that the man's throat was slashed and the woman received multiple stab wounds to her stomach. Both were presumed to have been murdered around two in the morning. Forensics was still working the scene.

"Jesus," Leonard said quietly. The word fluttered away as quickly as it sputtered from his mouth.

As the story continued, Leonard found his head beginning to ache. Sharp pains like pinpricks assaulted the area between his temples. The pain wasn't on the skin but under it. Leonard pawed at his skull like a madman, wincing and shaking as he dropped to his knees. His vision began to fade, his room turning to splotched pixels of color. Suddenly, he was enveloped in complete and total darkness, no longer kneeling in his apartment, but somewhere else entirely.

Fifty-three

Janiya lay in her cell, eyes closed, drifting through stages of consciousness. She could no longer make a distinction between being awake and asleep. The room was too dark, and her mind was too traumatized to discern between the two. She constantly hoped for sleep, thinking she might wake up somewhere else, but every time her eyes opened, it was the same dark room that greeted her.

Her dreams were surreal. Every time Janiya closed her eyes, she was transported to places that she'd never seen before, places she hadn't known her mind could even project. Sometimes she stood on the white sand of an endless beach she'd never been to, watching as waves tumbled into the shore. The warm water would rush over her feet, wash her toes with grains of sand, and give a slight tug as it pulled back to the ocean. Sometimes she'd be standing in a large field of grass, the brightest shade of green she'd ever seen. Goats wandered aimlessly, plucking at the blades and bleating to one another. She'd be transported atop a mountain, surrounded by blinding snow, but was never cold, even when the wind whipped and swirled the snow into violent flurries. Janiya would walk to what felt like the edge of the world and consider jumping, but never did.

She was constantly in this state of dreaming, even when awake, which made distinguishing between real life and dream life nearly impossible. There was one moment when she thought she was wide awake, when she appeared in a field of wheat, still stuck behind her cell's wires, staring down the scattered stalks of gold to a pond. At the water's edge, there stood a man and his daughter, fishing the depths. This particular dream stuck with Janiya because it seemed so real. When the man met her eyes, it was like he could see her, like he wanted to say something, to reach out to her, and then he disappeared. The image of his slack jaw and head of red hair had seared itself on Janiya's brain. She hadn't stopped thinking about him since. It was ridiculous, Janiya knew, to fixate on a dream, but that's all she had.

The concrete floor pressed cold against Janiya's back. She lay there, thinking about thinking, counting the rise and fall of her chest as her lungs worked tirelessly to keep her alive. It was a funny notion, she thought, that the body kept itself alive even in such shitty circumstances. Lungs couldn't determine if the life they gave breath to was worth it; they just did their job. The cells in Janiya's body understood nothing but survival. Even though she wished she were dead, wished that she would pass away in her sleep, her body kept on working.

Janiya felt herself beginning to drift. Her eyes rolled to the corners of their closed lids. She was floating into unconsciousness now. *Please*, she hoped, *please be the time when I wake up away from this cell.*

When Janiya came to, she was standing in a room she had never been before. It was someone's home. Barely used furniture cluttered a living room, encircling an unstained coffee table. Every piece was directed towards a television set, which aired a news station. The walls looked

250

old but were well taken care of, housing cheap art and a few potted plants. It was a nice enough place and smelled of breakfast.

Janiya hadn't eaten in what seemed like days, and the scent nearly drove her mad. In search of the source of the smell, she paced the house. Around a small dividing wall she found a kitchen, where sausage links and eggs simmered and a big pot of coffee steamed. The smell made her ravenous. Janiya's stomach rumbled, sending her lunging towards the skillet like a starved dog. She had never been so hungry.

As she snatched a handful of the sausages and began stuffing them into her mouth, Janiya heard a voice call from behind.

"Hey."

She turned to see a man standing in the kitchen. He was black and moderately handsome, but nothing special. His face was clean-shaven, and he dressed like an accountant. Really, he was quite unremarkable but looked intense, driven. His young eyes, peering into Janiya's, burned with a mixture of emotions.

Suddenly, the two were taken away from the kitchen. In an instant, they were standing in a chamber of darkness, one that wasn't quite the cellar, or quite anywhere at all. It was, unexplainably, an empty void. Surrounding the two was nothing, just an endless sea of black. There was a single, bright shaft of white light boring down on them from above, from nowhere. The man's eyes bounced, shifting frantically, confused. For a second, he looked like he was going to speak, but didn't, so Janiya started.

"Well, this is new." She began to walk, laughing as the cone of light followed her like she was pacing a theater stage. She sounded crazy, laughing like that, even to herself.

When she stepped through the emptiness, her feet made no noise, as though they were floating through the vacuum of space. The man drifted behind, cautiously. He was observing her, probably scared, definitely bewildered. Janiya wondered where her mind had pulled this projection from. She had never seen this man before as she had never seen any of the things in her previous dreams.

This man reminded her of the red-head. The way he looked at her made him seem real. Janiya might have been able to reach out and grab hold of him – that's how real he felt. She might have been able to tell him that she'd been kidnapped by some God-crazed lunatic. If only she weren't dreaming, she might have used him as a means of escape, to help her leave wherever it was that she and the other children were being stored.

"What's your name?" Janiya stopped and asked, looking across the blackness to where the man stood. Face clouded, he rubbed his eyes and pinched his skin. At that same moment, Janiya realized she still had a handful of sausages. They felt incredibly real in her palm, and when she put them in her mouth and chewed them up, they had a taste and a texture. *How strange,* Janiya thought, but was so hungry she didn't question it.

"Leonard," he finally answered. His voice sounded unsure of itself like he had just woken up from a thousand-year nap. It was more of a tremble than a response. The words vibrated through the void in an almost tangible wave of sound.

"Hello, Leonard. I'm Janiya."

The mention of her name was like a shifting fault, causing the void to quake. It shook, and then began to collapse upon them. The blackness, seemingly endless before, was now shrinking like an imploding star. The shaft of light shot up through the void above them, disappearing completely and leaving them sightless. Suddenly, they were back in the cellar. Janiya was back in her cage. The man, Leonard, was standing in the center of the four cells, staring in disbelief.

His eyes darted along the walls of the children's home. Unable to see as well as the children could, unadjusted to the darkness, Leonard stumbled forward with his palms out in front of him. It would have been a funny sight under different circumstances.

"Leonard." Janiya laughed from her cell. Just as the stranger's eyes shot towards Janiya's and locked on to them, he was gone. All that was left was the cellar, the children, and the ever-present *drip-drop* of water.

Janiya moved to the edge of her cage and wrapped her fingers around the thin wires. She shook the mesh as hard as she could, and at the top of her lungs, she screamed. It was an ear-piercing, guttural screech, birthed by the pain of realizing that she would never again be free. Her only escape from the cellar would be in the form of dreams.

Fifty-four

Leonard, head throbbing, stood in his kitchen scratching at his eyes, wondering if what he just witnessed was real. He had seen the girl, had been within arm's reach of her, trapped in some empty hall of darkness. He had seen her in his kitchen too, and inside what appeared to be a cellar of some sort. There were others in the cellar, three children along with Janiya, all locked in cages. He must have dreamt the whole thing. The last thing he remembered before passing out was watching the news and seeing the report about the murdered couple. From there, his vision went black.

In his staggering contemplation, Oliver came to Leonard's mind. He needed to contact him. Just last night, Oliver had described a similar happening, that he had seen Janiya and the other children. Was it possible, Leonard wondered, that he and Oliver had dreamed of the same place? As crazy as the idea seemed, Leonard felt a twinge of belief. He had been in a whirlwind of turmoil since his arrival in Clyde County. Reality itself was beginning to lose form. Leonard could no longer determine what it meant for something to be or sound crazy.

The reporter hustled through his apartment in search of his phone. On the screen was a missed call from Jennifer, along with a voicemail and a text from her that said, *Call back when you can*. As much as he wanted to ring her, he couldn't. Leonard had to contact Oliver first. He had to know if they had seen the same place, the same children. It was possible, Leonard thought. They'd already seen the same boy, who happened to be dead. Maybe Leonard and Oliver were linked in some way.

The phone rang three times before Oliver answered. "Hey, what's going on, Leonard?"

"Oliver. Last night you texted me, saying you saw the girl, Janiya. You saw more children too. Where were you? The place they were kept in, what did it look like?" The sound of his own voice caught Leonard by surprise. It was frantic and rushed. His heart was thumping like a stalked rabbit's. He needed to calm down, to breathe, to relax. A racing mind wouldn't help him in any manner.

"Well," Oliver said slowly on the other end. His mind seemed to be searching for an exact recollection of the event. "I was just fishing with my daughter, as I explained in the text. We were having a good time, laughing and talking, though we weren't catching any fish."

The Southern man and his storytelling. Oliver sure knew how to drag out a moment that didn't need to be dragged.

"Anyway. We're fixing to leave 'cause Becca finally caught something, when I look up the hillside, and I see the boy again. Looked like God, arms stretched to the sky and all that. Scary as hell he was, only this time, I had a different feeling. Almost like a familiarity with him. Like I'm getting to know him or something. I mean, I was still frightened by him, don't get me wrong, but not as much as usual. So I try to just brush him off like I ain't see him. Then I see a flash."

"A flash?"

"Yea. Then my vision went black, and suddenly, I wasn't at the fishing hole no more."

"Where were you?"

"It was brief, not more than a few seconds, but I was standing in some cellar or something. It was dark and eerie as can be. There was just a feeling about the place. It felt heavy in a way I can't even explain. Ugly sight it was, and cold too, all concrete walls, reeking wet with mildew. There was shelving, like it was a storage cellar or something, holding paint tins and gardening tools, but that wasn't the only thing it was storing. There was also them kids. They all looked like Robert, with pale little bodies, so white they could be seen in the near pitch-black room. It was horrifying to see them, three like that, looking all kinds of sick, malnourished and mistreated. Then I saw another child. A girl. It was the one who was taken just recently. I knew it was Janiya as soon as I saw her."

There was silence on the line for a moment. Leonard heard Oliver swallow from the other side of the phone. His voice was vibrating with unease. Leonard was uneasy as well, because the place Oliver was describing fit the place he was just transported to.

"The girl looked right at me, Leonard. Like she could see me. Like she could have reached out and touched me. Or I could have touched her. Like, er, I don't know. I wonder if I could have pulled her from that cage, had I been given more time, but before I could count to ten, I was back at the pond, standing by my own girl, like nothing happened. My daughter didn't even seem phased. She just laughed, like I didn't go nowhere at all. But I swear, it felt real, as real as seeing that boy. And I know that you know what it's like to see that boy."

Leonard stood there, thinking of what to say, how to respond. His mind was tangling in his pounding head. The ache splitting Leonard's temples grew worse with every word Oliver uttered. It was as if Leonard's brain was swelling inside of his skull, pressing against the bone.

"I saw the same place," Leonard finally said. "Just now. No more than a few minutes ago. At least I think it was just a few minutes. It was like I was dreaming, but also not dreaming. I can't explain it."

"You saw the cellar? The children?"

"That, and more. I also saw Janiya in my kitchen, rummaging through the food on my stove. And then I saw nothing."

"Nothing?" Oliver sounded confused.

"Nothing at all," Leonard said, searching for words to describe the void he was taken to. "It was literally an emptiness. Nothing but hollow darkness. Janiya and I were standing in an endless void of black. I can't explain. There are no words to describe *nothing*, *nowhere*, but that's where we were. We were nowhere at all."

Again, silence.

"And then?" Oliver eventually asked.

"And then we were in the cellar. The girl spoke, and the void collapsed. Next thing I knew, we were standing in the cellar, and she was in a cage, as were the other kids. My experience was like yours. I only had a few seconds to examine the place. I was looking around when I heard Janiya say my name. She said, *Leonard,* almost like it wasn't a real name at all. Like she was just playing a game. And she laughed. Then I was back here, back in my apartment."

"Wow," Oliver said. The heavy falls of his breath echoing through the phone. It was an uncomfortable sound, but everything about the last twenty-four hours was uncomfortable. "Did you have a headache when you came to?"

"Yea, I have one right now actually. Like I woke up from a binge."

"That's how I felt after I left the cellar. Mighty painful, isn't it?"

Leonard didn't answer. He didn't need to explain, as Oliver already knew how painful the aches were.

"What if we ain't just seeing things, Leonard?"

Fifty-five

Like a fly in a web, the notion that there was connectivity between everything stuck in Leonard's mind. Ever since his phone call with his Oliver, Leonard couldn't stop thinking about the statement.

What if we ain't just seeing things?

Was it so crazy to think, in their dreams, their visions of the children, they were actually being transported somewhere? The two men might not have been physically taken to the cellar, but their minds were. Leonard knew with great certainty that *when* he found the children, the cellar would be where he'd discover them, and it would look exactly how he and Oliver had dreamed it.

Parked outside the South City Helping Hand Home, Leonard thought about the investigation and the way he felt when he had looked at Janiya in her cage. Something in her eyes told him he was close. He had been losing confidence in himself, but not now. Now he felt like he was on the doorstep.

After returning from the cellar, and taking his call with Oliver, something urged Leonard to investigate the murdered girl. He thought the best place to start would be her former place of employment. Observing the building, Leonard spotted plenty of cameras on the walls. This was probably to keep an eye on escaping residents. They were a good sign because if none of the employees could help him, the cameras might. It was a stretch, but so was everything.

Before he went in, Leonard looked at the clock and realized he had to make a call.

"Detective Baumgartner," a sharp voice said into the line after a few rings.

"Good afternoon Detective, this is Leonard Beard. I've been trying to reach you. This morning you left me a voicemail. Said you'd be free around this time. Do you have a couple minutes?"

"A few," he seemed disgruntled, "let's make it quick."

Leonard put the phone on speaker so he could write on his notepad. "You are the leading detective on the Janiya Peters case?"

"Yes."

"So you were on scene the night of the abduction?"

Baumgartner responded strongly, "There has been no affirmation of an abduction Mr Beard. What makes you say that Janiya was abducted?"

"I was told by eye-witnesses that Janiya was thrown into the back of a van the night she went missing."

"Eye-witnesses?" Baumgartner asked in annoyed disbelief.

"Yes," Leonard realized his tone was overly firm so he eased up. "I spoke to two people yesterday afternoon who said they saw the entire thing."

"And who were these *witnesses?*"

"One is named Cat, and the other is a man whose name I didn't catch."

"Cat and a nameless man," the detective exhaled again and laughed. Leonard grew red with embarrassment. "You talking about the homeless couple? Ha! What a crock that is."

"I don't think we can just throw their story out like nothing, just because they're homeless."

"Who said we are?"

"Well, the laughter made it seem so." Leonard was sweating. He felt like he was back in journalism school, like he'd never interviewed before. "So you know about the gray van and the man who took her?"

"I know what Cat and the nameless man said about the gray van and the kidnapper, yes."

An awkward silence hung between them. Leonard felt a like a fool. He sat a second and listened to the hum the AC in his car before asking, "Are you going to do anything about them? The van and the kidnapper? Because I haven't seen a word about it on the news. And the witnesses also said that you told the other officers not to—"

"Stop, Mr Beard. Just stop."

"Stop what?"

"Look, this is an active investigation. I don't have to tell you what my motives are for keeping this quiet. Take heed when I say, don't try and come forward with this shit about a van or an abduction. I don't know exactly what happened to Janiya yet, but I'm real close. I deal with enough of you reporters running around and fucking things up. I don't want this case to be one of them. Do you understand?"

Leonard could only stare out the window towards the Helping Hand Home. His mind was blank from shock and anger.

"Silence is consent. Now if you get any *real* information, you'd best contact me before anyone else. I mean it. You contact me first, Beard." Baumgartner said and hung up. The command in his voice made Leonard feel like nobody, like less than nobody. He was just an ant looking up at a boot.

Clouds swallowed the sun. Leonard took observance as he crossed the parking lot to the home. The temps weren't hot, but the air was sticky. Leonard's arms glistened with moisture and his pants stuck to his legs, but it was better than cooking under the usual rays.

Inside, the home didn't offer much of a saving grace from the weather. The air was warm, keeping at about seventy-eight degrees. Probably because the halls were riddled with people on the last leg of their life. The elderly were scattered everywhere, coughing into handkerchiefs, playing backgammon, and watching daytime television. The place even smelled old. It brought Leonard to thinking about his grandma again, specifically her car, a Buick even older than she was. The thing possessed the same odor the home did and was constantly hot. Leonard could recall, with great clarity, sticking to the leather chairs in the summertime. Wearing shorts was torture. His thighs would bond with the leather like it was some sort of adhesive. Peeling them away when they reached their destination was always miserable.

Looking around made him miss Grandma, and miss the dollar bills, and her sweet, slow voice, and even the cheek kisses. Luckily for her, she never saw a home like this. She passed suddenly of a heart attack at the fine age of seventy-three. Thinking on it, Leonard wasn't sure there was ever a fine age to die.

"Can I help you?" a voice asked in a mechanical tone of kindness. Leonard turned to see a lady in pink scrubs standing beside him. She was incredibly short, which was probably why she caught Leonard by surprise.

"Um, yes, actually. I'm here in regards to Brianna Kellerson. I'm a reporter for a local agency, and was wanting to ask some of the employees a few questions about her."

The caretaker's eyes began to fall, her cheeks sinking right along with them. Leonard scanned her uniform for a nametag but found none. That was an odd choice by the home, he thought. Most of the residents' minds were deteriorating, why wouldn't the staff wear something that helped them discern between the caretakers?

"I'm Leonard Beard, by the way. What was your name?"

"Claire," she responded, still shaken at the mention of Brianna's name.

"I'm sorry about what happened, Claire."

"It's okay," Claire responded, although it wasn't. Nothing about the last week was *okay*. "What can we help you with, Mr Beard?"

"I really just wanted to ask a few questions. Get a feel for how Brianna was as a person. See why someone wanted to ... you know."

"To kill her," Claire said bluntly.

"Yes. That."

"Well, there's about five caretakers, other than myself, on duty right now. You can ask me whatever you want, though I'm not sure how much help I'll be. I'm not sure how much help anyone will be for that matter. Brianna was such a sweet girl. She never did a thing to make anyone mad. Always thinking about everyone but herself."

Claire began to well up. She tucked her head into the crook of her arm for a moment. Leonard watched, awkwardly, like the stranger he was. He didn't know if he should try and say something to comfort her or just continue standing there. He chose the latter.

"Follow me. I can't talk right here, in front of everyone. I need to sit down."

The caretaker turned and moved down a hallway. Leonard followed close behind, continuing to observe the residents as he passed them. When they approached a door, strictly meant for employees, another caretaker passed by, pushing a man in a wheelchair. Leonard looked him over. His skin was a yellowish-gray and hung loosely around his face, like the bones in his skull had shrunk with time. His eyes were doll-like, cold and motionless.

Leonard nodded at the man and then looked at the other caretaker.

"Hello," he said.

"Hi," the caretaker returned with a smile.

She continued to push the chair, but as the man passed Leonard, he began to mutter something, inaudible at first, but then clearly, "You." The man lifted a thin, shaking finger, pointing at Leonard's chest. Then again, "You."

"Me?"

"The devil is in you, boy." The man's voice was like the cracking of a whip, sharp and harsh against the ears. "I can see him, burning in your soul."

Leonard stood aghast, staring at the old man. Claire had stopped walking and turned to face the proclaimer.

"Oh, stop it, Manny," the unknown caretaker said.

"I'm sorry, Leonard." Claire jumped in from behind. "He tends to speak off the rails sometimes. Come on, let's get to the break room where it's quiet."

Leonard kept following his guide, but his eyes were fixed on the man in the wheelchair.

What the fuck?

Fifty-six

None of the caretakers were much help in contributing to Leonard's investigation, though they were very willing to share their testimonies. Through six teary-eyed conversations, all Leonard had learned was that the murdered caretaker was an incredibly nice woman who had no enemies. Leonard was starting to suspect it was the boyfriend, Angel, who was the reason the couple was murdered. None of the caretakers, Claire included, could say much about him, other than that, if Brianna chose to be with him, he was probably a saint.

Leonard now stood in front of a television set, looking at camera footage from the night of the murder. Neither he nor Claire, who was showing Leonard the film, knew if what they were doing was legal or not, and neither cared to know. They had already breezed through the footage from during Brianna's last shift. It offered nothing of interest, so Leonard suggested skimming the previous two days' worth of film to see if anything might pop out at him. He didn't expect to find anything. Really, he was just scratching and clawing for a clue that might help him reach the children.

The footage only showed areas of the parking lot and the backside of the building. There was no need to film the inside of the home. The cameras were installed to ensure that residents didn't escape and get lost out in the streets, Claire explained. The footage was blurry but better than the power plant's, and even with the advances of modern technology, it was black and white.

Together, Leonard and Claire fast-forwarded through hours of film. There were countless images of men, women, and children, moving in and out of the home's doors, their legs moving rapidly under the film's expedited viewing mode. Leonard watched with a keen eye, mainly focused on the parking lot. He was growing tired from focusing his eyes on a single point for so long. Both were exhausted, on the verge of shutting off the film, when Leonard spotted something.

"Pause the footage," Leonard demanded sharply like the world might end if Claire didn't halt the camera at that exact instant.

"What is it?" Claire asked, pausing the camera.

"There." Leonard pointed at a fixture in the parking lot.

"What about it?" Claire asked.

Leonard didn't answer. He couldn't tell her everything he had experienced over the past couple of days. He couldn't tell her why he was transfixed on a minivan parked in the front row of the home, looking like a beacon of light under the black and white storm of static. He couldn't have possibly explained what he was thinking or feeling. He could only ask her to roll the camera back and watch who stepped from the driver's side door.

"Just play it, please. Slower this time. At regular speed."

Claire, wearing a mask of confusion, did as he asked. She clicked *play* on the monitor, and both of them watched a man step from the van. He was tall and slender, with a severely dark head of hair. His face, though blurred in pixels, looked clean-shaven and narrow. By all accounts, he looked normal. For all Leonard knew, he was normal. There was no way of knowing if this was the man who had stashed four children in a cellar somewhere or murdered Brianna Kellerson and her boyfriend, but for the sake of the investigation, Leonard had to act like he was.

"Do you know that man?" asked Leonard, still watching as the stranger crossed the parking lot. He was dressed fancy, too much so for the ragged heat of the city, but that wasn't necessarily a red flag. It just meant he liked to dress nicely, or he had a job that required him to do so.

After some consideration, Claire said, "Yea, I know him. His name is Manfred. He's in here about once or twice a week."

"Really?" Leonard asked. His heart began to jump. "Who does he visit?"

Claire looked strained. Leonard knew she wasn't allowed to tell him that kind of information, but she probably wasn't allowed to show him camera footage either. What they were doing was wrong, but they were doing it in order to possibly find a murderer, a kidnapper. Leonard hoped this sense of higher service would force Claire to bend the rules just once more, but she wouldn't.

"I can't tell you that. I'm sorry." She shook her head. Her face showed that she truly was sorry, and also a little guilty, like she was letting a murderer walk.

"That's fine," Leonard said, looking back at the screen. It continued to roll, showing more visitors streaming in and out, but Leonard only focused on the parked vehicle in front of the home. The license plate was hidden behind some shrubbery in the divide that separated the parking lot from the drop-off lane. There was nothing Leonard wanted to see more than that plate number, but he never would. Eventually the man, whose first name was all that Leonard knew, crept back across a moonlit lot and into his van. The lights turned on, and the van pulled away, leaving Leonard agitated. He had to find out what his last name was, and who he visited in the home.

"I really am sorry, Leonard, I just don't want to jeopardize my employment."

"It's fine, really, but I have to ask, is there one more thing you could do for me?"

"Sure, depending on what it is you're about to ask."

"Can you replay the footage from Brianna's last shift?"

"Well, I guess so, since we've already watched it. What are you looking for?"

"I don't really know," Leonard lied. He knew exactly what he was looking for. He hoped to find that man again. In Leonard's stomach, something churned, telling him he would see Manfred at some point during Brianna's last shift.

Claire searched through the footage history and again, played the film they'd already exhausted their eyes upon. Leonard watched the screen in forwarded motion again. He watched the lot intently until he found what he was in search of. The slender man walked out into the parking lot sometime around seven o'clock, but he disappeared into what looked like a black Lexus this time.

Leonard continued to watch with cautious eyes until he saw Brianna walk out of the building. It was like watching a ghost. She bounced, her body still full of life, towards a Corolla. When she ignited the vehicle and backed out of her spot, leaving the view of the camera, Leonard kept his steely gaze. He was waiting for something – hoping for something, really.

Not more than ten seconds after Brianna's vehicle disappeared from the lot, a black Lexus crossed the field of view. Leonard watched the vehicle drive down the drop-off lane, making sure to write down the plate number. As soon as the last digit was etched onto his notepad, images began to flash across Leonard's mind. Images of the children, the cages, the cellar, and then a vivid recollection of the man in the wheelchair – the one who shouted at Leonard just hours ago.

By the time Leonard's vision steadied, the lot was empty. The Lexus had disappeared in the same direction as Brianna's Corolla. Leonard's chest began to ache with excited anticipation. He needed to find out more about Manfred.

"Claire, thank you so much for helping," Leonard said, his heart still seizing.

"No problem, though I'm not certain it helped much. All we did was watch people walking in and out of the building."

Not quite.

Leonard wished he could explain everything. If he could have just told her the truth of the story, in a believable fashion, Claire might have told him the man's full name and who he came to visit, but there was no way Leonard could accomplish the task.

"One last thing," he said.

"What is it?"

"Manfred, does he come to visit the man in the wheelchair, who we saw in the hallway earlier?"

Claire didn't respond, but her face revealed everything Leonard needed to know. Judging by her expression, the answer to his question was undeniably, *yes.*

Fifty-seven

"My children," Papa said.

He stood in the center of the cages, underneath the dim light, holding a tray that contained four bowls. His body was slender and lined with elegant clothing. The hair atop his head, as dark as the cellar walls, was combed neatly over his narrow skull. The clean-shaven skin around his cheeks was tight. Every inch of his face was thin, throwing shadows underneath the rigid angles. His eyes were small and rich with emotion.

Janiya hated everything about this man.

"I have brought you all breakfast," he continued, voice filled with elation. He sounded as though he had just won the lottery. A wide smile was fixed upon his face, chiseled into the bone by some unknown sculptor. He looked manic – evil, in its purest form. Janiya gagged at the sight of him and considered vomiting through her cage's mesh. Some of the bile might land on the fancy shoes of her kidnapper. That would be a perfect scenario, but more likely, she would just ruin her cage and be forced to fester in the scent of her own puke. In both scenarios, *Papa* would likely throw her against the concrete floor or smack her up and down.

Janiya rubbed the bruises left under her skin from his last visit. Remembering his strong hand around her neck and the way he tossed her so casually to the floor made Janiya decide against vomiting. She sat at the back of her cage, calmly watching through the links as the man distributed bowls to each child. He served the others first, finally settling in front of Janiya's cell, holding a bowl of food that was hardly food. It looked like something a cat might eat, wet and brown, stinking of some undeterminable ground meat and vegetable medley.

"If I open your cage, are you going to be a good little girl?" asked the vile man, voice maliciously smooth. Janiya wanted to spit in his face but knew what the repercussions for that would be. She remembered him saying the others would not eat until she cooperated. She didn't want them to suffer, and her stomach yearned for food, aching from hunger pains, so much so that even the slop in the bowl was appetizing. Looking at it, Janiya decided she would be a *good little girl* if that's what it took to survive. She didn't want whatever had happened to the former Number Three to happen to her – not yet, at least.

"Yes," Janiya replied, feeling like an insect.

"Yes, what?"

After some hesitation, Janiya answered, "Yes, *Papa*."

The sound of the word leaving her lips made Janiya cringe. This man was not her father, not her papa, not her caretaker, not God's descendent, not a fucking thing. This man was nothing but a stain on humankind's history.

"Very good."

He pulled open the cage and slowly lowered the bowl. Janiya knelt at the back, wanting to be as far away from him as possible. She watched his beady eyes, black and soulless, as they stared into her own.

They glinted as he smiled at her. If she wasn't so weak and hungry, Janiya might have lurched towards him and clawed at his pupils. Maybe she could pluck an eye from a socket before he knew what was happening. God, she hated him, but she was hungry. Her empty stomach growled and her mouth watered for the unknown hash.

"Oops," the man said as his hand neared the concrete floor. Unsure what he was talking about, Janiya offered a befuddled gaze. Her kidnapper smiled and turned over his wrist, dumping the meat onto the concrete floor. Her stomach cried out in agony as he closed the cage, leaving the overturned bowl behind. The spilled contents mocked Janiya, who felt like crying and screaming and dying.

"I am so terribly sorry, Number Three. I forgot how heavy those wooden bowls can get. Please, do forgive me."

The man looked down, wearing a face that read, *You better say something. You better be a good little girl.*

Janiya glared as she said, "It's okay, Papa."

The man perked up with her words, like he had just received a shot of testosterone in his ass. He strutted around the cellar with a peacock's gait, basically prancing. The bounding happiness was more horrifying than when he was enraged. It meant he was getting what he wanted, which sickened Janiya.

"Now eat up," the man said as he skipped to what looked like an old fridge. From it, he snatched four bottles of water, which he distributed to each cage. When he stood in front of Janiya's cage, he spoke again. "I said, *eat up.*"

Wanting no more abuse, and even more so, no more attention from the man period, Janiya did as commanded. On her hands and knees, she crawled to the mush and began picking it off the floor and putting it in her mouth. It tasted of concrete and smelled rank. Janiya gagged but forced the food down her throat. After a few bites, she found the meal growing more and more bearable. Her hunger far outweighed her desire for a nice meal of sausage links, like she had eaten in her dream with Leonard. The floor meat would have to suffice.

"So good!" the man bellowed with cheer. "You are learning quickly, Number Three. You are doing so very well." He turned to face the others. "And you all. Thank you so much for steering her towards acting with some dignity. I half-expected another outburst, but she has proven me wrong, and I thank you three for that. I don't know why I ever doubted you all, my beautiful children. Such gorgeous children."

Janiya muted the man by thinking of her siblings back home, her real home. She tore off the bottle cap and began drinking her water. The feel of it against her lips was like nothing she'd ever experienced. Never before had she gone so long without drinking. She didn't even realize she was so thirsty until she held the bottle between her hands. Now, as the water poured down her throat, Janiya understood what it meant to be without.

"I want you to finish your meals and savor your water. I have been out all night, doing the Lord's work." The man spoke in his typical prophetic fashion. "I must go and clean myself. Wash myself of the world's filth. After, I will return to you."

He held out his palms as if to say *sorry*. The other three children groaned. They did not want him to leave. Janiya longed for nothing more. The sight of him made her body shrink.

"I will have a message prepared when I come back." He looked at Janiya. "Hopefully, when I return, you will begin to learn what it means to be a part of the prophecy; to be one of the four."

Janiya nodded and smiled as best she could. She wondered what her teeth looked like, what her breath smelled like. Was her hair ragged beyond repair, stained with whatever grime existed on the concrete floor? How badly did her body stink?

"I am looking forward to delivering the message to you, Number Three. The others have grown accustomed to hearing the word of God, the *true word*. But I must believe that you have never heard anything containing a shred of truth."

He stopped his speech and chuckled. It was a type of scoffing laugh, like he knew something that society didn't. Really, he was just an asshole who knew nothing. Unfortunately for the other children, this man was all they'd ever had. They couldn't compare his detestable acts to those of a good man, or his messages to those of a good preacher. Every word that left their papa's mouth was like a nugget of gold to them. Even at that thought, Janiya had to correct herself. They probably didn't know what gold was, or the value of it. All they knew was the frantic words of a madman.

"I will be back in no time. I expect your bowls and your cages to be clean upon my return," he said, moving to a shelf in the corner. He retrieved and distributed a hand towel, wet with some cleaning agent, to each cage. "It will also be our time for hygiene. Please hold your bladders until then. Goodbye, my children."

The man disappeared to the top of the staircase, closing the cellar door behind him. Janiya laughed to herself as the room returned to a mask of darkness. She thought about how Number Two believed the door was a portal to some other world. How did he even understand what a portal was? Had their papa told them?

"Thank you, Number Three," Number Four said.

"Thank you for what?" Janiya answered. Every time she spoke, the sound of her own voice startled her. In the dark vacancy of the cellar, every noise was altered.

"For not causing a fuss. For helping us eat."

"Don't thank her," Number One ordered from the confines of his cell. "She did nothing but behave as she should. She should be thanking us, for not telling Papa that she was spreading falsities in his absence; or that she was trying to lead us astray from the righteous path, talking about her other world like it was something great. And she should be thanking Papa for allowing her to eat and drink. His mercy is the only thing that keeps her alive."

Number Four answered carefully, "You're right, Number One. You are always right."

At that moment, Janiya wished she knew how to pick a lock. The brainwashed child, Number One, made her want to peel the skin away from his bones. He was like a miniature version of their papa. Janiya wanted to break from her cage and into his. She wanted to drive her fist into his pale chest, and again into his pale chin, until he realized the real truth, that the cellar was nothing but a prison. It wasn't a world of their own. They weren't training to fulfill a prophecy or to rule the world. They were just rotting and waiting to die.

"Don't listen to him, Four. Number One has no idea what he's talking about. He is an idiot. All that he knows is this Goddamn cellar."

At Janiya's taking of God's name in vain, the three others gasped.

"You—" Number One began to stumble for words.

"Me," Janiya responded. "Me. What about me? What have you got to say?" Her words echoed through the cellar. She could feel her body growing hot.

"Don't you dare," commanded Number One, his voice shaking with anger. The fact that he truly believed in the prophecy made Janiya even hotter. She was mad at the child but furious with the kidnapper. He had taken these children's lives, and now, he had taken Janiya's.

"I will do what I want," Janiya answered. "You don't command me."

One began to scream out another demand but was interrupted by Number Two, the curious boy. "Please, just stop." Two spoke softly.

"Silence, Two," Number One ordered.

"No." Two replied.

"That's right. You don't control any of us." Janiya said.

Four spoke up. "No, One is right. We should all be silent and wait for Papa. And you should consider thanking Papa for your meal, Number Three."

Janiya thought she might explode. The way the other children spoke was as tormenting as their papa. The four children's words collided, mixing together in a heated cacophony of adolescent voices, making what was being said undeterminable. Janiya's head began to hurt, and her mouth grew dry with exhaustion from debating, but she kept on with the shouting match.

"Please, just stop!" Two screeched, silencing the others.

With the high-pitched belt of Two's demand came a piercing ring like a bomb had just exploded in the cellar. The sound bored through Janiya's ears and into her head, sending shocks of pain through her body, forcing her to her knees. She plummeted to the floor, and her hands shot up to form cups around her ears. This was an instinctive motion. Her body was trying to silence the ringing, but it was impossible.

She writhed in pain, closing her eyes until the dim light of the cellar came to life and illuminated the cages, flickering upon the rattling steel. Janiya looked around to see One and Four curled in the same position as her. They lay on the floor, hands pressed to the sides of their heads. Two was standing still, looking scared and confused. It felt like one of the dreams, but Janiya knew it wasn't. She was actually there, in the cellar, in her cage, watching the strange phenomenon unfold.

After a moment, the ringing stopped. The cages silenced and the children's hands fell from their ears. All was back to normal, except for the overhead light, which slowly faded back to darkness, shedding a gently disappearing brilliance on the four children who shouldn't have been where they were.

Fifty-eight

"Are you serious? After everything, after a week almost, that's all you've got to tell me?"

"Well ..." Leonard hesitated, too afraid to tell the truth and risk sounding insane.

Janine stood in front of him, wearing a sharp, discontented look on her face. Apparently, what Leonard had gathered so far wasn't quite cutting it. He had told the true story of the boy and everything that happened in Clyde County, save a few seemingly unnatural details. He even shared his theory about Manfred, and how Janiya and Robert Banks seemed to be connected, but it was clear that Janine either didn't believe the story or wasn't interested.

Leonard shriveled in his chair. Janine was an intimidating woman. Everything about her was fierce, from the blonde hair she pinched into a tight bun, to her slim-fitting suits and tall heels. Her voice carried a pitch like a hammer, driving a spike into Leonard's head with every word she spoke.

"Just get out of my office and back out in the streets. I don't want to see you in here again until you have something I can actually publish. All of this conspiracy nonsense is worthless. Find something we can use, and find it fast."

"I'm going to have something by the middle of next week. I promise."

Janine didn't reply. Her head just turned to her computer in dismissal. She couldn't even be bothered to look at Leonard any more, and he was fine with that. All he wanted to do was escape her office and get back to work.

"Have a nice day," Leonard offered as he left Janine to stare at her computer screen. Her fingers clicking the keyboard was the only response he heard as the glass door closed behind him.

Just over three hours later, Leonard was in Clyde County, parked up in front of the feed store. It was just after closing time, but Oliver, who was standing behind the counter, thumbing aimlessly through a magazine about bow hunting, knew he was coming. Leonard looked through the window and thought about how in another world, in another time, he and Oliver probably would have never even considered speaking to each other, but now, they were making plans to solve a murder-kidnapping together.

Leonard made his way from his vehicle and into the feed store, smelling the grain as he ran his palm over the canvas sacks piled waist-high.

"You finally made it." Oliver looked over his magazine. "How was the drive?"

"As boring as ever."

"Is it still just cornfields and trees?"

"Still is."

Oliver reached out his hand, which Leonard took in his own. The clerk's palm was rough with callouses, far different from Leonard's, whose fingers spent most of their time pressing keys and scribbling in a notepad.

"I'd offer you a beer, but I've been taking the last couple of days off from that," Oliver shared. "Been trying something different, for my daughter. Only have one with dinner now."

"Oh, that's alright," said Leonard. "I'm glad to hear that. I bet she appreciates it."

"I hope she does. I can't go drinking my life away, thinking it'll bring her mom back. That won't do no good for nobody, I finally realized."

Leonard shook his head and asked, "Do you still smoke?"

"Been trying to slow that down too, but it's harder. I'll have one if that's what you're hinting at."

"That's what I'm hinting at."

They walked outside and made their way to the tailgate of Oliver's truck. Sitting on the bed, they watched the cherry-tips burn through the darkness, neither knowing exactly why they needed to meet each other.

"I think I know who the kidnapper is," Leonard said after some time, his cigarette half-smoked.

"How?" A warm wind howled through Napoli square, causing strands of Oliver's hair to fall over his face. Smoke poured from his lungs as he brushed it away.

"I had a feeling, after being taken to that dream and seeing Janiya, that I needed to investigate a murder that occurred in St. Louis," Leonard answered. "While doing so, I was able to watch some security footage. The film was simple, just showing a parking lot, but I saw a man stepping out of a van."

"A van? Was it gray?" Oliver nearly gasped, his white skin losing color it never even had.

"Yea." Leonard took a drag. "Well at least it looked gray. The footage was black and white, so it's hard to tell exactly. And I know, it could have been literally anyone's, but get this. After I saw the man, I had another vision. It was brief, but I think it confirmed what my belief was."

Leonard rubbed his eyes. Hearing the story come from his mouth made the whole thing sound absurd. In his head, he knew that Manfred was the kidnapper, but when spoken out loud, the theory sounded ridiculous. He was willing to go all-in on a suspect, simply because he had a vision after seeing him on a security camera.

"I know it sounds crazy, but I promise you, it's him."

"Everything about this mess is crazy," Oliver said. "I don't think betting on a hunch is that absurd. I mean, hell, we've both been seeing things. Who's to say we ain't being led to these children by some higher power or something?" Oliver smashed the end of his cigarette on the tailgate and flicked the butt in the direction of a trashcan. "What all do you know about this guy?"

"Enough," Leonard bragged. "I know what he looks like, his name, the vehicles he drives, and even where he lives."

"You know where he lives? Goddamn, Leonard, you've been doing some real investigating, haven't you? How'd you find all that out?"

"A buddy of mine from college, a tech genius, working for Boeing now. All I had to do was give him a first name and a license plate, and he did the rest. Our kidnapper's full name is Manfred John Phillips III. He works as an accountant for a brokerage firm downtown. Doesn't have much of a history online, and seems pretty normal by most accounts, but I learned that the guy's dad has brain disease. I think that could be an underlying reason for Manfred's psychotic tendencies."

"Jesus, it all seems so real when you give a name to the guy." A moment passed before Oliver asked, "What are you going to do now? You going to call the cops or what?"

"And tell them what, exactly? I don't have any real dirt on him. There's nothing I could say that would warrant an arrest or even a search of his property. All I have are visions and dreams, which only you and I have experienced. I think that's why I needed to talk to you – because you wouldn't think I'm crazy. Besides, I talked to the leading detective for Janiya's case and he basically told me to fuck off until I have real information, whatever that means."

"So, what you're saying is …" Oliver paused and looked Leonard in the eye.

"I think I'm saying," Leonard started and swallowed. "I think I'm saying I need to investigate Manfred Phillips myself. I'm going to visit his property. I Googled it, and judging by the satellite images, it looks like he's got quite a bit of land. Plenty enough to house some children."

"What?" Oliver's voice was sober. "You're going to go snooping around a murderer's house by yourself?"

"I don't see any other option," responded Leonard, sure and calm.

Oliver sat back on the tailgate, supporting his body with the palms of his hands. His face looked worried. Leonard was worried too. Every word he had said cemented the fact he would be wandering into a murderer's home, alone.

Fifty-nine

Jennifer opened the door, wearing shorts and an oversized t-shirt with the word *SEMO* plastered across the front in red letters. Her hair, dark and silky, fell lazily over her shoulders and eyes. Leonard smiled when he saw her.

"Hey," Jennifer greeted. Her breath smelled sweet with wine. A long-stemmed glass was in her hand, nearly empty.

"Hey," he said right back, eyes shifting to her feet. He felt bashful for some reason. It was probably because of the way he last left her, combined with the fact he was staring at her now, enthralled.

"Well, come in. You don't plan on standing out there all night, do you?"

"Actually, I quite like it here. Was thinking I'd just stay on this doorstep and watch you all night."

They laughed awkwardly as Leonard entered the apartment. The smell of cherry and spices radiated through the home from a candle which rested on the kitchen island. The scent was nice, and so was being back in Jennifer's home.

"Wine?" Jennifer asked as she poured her glass to the brim. It wasn't exactly wine etiquette, which made Leonard smile.

"Sure."

Jennifer fetched another glass and poured the rest of the bottle into it. Leonard walked to the kitchen island and leaned over it.

His counterpart handed him the glass, its contents grainy with sediment.

"Thank you."

"Yea, yea. I was getting it for myself anyway."

They stared at each other a moment, laughing awkwardly.

"I'm sorry I left you the way I did," Leonard began, his voice slow. "I should have asked you to come to St. Louis with me. Or I should have—"

"Kissed me?"

"Yea, I should've done that."

"Yea, you should have." She shook her head and gave a crooked smile.

They drank.

"I just …" Leonard searched his mind for the right words to say. "I just wasn't sure what to do," he admitted. "I was a little scared of pulling you into the middle of my investigation. It's my first one, and I didn't want to ruin it. I now realize that was pretty stupid."

"You're right. That was pretty stupid," she joked.

"Look, I know it was just a few days together, but it was good. You're the only bright spot on my visit to this town." He wanted to curse Clyde County. He hated the town but didn't want to drag Jennifer's home through the mud.

"Stop." Jennifer halted his rant and drank from her wine glass in a casual manner. In that moment, she seemed much older than

Leonard. Not in physical age, but in maturity. He felt like a little boy again, in his first relationship.

"I still like you, Leonard. I'm not mad at you." Jennifer smiled. The way her bottom lip sunk when she did so made Leonard's knees wobble. "I get it," she continued. "We literally just met each other. Don't make things weird, you creep."

The candle on the island flickered, casting shadows over Jennifer's smooth face as she grinned at him. They danced under her nose and across her cheek. Standing in her sleepwear, halfway to drunk, she was stunning. Leonard felt guided to move to her and kiss her right then and there. Maybe after they pulled apart, he'd hoist her up onto the island and continue down each inch of her body.

Painfully, he avoided the urge.

"Well, I'm glad you weren't mad. And I'm sorry for being such a creep, as you like to put it."

"Eh, you're not so bad. I'm just glad you called back after getting my messages."

"I would have sooner but I had another asshole cop to talk to." Leonard pushed his glass, now just sediment and backwash, towards the center of the island. "I don't know why they all hate me."

"I could give you several reasons why."

They laughed, and Leonard finally moved to her. One hand fell to the small of her back while the other braced on the island. He needed some sort of support, or he would have burst.

Sixty

The sponge pressed into her back, moving in gentle circles. The soapy water felt nice against her skin. Number Four had always enjoyed these baths. She enjoyed the time out of the cage, enjoyed the way the coolness of the cellar was met by the warmth of the water, and she especially enjoyed the time spent alone with Papa. He stood behind her, a hand on her shoulder while the other massaged the soap into her skin, ridding her of the Earth's filth.

"Now turn around," Papa said, nudging her easily. "Arms up."

Four spun and hoisted her arms towards the ceiling. Papa smiled at her and ran a hand through her wet hair. His fingertips felt good against her scalp.

"How are you settling along with your new friend?" he asked.

Four looked over his shoulder, down the dark corridor of the cellar to the dimly lit cages. She could see Number Three sitting on the floor, trembling, wet and cold and crying. The new girl had already had her time with Papa. It didn't seem to go well. Three had whined the whole time, but from her spot in her cell, it was hard for Four to see exactly what had happened. Three wasn't used to her new life yet, but she would learn.

"I have enjoyed her being here," Four smiled. "It's nice knowing another girl, like me."

"Good. I'm glad you like her, but she's not anything like you yet, little darling. Three still has a lot to learn."

Four nodded and closed her eyes while Papa washed over her face. When the soap cleared, she said, "She will."

"I hope so," Papa said and squeezed out the sponge over the drain. "Here, dry off."

Four took the towel from Papa's outstretched hand. She rubbed it over her head and body until she was completely dried, then offered it back. Papa took the towel in his hands and pressed it to his nose. He sniffed and nodded his approval.

"Here you are," Papa handed over a new set of clothes. White t-shirts and white shorts were all they were ever allowed to wear. *White is the color of angels,* Papa told them a long time ago.

"Thank you, Papa," Four said and dressed herself. Once clothed, she placed her palm in his and they walked back to the cages.

Number Three looked at Four as she crawled back into her cell. Three's eyes were angry and scared. Her new clothes were already stained from the ground. Her body, which Four noticed was bigger and more developed than her own, was trembling violently. Three's arms were hugging herself. She looked like one of the crazy people that Papa had always told them about.

"Good," Papa proclaimed cheerfully. "Now that we're all clean and we've all went to the restroom, let us begin our message."

Sixty-one

At the edge of her cage, Janiya numbly sat. Her eyes were sunken, staring a hard look of hatred at the man who had ruined her life. *Papa.* God, what a thought that was, that a man with white skin and slick, straight hair was her Papa. The thought made Janiya's insides capsize.

He had come about thirty minutes before, though Janiya had no way of telling the time. It at least seemed like thirty minutes, but everything that happened in the cellar was stretched, elongated, due to the agony of imprisonment. Misery made time stand still.

It had been cleansing time. Papa made them go one-by-one to the back of the cellar. They'd passed by the shelving and a few doors that led to God knows what, before stopping over a wash bucket and a drain. Papa ordered her to strip off her clothes and he bathed her himself. It was mortifying. Janiya tried to put up a fight. She said *no* when he told her to undress, but was dealt a hand across her jaw. When he placed the sponge against her skin she retreated, but was met with a strike to the side of her head. There was no escaping the *cleansing.* God, it made Janiya sick. Papa made her sick. The way he touched her made her sick. The way he took the towel and pressed it against his face made her sick.

Fuck.

The man was wearing a thin robe now, woven a translucent shade of purple, draped over his shoulders. It fell to the dirty floor like the train of a bride's gown. Janiya shook, rocking herself back and forth as she watched grime gather on the robe while the man turned in circles, preaching nonsense about prophecies and a God who didn't exist. Every mention of a higher, divine being made Janiya turn ill. God couldn't have been real because if He or She was, there wouldn't be kids locked up in a cellar. There would have been some intervention by now. Papa would have been struck down by lightning or whatever Gods used to kill bad men. The cellar door would have sprung open, and the cages would have rotted to pieces, leaving the children free. This, Janiya understood, was evidence that God was a myth, a tall tale, told by people who had the luxury of believing in such a thing.

"I am told, by word of angels, that your time is coming soon, my children," Papa said, waving his arms towards the ceiling as if heaven stood just beyond the dim light of the cellar. "Soon you will be free of your cages, and the prophecy will begin. You will walk from the darkness of the cellar and into a true darkness, which eats the world. This plague of lightlessness is what you have been preparing for all of your lives. For the world, what lies beyond this place, your home, is full of shadows. There is no goodness left, but you four, you will be the light. You will be something that I, and so many others, could never be."

Janiya wondered if he truly believed what he was preaching. If he did, he was a Goddamn idiot. There were plenty of good people in the world. Her little brothers and sisters, and her mother were good. Jacky was good. Her favorite teacher, Mr Shepard, was good.

Everything wasn't dark, and the children hadn't been preparing their entire lives for anything. Janiya certainly hadn't. She couldn't have been in the cellar more than three days, based off of how much she'd had to eat and drink. The man was probably just preaching this message to instill hope in the children, hope that they would one day be free of their cages. Janiya knew this was a lie. The children would never be free. They would live in these cages until they were old enough to fulfill the man's needs in a manner that didn't involve verbal messages, but instead, involved a more sinister, physical touch. Shivers crawled like spiders up Janiya's spine. She wondered if, at age thirteen, the children were old enough already to fulfill *Papa's* needs in that way. She had only been there a short time, so she couldn't know if he fucked them or not. Judging by the way he bathed them, she suspected he did.

Janiya squirmed in her cage, eyes shifting across the dimly lit room to Number Four. The girl was sitting cross-legged at the foot of her cage, elbows on either leg, hands supporting her head. Her pale skin was yellow with bruises in countless places, up and down her arms and legs. The girl's hair looked like the frayed end of a rope, waving above her head in some places and falling to the floor in others. She didn't even look real, like someone drew her. Janiya couldn't tell just by looking at the girl what their kidnapper had done. Perhaps some of those bruises came from Papa's grip, but more likely, they came from lying on the concrete and rolling over on the rough floor.

The boys, One and Two, appeared just the same. Their hair was long and dirty. Their skin was white and bruised, each child horrifying to look at, especially their eyes, which were glazed white and hollow. It was a wonder that any one of the children could see through those things. Being in darkness for so long must have altered some of their physical features. It definitely affected their skin and their vision. Janiya didn't fear she would grow pale, but those eyes – she desperately wanted to avoid crossing into that threshold. She couldn't imagine what it would be like to lose her sight, or at best, only have the ability to see well in the darkness. Both would be horrible adaptations.

"The end of time, as we know it, is drawing near," Papa's preaching continued. Janiya had been drifting in and out of attention as his words meant nothing to her. She only sat still and acted as though she cared, so as to not receive more beatings.

"Soon, the blue sky will turn dark, and the trees of the Earth will catch flame. The seas will dry up, and the roads and buildings will crack. All will crumble, leaving nothing behind. When this day comes, it will be you four who rebuild the Earth. You will bring light to the dark skies and water to the empty oceans. Those who survived the turmoil will look at you as Gods, but it won't be so. You will still be my children, though I will be long gone by then, but by any means, you are God's children. It is important that you understand that. You cannot let power and conceit consume you as it has the rest of the human race." Papa's face twisted in disgust. "It is in these moments of mental warfare that you must remember your mission and keep faith; keep strong."

Janiya considered asking what the mission even was, how exactly they were going to save the planet, but didn't want to be struck. The man was just speaking poetically, preaching with a romantic vagueness about things that would never actually happen.

"Papa," Number Two spoke, interrupting the message. The man turned, his robe slicing through the air in dramatic fashion. Janiya hoped he would trip on it.

"Yes, my child?" he said kindly, but his face said otherwise.

"What about Number Three?"

"What about her?"

"Well, she hasn't been here her whole life. She hasn't been preparing. Not like we have. Is that part of the prophecy too?" Two's voice seemed to shake with fear, but his concern for truth outweighed his concern for being backhanded.

"Oh, but she has," Papa replied, his voice as smooth as ever. *Christ, he never missed a beat.*

"How has she, if she hasn't been here?" asked Two.

Janiya couldn't wait to hear the response. She looked at Papa. His eyes were flaming, narrow, but his demeanor was still calm and prophetic. "She has been training beyond the portal. She has been living in the world above, the same world that you will one day rule. The prophecy states that there will be one, one girl, who bridges the divide and acts as a guide for the others. Number Three understands how to navigate the land beyond this home, and will one day show you all how to do so, leading you by the hand through the pits of blackness. Her vision enables her to see in the light, and her wisdom is an expanse, far greater than your own. She will be your beacon, once your time has come." Papa glared at Janiya, eyes full of hate. "But beacons can be damaged, lights can go dark, and even guides can get lost. So that means it is up to you three, my children, my first loves, who possess the ability to see through the darkness, to ensure she stays afoot on the path of righteousness."

"Yes, Papa. We will do our best," Number Two answered in a sort of quiver. He seemed hungry for more information but was too afraid to ask for a scrap, too scared to question the powerful entity known as Papa.

"Your best will not be good enough. You must do better than your best." He glared at Janiya. "This one will be your guide, yes, but she will do everything in her power to stray you from the Lord. Your journey will be long, and it will be strenuous, but if you stay in the light of the Lord, you will see Number Three come to find peace with our ways."

"She will never lead us astray," Number One shouted with a certainty that Janiya would never share.

"That is the very attitude that you should have," answered the boy's papa, "that *you all* should have."

He rotated around the room, looking every child in the eye, the tail of his robe gathering dirt from the floor. The jet-black hair on his head stayed put like it had been etched in stone. Small beads of sweat had begun to gather on his forehead. Janiya, while looking at the deranged man, was beginning to understand that he actually believed what he was preaching. He actually thought he was a servant of God. What an absurdity, she thought, and began to tremble.

Papa made some final statements, distributed more water and some fruit cups to every cage, and then disappeared to the world above, once again leaving the children in darkness. Janiya sat still and listened to the beating of her own heart. She fought the urge to devour the pineapple and cherry medley in one large gulp. Her stomach pleaded for her to do so, but she needed to savor it, along with the water. The previous bottle she was given was consumed in less than a few seconds. Janiya wouldn't make that mistake twice. She didn't even know when Papa's next visit would be, so she needed to salvage every morsel.

In the darkness of her cage, Janiya decided to not drink the water at all for a while. She sipped the juice from the cup and left the fruit in the plastic. This ration would be her supper later on, or breakfast, possibly even lunch, depending on what time of day it was. Janiya didn't know, and she no longer cared. She just wanted to survive.

In her younger years, Janiya had seen reports about missing children who were held captive, and wondered what it would be like. She wondered how they could survive for ten or twelve years. She wondered why they wouldn't try to kill themselves or to escape, but right then, while she sat on the cold concrete, sipping peach syrup from a plastic cup, Janiya realized they didn't do so because it was basic human instinct to stay alive, even when in the worst circumstances imaginable. The brain would do all that it could to adapt and keep its host breathing.

Janiya shook, cold with sweat and deathly afraid. She thought about her captor, and the seriousness in his face when he preached. Papa really did believe every word he spoke. He thought he was a man of the Lord and that abducting children was God's work. Janiya couldn't decide what was worse: being captive to a religious lunatic, or being captive to a madman who kidnapped just for the fuck of it. Both seemed equally terrifying.

Slowly, Janiya finished the fruit juice from her cup, leaving the handful of preserved fruit pieces to reside in the plastic until she was ready for them. She then crawled to the back of her cage and took rest against the cold wires. When her head touched the steel, she began to sob.

Sixty-two

Oliver awoke in the middle of the night, in a room that wasn't his room. There was no ceiling fan, no closet where he kept his boots, and no picture of Lela and Becca on the nightstand by the bedside. In fact, there was no bedside at all. Oliver sat up and found he was laying on the flat, empty ground of a vacant warehouse of darkness.

Encompassing him was a blackness so vast and empty, if he were to scream, his voice would have been swallowed by the absence. The only light that shone was a single tunnel of brilliance which fell in a bead upon Oliver, from nowhere and everywhere all at the same time. There was nothing else in the vicinity. There were no objects, and there was no sound. The emptiness was so great and quiet, Oliver could hear the blood moving through his veins as it rushed to his beating heart. His breath misted before his face, but the temperature wasn't cold. It was as if temperature didn't exist.

Oliver stood, spinning in circles, taking in the expanse. It was indeterminable just how large the area was. There were no objects to gauge depth or distance; only nothingness.

After some time taking in the space around him, Oliver began to walk, with no particular direction in mind. His footsteps against the black ground made no noise but sent ripples of vibrations through his body. It was a strange sensation, one that made him feel as though he was walking on water.

"Hello?" Oliver shouted, his voice muffled, dissipating in the air like it was trapped in a vacuum. "Is anyone there?"

He looked back and forth, but there was no response. A twinge of unease began to stir in Oliver's chest. This experience, Oliver thought, must be what death feels like. It felt like the dimension between life and death. The thought sent Oliver into a panic. When Leonard described his journey to a void, there had been another person, but Oliver was alone, so very alone. What if he never woke up? What if this was his eternal resting place, this plain of nothing?

Afraid, and not knowing what else to do, Oliver began to jog through the darkness. Everywhere he went, the light that bore down from above followed. With every footstep came a heaving breath and an accompanying mist. He began to sweat, even though there was no temperature. Once he started, he found he couldn't stop running. His human mind, unable to grasp the situation, told him that there must be an end. Somewhere, after some time, Oliver would find the edge of the abyss.

Vibrations continued up his legs as he moved. He was buzzing now, continuing to run, his mind racing right along with his feet. The sound of his pillowing footsteps against the ground, which wasn't really the ground, made concert with the wheezing lungs in his chest. He was tired, but he also wasn't tired. The organs of his body made efforts to expel him forward, but it seemed to Oliver that he could run until time ceased to exist, like he had an endless energy.

He kept moving, running towards nothing until he saw something. Startled, Oliver stopped in his tracks, his lungs almost immediately recovering from the exertion. Across the vast blackness, far off in the distance, there shone another shaft of light. On what, Oliver couldn't quite tell, but he intended to find out. He turned and continued his trot towards the other ray of brilliance.

He moved towards the light for what seemed like an eternity. His legs and arms cycled on, but the light barely grew in size. After some time, Oliver thought to wonder if he was imagining the damn thing, but he kept on moving. He churned forward until the object the light shone on finally became clear.

Curled into a ball on the floor of the void was a girl. Her skin was black, covered in grime. Her hair was tangled and fell across her knees in frizzles. She was crying. It was a heaving, sobbing, ugly cry – the kind of weeping that occurred only when someone had experienced loss or had given up on something. These were the kind of tears Oliver shed when Lela died. These were the tears of a girl who had been taken from her family and friends, of a girl living in a cage.

"Janiya?" Oliver asked as he slowed his pace.

The girl peeled her head away from her knees and looked at Oliver. The skin around her eyes was puffy from crying. In that moment, she looked much younger than thirteen.

"I … I've seen you before," she said. Her voice sounded much more powerful than Oliver's like she was familiar with this place.

"Yes. And I've seen you as well," Oliver answered. He wanted to sound kind, but he was both shocked and afraid. He hoped his own emotions didn't carry over and infect the girl, who might not even be real. He still didn't understand what was going on. There was no way to understand.

"Who are you?"

"My name is Oliver."

"How do you know who I am? How do you know my name?"

"Because you were kidnapped," Oliver said as gently as possible, thinking the reality of her situation might crush Janiya. It didn't. "I know your name and who you are. And I know the man who is going to find you."

Janiya shook her head. "Are you real?"

Oliver stepped forward, the light above his head merging with the one above hers. The white lights shimmered off his skin, which looked fake under their radiance, almost plastic. "I am real, I think. Are you?"

Janiya nodded and wiped her sobbing eyes. Both were stricken by the bizarreness of the void. This place, their dreams, everything over the last week, defied reality.

"Is it only one man looking for me?" she asked.

Oliver shook his head. "No. There are others, but my friend is going to be the one who finds you."

Janiya stood. Her body looked wrecked. She turned away from Oliver and walked a few steps. Her light followed her, splitting the cones once more. Oliver scratched his cheek and pinched the skin, wondering if all this was just a hallucination. *No,* it couldn't be. Leonard had seen the same place, had seen the same girl.

"I think I know your friend," Janiya said, turning back towards Oliver.

"I think you do too. You've met him here before."

"Is his name, Leonard?"

"Yes."

As soon as Oliver answered, the floor began to shake. The lights above shrunk, narrowing upon their heads. Both residents of the void were startled, unsure what was happening. It was a new experience for each of them.

"What's happening?" asked Janiya. "This isn't like last time."

"I don't know," answered Oliver.

The shaking was violent but brief, an eruption of low magnitude. It quickly ceased and the lights above expanded to their original size, only now, there was a third light. Another shaft broke through the darkness and illuminated a man who was no stranger to this place.

"Leonard," Oliver and Janiya said in unison. Each were equally shocked to see the reporter, who was stunned himself.

"Oliver? What are you doing here?" answered Leonard, eyes agape. All three stood still, in a wash of bewilderment.

"Janiya," Leonard finally broke, "is this really you?"

"Yes," she answered. Her voice was weaker than before. The strength in it gave ground to the anguish in her mind.

"Do you know where you are? Not this place, but the real place, the cellar. Do you know where that is?"

Janiya shook her head, *no*. Oliver stood by silently, watching the two. This experience was the most unusual thing he'd ever witnessed. He brought his hand to his hair and plucked one out. The single strand gleamed beneath the light. He was still real. He was really standing there, in the darkness between worlds. He was positioned between dimensions. Was this purgatory? His sweat started again. Oliver had never been so scared, nor so excited.

"I have no idea where I am," Janiya answered.

Leonard said urgently, "Who has you? Do you know his name, what he looks like?"

"I don't know his name. The others call him Papa. He thinks he's doing the work of God, but he's evil. He says that he's fulfilling some sort of prophecy, but it's bullshit. He's crazy and he's white, as white as you." Janiya pointed to Oliver, who stepped back when her finger shot towards him. Janiya continued, "He's tall and skinny, with black hair. And his eyes are as small as marbles and dark. He's disgusting looking."

Leonard stepped closer to Janiya and knelt before her, bringing his eyes to meet hers. Her voice had started trembling. She was visibly shaking. Leonard reached out and placed a hand on her shoulder, but as soon as he touched her, the floor began to move again. The tunnels of light flickered until they shot up, reeling away to the ceiling that wasn't a ceiling. They were left standing in complete darkness.

"No!" Janiya shouted. "I don't want to go back. Please, don't let me go back."

The void continued to shake, knocking all three of them to the ground. The next thing Oliver saw was the walls and the cages of the cellar. Three other children, as white as the comforter on Oliver's bed, looked at him and Leonard. Janiya was behind the wires of a cage now, screaming and rattling the steel that entrapped her. The floor and walls were still shaking.

"Devils!" a voice proclaimed with authority. It was one of the other children, a boy. His white eyes burned with hate. The bruised skin under his shoulders was woven tightly around a malnourished frame. He looked exactly like the boy Oliver found tied to a tree, only this boy had life in his lungs and fire in his eyes. A finger pointed through the cage directly at Oliver and Leonard. "Devils, both of you!" the boy spoke again.

Oliver's jaw sunk. He didn't know how to react, how to respond. He still didn't believe this was actually happening. This, he thought, had to be a dream. Maybe the void was real, maybe, but this cellar, this was certainly a figment of his imagination.

The walls began to crumble and collapse. Oliver knew he was going to be taken from the dream and back to his home, to his bed, where there stood a picture of his lovely family on his nightstand. He knew this because he had experienced it before, and while looking at the cellar-children, Oliver realized he couldn't wait for the transportation to occur, to wake up away from where he was.

The last thing Oliver heard before the world collapsed was, "Don't worry. I'm coming for you."

When Oliver opened his eyes again, he was back in his house. His head lay against his usual pillow, and his eyes were staring at the usual ceiling fan. Starlight stole through the usual slits in the blinds over his familiar windows. He was back in the real world. He was back home.

Oliver sat up, his mouth bone dry and his head throbbing. He had grown familiar with the latter symptom, which seemed to occur every time he had a vision of one of the children, but this time it was worse than ever. It felt like someone had taken a nine-pound hammer to his skull. He pressed his palms against his temples and groaned. Before his pain subsided, a blue light cast from the phone on his nightstand. Someone was calling.

Head still aching, Oliver brought the phone to his ear and said, "Leonard?"

Sixty-three

When Two thought about the one who called herself Janiya, he couldn't imagine her being a part of the four, or part of the prophecy at all. She seemed different. She was not good, nor bad, but something else entirely: an in-between. Two wondered, if the new girl was a representation of the outside world, of everything that Papa had taught about their whole lives. If she was, Two didn't understand why Papa was training them at all. She wasn't a vile person, full of darkness, who needed to be brought to light. She was just a girl. Obviously, she was connected to the prophecy now, but before, she walked through the world beyond. She didn't fall victim to the ways of that world that Papa had always warned about. Janiya was innocent and pure, just as Two and his cellar mates were. That had to mean that others who walked the world above were like her. That meant the world wasn't completely dark and in need of saving.

The thoughts in Two's mind were torture. Every idea that formed was a contradiction of all he'd ever known. Doubt was taking shape. His body grew cold at the thought that everything he'd ever been taught was a lie, or at the very least, a misinterpretation of the truth.

Maybe Janiya was right. When she arrived, she spoke ill of Papa. She said he was a liar and a thief who stole children from their families. The girl who now sat across from Two's cell, whose skin looked different than his, whose hair was different, and whose attitude was vastly different, said she had her own family, that she didn't always belong to the four.

Two trembled and rubbed his arms. Chilly bumps had formed over the skin. He couldn't imagine what it would be like to be in Janiya's shoes, to be taken from her family. If Two was taken from the four, from Papa, he would no longer want to live. His home and his friends, One and Four and the former Number Three, were all he'd ever known. Being taken away from them would be devastating.

Two sat back in his cage. He was beginning to understand why the new girl acted the way she did. He couldn't blame her for taking rage against their papa. He couldn't blame her for anything. She was just a girl, who had been stripped of her life, a life that Two couldn't even try to comprehend. He knew nothing beyond the wires of his cage and the walls and shelves of their cellar home.

As the sense of doubt mixed with a remedy of countless other emotions filled Two's body, he began to think of Number Four. He thought about her beautiful skin and thick curls of hair. He thought back to the last time they were let out from their cages for a message, about fifty or so visits from Papa ago. They had been allowed to sit on the concrete together and share a meal while Papa preached. That was the last time they had touched. Two had sat next to Four, as he always did. They crossed their legs and ate cold soup and bread. Two knew how much Four loved bread, so he gave her his. When he did so, she placed her hand on his thigh, only for a moment, but a moment was all Two needed. The feel of her hand against his skin was the single greatest sensation of the boy's life. He had thought about it every day since. There was nothing he wanted more than to feel her touch again.

At the thought of his love's hand against his skin, Two remembered the itch that plagued him. The previous few days, starting about the time Janiya was brought in, there had been much to distract him from the infection. Presently though, his need to scratch had been flaring. He didn't know what the source of the itch was. All he understood was that after his last visit to the holy room, the pain birthed. During the last cleansing time he told Papa about it. Papa responded by rubbing some ointment on it and ordering Two to keep from touching it.

Two moved to the front of his cage and grabbed hold of the wires, as was his usual effort to keep from scratching. His mind frantically bounced between thoughts. The flesh of his arms was still standing, rigid and cold. He looked at Four, who lay in her cell, nearly motionless. The sight of her legs sprawled out against the concrete floor nearly made him explode. His chest tightened. All he wanted to do was break through his cage and into hers. He wanted to press his lips against hers, and then against the skin of her chest, but both God and Papa would not approve of that.

While Two imagined kissing Four, the rift in the cellar expanded. Moments ago, before Two dove into his contemplation, the four had visitors. This wasn't the first time something like this had happened, but it was the first time since Janiya's arrival. Usually, the four would discuss the visions together, and with Papa, but after the last visit, there was only silence. That's what led to Two's internalizations. All he wanted was to hear a sound, a voice, anything but his own mind and the splash of water, but he would not be the first to speak. That duty belonged to One, or to Janiya. Two would not intrude upon their territory. He could only sit in silence, waiting for someone to make a statement. Eventually, Number One did.

"Who were those men, Number Three?"

Janiya took a moment before answering. Her tone was sharp. "How the hell should I know?"

"You know, don't lie to me. They were staring right at you like they had been talking to you."

"I don't who the hell they were. Why would I lie about that?"

Two watched through the darkness. One moved to the front of his cage. The boy wrapped his hands around the steel and shook hard, sending an ear-piercing rattle through the cellar. Two always hated when someone shook their cage.

"All you have done, since your arrival, is break Papa's rules. And you know what that means? You are breaking God's rules!"

Janiya moved to the front of her cage, but thankfully, didn't touch the steel. She just stood there, peering through the darkness at her opponent. Two knew Janiya couldn't see as well as he or the others could. It was obvious in her movements and the way she crooked her neck when she looked at something like she was focusing hard. Across the cellar, Four was stirring now, crawling on all fours to the door of her cage. Two nearly melted at the sight but stiffened again as the tennis match continued between One and Janiya.

"There is no God, you idiot. If there was, none of you would be here. You would be with your families. Your *real* families."

"You watch your mouth," One commanded. The conviction in his voice made Two tremble.

Janiya said something in response, but Two was stuck thinking about her previous statement. The girl claimed with such certainty that God was a myth. He wondered if what she said, all of what she said, had any truth to it. Had he once had a real family? Had he once had people who loved him and who he would have loved, just like Janiya? Was there really no such thing as God?

Stop. This is what Papa warned about.

"I will see to it that you are punished," One threatened. "I am going to tell Papa that you are full of deceit. I will tell him about what you are conjuring. That you brought unwanted guests from the world of darkness into our home, you wretch of a girl. You are just like them."

Janiya sat down. "Say what you want," she said with an indifference that struck Two. She didn't fear, nor respect, Number One. Two had never heard anyone talk to the boy like she did, but he also didn't know anyone, besides those currently in the cellar and their papa. "I will be getting out of here soon, and so will you, whether you like it or not."

"You are so full of de—"

"You will see what a real life is," Janiya cut the boy off, treating him with such disregard. Two could sense the anger boiling in his old friend. He knew the new girl was walking on nails. If she continued her trek, she would find her feet pierced.

One continued to serve threats, but Janiya retreated to the back of her cage. Two thought this was a smart tactic on her part. He didn't want to see the tension tighten any more, or the bond between the four would certainly snap. He just wanted peace, like the peace that existed before the girl's arrival. But strangely, at the edges of his mind, he wanted the disruption to continue. Curiosity inspired him to wonder: what if Janiya's deceitful tales weren't deceitful at all? What if her stories were real?

Two sat and stared at Four, who happened to be staring back at him. Their eyes met, sending surges of electricity through Two's body. He thought about what life would be like with this girl in the world from which Janiya came. He considered breaking away from the cage and going out through the portal with her.

What kind of world was actually out there? Was it full of darkness, like Papa had always said? Or was it a world of beautiful equilibrium, like Janiya told them?

Two scratched his leg. At that moment, all he wanted was to know the truth.

IV

"In the city I found her,

The narrow-streeted city.

In the market-place I came upon her,

Bound and trembling,

Her fluted wings were fastened to her sides with cords,

She was naked and cold,

For that day the wind blew

Without sunshine."

– Amy Lowell, *The Captured Goddess*

Sixty-four

Jennifer brought a cup of coffee to Leonard then moved back to the kitchen to continue cooking breakfast. The steaming liquid was like medicine to Leonard's troubled mind. He didn't go back to sleep after his visit to the void. He just lay there, head screaming, thinking about the children until the sun came up. He had to find them and do so quickly. Something in his gut told him that death was coming if he didn't hurry.

Leonard looked up from his cup to see Jennifer navigating the kitchen, making eggs, bacon, and English muffins. She wore a long t-shirt like a skirt over her underwear. He observed her for a moment, taking in the harmony of the morning, distracting his mind if only momentarily. He moved to her and wrapped his arms around her. The embrace was even more medicinal than the coffee.

"Stop, you." She smiled, still holding a plastic spatula which was coated in a layer of grease.

"I can't help it."

Leonard let her go and leaned back against the kitchen island, feeling the coldness of the counter against his bare back. Jennifer flipped an egg over, spoiling the perfect bulb of the yoke.

"Dammit. That one is going to be yours now, since you want to distract me."

"They'll all taste the same." Leonard shrugged.

Jennifer turned and they found each other's eyes. Her morning look, hair a mess and wearing no makeup, was just as pleasant as the night they went to the bar.

"You had a strange dream last night, didn't you?" she asked as she pulled apart the strips of bacon with a fork. Grease popped. Leonard was surprised by both the question and the sting of the grease that landed on his forearm.

"Why do you say that?"

"Because you were shaking so bad you woke me up. I tried to go back to sleep, but couldn't with you like that. And after you stopped, you crawled out of bed and started yapping in the other room. You kept me up all night you jerk."

"Sorry."

Jennifer laughed. "Was it Oliver?"

"Yes," Leonard admitted, "it was Oliver."

"Why'd you call him? Just to tell him you had another dream? Did you see the boy again?"

"Sort of."

"Why, sort of?"

Jennifer began plucking the bacon strips from the skillet and placing them on a paper towel. The grease soaked into the fabric, covering the entire surface in oil. Leonard thought about snatching one up and eating it but held off.

"Oliver was there," he said. "In my dream. Like, really there. I could see him, and he could see me. It was like we were dreaming the same dream at the same time."

Jennifer continued building the breakfast on two plates as if Leonard wasn't telling her about the strangest thing that ever happened to him. She was careless. Watching her made Leonard long to be careless again.

"The girl was there too. All three of us were there, and all three of us could see and talk to each other. I've never experienced anything like it."

"What did you talk about?" asked Jennifer in a tone that sounded similar to a mother asking her child about an imaginary friend. Leonard didn't mind. He knew he sounded crazy, and he knew that Jennifer was just trying her best to sound like she believed him, even if her acting was horrible.

"I asked about her kidnapper."

"And?"

"The man who Janiya described fits the description, almost exactly, of the man from the camera footage."

Breakfast was finished. Jennifer took the plates to the kitchen table. Leonard followed, eager for a response. He needed to hear the sound of her mother-like voice. He needed confirmation, even if fraudulent, that he wasn't a lunatic.

"Well, what does that mean?" she finally asked.

Both of them sat at the table, but neither started eating.

"It means that I'm right. The man I saw, he's the one who took them. I knew it when I first looked at him, and I know it now. I had a feeling all along, something in my gut, and all my dream did was confirm it."

"So you're still going to search this guy's house?"

Leonard hesitated, sipped from his coffee, and eventually came to an answer. "Yes. How could I not?"

Jennifer didn't respond. It was clear to both of them that Leonard had to go. Four children's lives depended on him. If he didn't, they would continue to live in cages under the hand of a maniac. They would eventually end up hanging from trees, crowned with thorns, or become a part of some other cruel display.

"When will you leave?"

"After breakfast."

An air of silence waded through the dining room. Leonard looked down at the table, finding no courage to stare into the blue eyes of the woman across from him. A naked gleam from the sun's morning light shone off the wood. Leonard wished he were in bed, nestled against Jennifer's back, feeling her skin against his own. He considered the fact that last night might be the last night he would ever feel another body against his.

The remainder of the meal was quiet. All that could be heard was the scrape of forks against porcelain and the slow gurgle of coffee. Leonard had hoped this breakfast would be spent differently. Sitting in silence, he tried to place himself in Jennifer's shoes. To her, he probably sounded crazy. He was willing to risk his life off the basis of dreams. From that perspective, it did sound absurd, but Leonard wasn't doing so because of the dreams. They were only catalysts. The true driving force behind Leonard's actions was the children. Leonard couldn't live, knowing that four children existed somewhere in cages. Even if he was wrong, and Manfred Phillips was just a normal guy, Leonard was going.

Leonard washed the dishes after the meal was through. Jennifer remained at the dining table, watching him. As he scrubbed, he could feel the burn of her gaze upon his back.

"I'm sorry I have to go," Leonard said, hands still bathed in the hot water. A wash towel instinctively moved in circles across the plates.

"I'm coming with you," she said as Leonard was turning away from the sink. "Even if you're a creep, I can't let you go alone."

Leonard looked at her, shaking his head with a laugh. He didn't contest, though he wanted to. He knew he had no choice in the matter. She was going to come to the city with him, but she wasn't going to Manfred's house. He could make certain of that.

Sixty-five

The day passed slowly, even with Jennifer's company. Leonard knew it would. The anticipation and the anxiety of knowing what the night held slowed time. Every minute stretched, feeling like hours, but all Leonard could do was wait and let the day elapse.

They'd made the drive to St. Louis and now sat in Leonard's apartment, watching mindless reality TV. There were no drinks to be had, save water and coffee. Jennifer was on the couch, a blanket draped over her, one leg hanging off the edge. Leonard stood at the divide between his living room and his kitchen, watching her lay there, staring blankly at the TV. Something about her sprawled out in his home seemed right, like she was supposed to be there, to be a part of his apartment.

The window blinds were separated, exposing the interior of the apartment to the dying light of the city sun. A mix of tangerines and violets spread across a cloudless sky. Only a single star had formed, near the horizon, bright and bold. The city at dusk was something that Leonard often took for granted. It was beautiful. *Tonight*, he thought while looking at the daylight fade, *is as fine a night as any to die.*

A hand on his shoulder pulled Leonard back to Earth. "Nice, isn't it?" Leonard asked, welcoming the distraction.

"Almost as nice as the country sky."

"Almost," answered Leonard, though to him, nothing could beat his city's sunset.

Neither of them said anything for a while. They stood there, Jennifer holding Leonard and resting her chin on his shoulder, each watching the motions of the sky. The sun dipped low, towards the horizon, setting the Earth ablaze in a wash of mahogany light. In what seemed like a breath, a blink, the time it took to place a soft hand on a shoulder, the sun was gone. Only traces of its existence remained, in dim needles along the horizon. The last leg of light fought back the darkness for as long as it could, but eventually, was swallowed entirely.

Lamps and overheads began to flicker on across the cityscape. Artificial yellows and whites popped up in windows and along streets, blotting out view of the stars. This was the part of the night that Leonard didn't appreciate so much. He turned into Jennifer, who remained behind him, silently holding him in her warm embrace. Though smaller than Leonard, she seemed large in that moment. Leonard felt he could get lost in her. He could bury his face in her arms and never find his way out.

They moved to the couch, and like the discarded sun, fell gracefully onto the cushions. The blanket that had covered Jennifer's shoulders was now underneath her. Leonard was on top, gently running his hand along the side of her body. Her dark blue eyes stared into his. Leonard brought his lips to her neck, where he could feel the warmth of her breath against his own. At that moment, he felt like a spring flower, one morning dew away from blooming.

He needed this. It might be the last time he'd ever feel another person's embrace; to feel what it meant to be human, to feel alive.

The shower ran. Leonard listened to the water spraying as he quickly dressed himself in the connecting bedroom. He had to move with haste, to escape before her shower was through. This was the only way he could spare Jennifer the trip to Manfred's house. As much as she wanted to help, Leonard couldn't let her.

Dressed in black pants and a black t-shirt, Leonard stood in the bedroom, waiting just a moment longer. He was calm and unmoving, ear craned towards the bathroom door. He listened for movement inside and fought back the urge to burst through the door. He wanted to see Jennifer one last time, to feel her skin against his fingertips just once more, but couldn't. As the water continued to pour, Leonard reluctantly stole away from the bedroom and out through the front of his apartment.

A hot, heavy humidity hugged him as he moved to his car. Once behind the driver's seat, he pulled up the address that his tech wiz friend had sent him just a few days ago. The screen on the dash of the car lit up and a computerized voice read off the address. He would arrive in approximately thirty-two minutes.

Sixty-six

I'm going.

Oliver fixated on the text from the quiet comforts of his security office. Though the weather was warm and muggy, a chill started up his skin. It was from Leonard. The reporter was going to Manfred Phillips's house, and if he didn't text Oliver by six in the morning, Oliver was to call Detective Baumgartner and give him Manfred's address. It was really happening.

Outside, the artificial lights of the power plant poured in through the square window. Oliver could feel the intensity of their brilliance on his cheek. *Friends* reruns played on the TV behind him, as always. A pen sat on the opened logbook on the desk, as always. There was no life outside the security box, save the slow groaning of the body of steel he was sworn to protect, as always. Everything was as normal. It was an ordinary night.

Unease set in upon the lonesome man in the lonesome office. Oliver thought about Leonard and about the children. What was going to come for them tonight?

The thoughts consumed Oliver. Even Joey Tribbiani couldn't silence the noise in his head. He hadn't known Leonard for very long, but the thought of a man, one who Oliver considered a friend, going into such a place alone was tormenting. If Leonard died, Oliver would bear some of the blame. He was probably the only person who knew where Leonard was going and why, but instead of helping, he was sitting in an office chair, three hours away.

Oliver stepped outside, beginning to feel cramped in the office. The door closed behind him shut off the sounds of the TV and introduced him to the peace of Clyde County's midnight sky. The plant creaked and groaned as usual, and the roads were quiet. Beyond the fields and banks of trees, Oliver listened for the train yard, hoping to hear the soft chug of a freight, but found nothing.

Pulling out his phone, Oliver glanced at the text again. He hadn't opened the message, so the bar, consisting of only two words, stretched across the screen. The words glared at him, ominously, saying more than just, *I'm going.* They said, *You should be here too,* and Oliver knew he should have been.

Oliver was lost in his reverie until a voice called out. The words surprised him, as did the tone. It was a mousy, gentle voice, drenched with conviction and varying in pitch, caught in the awkward stage of adolescence.

"He is going to die tonight."

Oliver, alarmed at the sound, spun to face the intruder. There, standing about three feet from the security guard, bare feet planted against the concrete, was the rail of a boy who Oliver had discovered hanging from the oak. His hair was the same, as was the blood on his face, the crown on his head, and the emptiness in his eyes. Everything was just the same as when Oliver originally found him.

A little stunned and a little scared, Oliver responded, "Who is going to die?"

Without a hitch, the boy answered, "Your friend."

"How do you know?"

"Does it matter?"

Oliver stared into the hollow eyes of the boy. The person, or being – he wasn't sure what he was – before him was only a youth old but seemed ancient. It felt to Oliver like he was staring into the face of God.

"No, I don't suppose it does." Oliver reached into his back pocket in search of his pack of cigarettes, but the pocket was empty. He must have left them in the office.

"Is Manfred the one who did this to you?"

The boy stepped forward. The yellow lights of the plant shone down on his angled frame, wrapped in a stretch of pale skin. He looked like a ghost, and that was because, Oliver considered, he was a ghost.

"I think you know the answer to that, Oliver."

The sound of his name leaving the boy's mouth was haunting. This had to be a dream. The whole experience seemed even more surreal than the visit to the void.

"Why is he doing this? Why did he do this to you? To the other children?"

Robert did not answer. An eerie silence set in upon the plant. Even the steel contraptions ceased to moan through their work. The air was a soft spell of nothingness. Oliver had never wished for the sounds of trains or highway traffic more than at this moment while he stared into the face of God, or the devil, or something else entirely.

"Are you going to help him?" Robert finally asked.

Oliver opened his mouth to respond, but the boy turned and walked away. For a moment, the red-haired security guard considered following but rejected the notion. He simply stood aghast, watching as the child disappeared into the darkness beyond the fence line.

A moment of quiet consideration passed before Oliver started running towards his truck. Never before had he carried a gun to work, and this night was no different. He would need to get one before heading north, which meant he would need to go home. That would add some time to the journey, no doubt, but it would be worth it. He couldn't face a murderer, a crazed child abductor, with no protection.

The old beast rumbled to life when Oliver placed his key in the Ranger. Rust shook from the steel and scattered across the pavement as he sped away from the plant. Out of the rearview, Oliver watched as the monolith of concrete and steel shrunk into the darkness. Surely, this would be the last time he worked security there. Possibly, he thought, it would be the last time he worked anywhere at all, barring how the night passed.

After twisting through the stretch of lane-less roads for about twenty minutes, Oliver was in his drive. The single-story home sat peacefully where it always had, looking as leisurely as ever. How careless this place was, with its white panel siding, stained a dark shade of green near the base, housing its black shingles overhead. This was Oliver's home, one which he built with Lela and Becca, one which he loved dearly, but the walls, the pane-glass windows, and the shingles cared nothing about Oliver. It was warm and cold at the same time.

Inside, the house was quiet. Ceiling fans spun, sourcing the only noise in the nearly empty house. Becca was sleeping. Oliver moved cautiously down the hall to his bedroom, tiptoeing so as not to wake her. He couldn't be caught. She would question him and try to stop him. Oliver knew there wouldn't be much trying. He would do whatever his daughter asked, even if it meant sacrificing four children and the life of a friend.

In his room, underneath a stack of miscellaneous junk, was a small weapons safe. Oliver displaced the junk and pulled the safe to his bed. After punching in the four-digit pin, the door of the safe swung open, revealing two handguns and several boxes of ammunition. Oliver grabbed his Sig .45 and two magazines that were already loaded. He briefly considered grabbing the other weapon as well but decided against it.

In less than two minutes, Oliver was ready to leave his home. He closed the safe and looked around the bedroom, wondering if it would be the last time he would stand there. On the nightstand by his bed, the picture of his family, of his wife, pleaded against him leaving. Oliver shook his head and crept from the room, back into the hallway. He couldn't turn away now.

As he moved down the hallway, Oliver continued to feel the strong pull of the photograph. Everything in him was saying *don't go*, but he knew he had to, so he kept trudging forward. He passed by the bathroom door and then by Becca's, stopping only for a second before continuing to the front door.

Once his palm was on the handle of the last obstacle, Oliver hesitated. Visions of the fishing hole, of laughing with his daughter by the water's edge, flashed across his mind. Visions of her bouncing through the puddles wearing her oversized overalls, and of her making macaroni art with her mother. Visions of her parallel parking in the empty school lot, giggling when she knocked over the orange cone that Oliver had brought from work. Visions. Visions of his daughter. He knew he couldn't leave now, not yet.

A moment later, Oliver was standing outside his sleeping daughter's door again. Inside, he could hear the gentle sounds of her snoring. He opened the door. It creaked ever so slightly, but not enough to wake Becca.

Peering inside, Oliver could see his daughter's face, illuminated by the dim blue light of the night sky. She looked beautiful. She looked like everything. She was life. What a wonderful young woman she had grown up to be. Oliver could feel the slashing of reality across his heart. A watering began behind the dams of his eyes. He couldn't stand there any longer, watching his daughter sleep, or he would certainly collapse.

A few heavy tears streamed down his cheeks as he closed Becca's door and made for his truck. He wondered, would that be the last time he'd ever see her? He wondered if four other children's lives would be worth the possibility of leaving his daughter parentless in a world so cold and miserable.

The answer had to be *yes*. Otherwise, he wouldn't have been in his truck, headed north.

Sixty-seven

2340 West Redbird Lane was smack in the middle of nowhere – not too far from civilization, but far enough to be surrounded by lightless streets and a thick Missouri wood. Leonard was parked about a half-mile from the driveway, which appeared to be a very long and narrow path of gravel, cloaked with a line of tall trees that stood like soldiers in formation. They completely hid Manfred's house from view, protecting him – guarding him.

Leonard had been sitting in his car for over an hour, just staring through the window at the dark wall of impenetrable woods. This time of year, the growth was like that of a jungle. It always amazed him, just how thick it became, but now it agonized him. Leonard wished it were thinner so he could see the home, see the full property he was about to break into.

After a few more minutes of waiting, of postponing the inevitable, Leonard stepped from his car, grabbing his phone from the center console. Overhead was a crescent moon and a canopy of stars which helped light up the road. It was nearing two in the morning, so there weren't any cars on the road, especially out in the middle of nowhere. The air was dead quiet; nothing could be heard but the crackle of falling leaves and nocturnal beasts. The reporter listened as he inched towards the driveway, every footstep feeling heavier than the last like gravity was stronger near Manfred's house.

Walking through quicksand for what seemed like an eternal mile, Leonard found himself at the base of the driveway. He stared up the slight hill, following the gravel path with his eyes as it bent behind the formation of trees, disappearing. The white rock and dust glowed beneath the night sky. Leonard stepped onto the uneven surface, feeling like a man walking the plank.

The home, which sat at the end of the long path, was enormous, made up of a mixture of stone and white siding. In front of the house were several stretches of garden beds, whose flowers were illuminated by the front porch light. A black Lexus was parked out front, but no minivan. This didn't discourage Leonard, who stood at the edge of the wood line, observing the scenery. The van was likely parked in the garage, or somewhere else on the large stretch of land. By the looks of the house, Manfred probably didn't like keeping the van out front, as it would diminish the grandeur of the property.

From his spot in the woods, Leonard could see there were multiple branches of paths leading around either side of the house. The property extended for quite some way beyond what Leonard could see from his hiding place. There was only one light on in the house from the look of it, shining through what appeared to be a living room window. Leonard didn't think Manfred would be awake so early in the morning, but he couldn't be certain.

After taking some time to initially examine the property, Leonard began to investigate deeper. He crept the edge of the woods, circling the house under the mask of darkness, hoping not to trip a motion light or whatever else might have been planted by Manfred. There seemed to be no life in the house. By all observations, the owner seemed to be asleep.

Leonard knelt in the woods behind the house, staring at a large back porch constructed of fine wood, housing a grill and a patio set. To his side led a path, well-worn and narrow, towards what appeared to be a building in the distance. Trees and shrubs lined either side of the path, obstructing Leonard's view of the structure in the distance, but he assumed it was a barn or stable of some sort. The dark construct looked like a gateway to hell. If the children were anywhere, they'd be there.

Cracking leaves and twigs beneath his feet, Leonard moved from the woods. He traveled slowly, swinging his head left and right, taking in the shadowed views. About fifty feet off the path, through a thin stretch of trees, Leonard noticed a pond. A little gazebo stood at the edge like a lonesome fisherman. The sight of the thing made Leonard wonder if Manfred had a family that visited and gathered there, eating barbeque from the porch's grill, skipping rocks across the water. Maybe little kids, similar in age to the ones trapped in a cellar somewhere, climbed on the roof and screamed, *cannonball!* before splashing into the muddy water. It was a disturbing thought that Manfred, who Leonard suspected was a kidnapper and a murderer, lived a normal life too. One where people loved him and cared for him. He certainly had a father, that much Leonard knew was true. Who else did he have? Who else did he love?

Leonard shook his head and kept moving, knowing he needed to focus. He couldn't get lost in his own head, as he always did. He needed to be mindless. He needed to be quiet and sharp. He needed to find the children.

After crossing the distance of the path, Leonard was standing in front of a two-story barn, constructed of aged wood, looking like it would leave a nice splinter if a hand ran along its surface. Leonard stood beneath the presence of the structure, staring up at it, feeling helpless and small. The building lorded over him, causing the fearful feelings in Leonard's mind to expand. The young reporter couldn't help but think he was mere feet from the answers he'd been searching for. All that divided him and the children could possibly have been just two barn doors.

With care, Leonard braced against the doors and pulled them apart. They were on tracks, and slid open with ease to reveal an empty room. Nothing but tall ceilings, load-bearing posts, and hay – lots of hay. The light on Leonard's phone shone on mounds of the yellow straw, baled up in small, square stacks. It was everywhere, to the ceiling even in some places. Lining the walls were six glassless window cut-outs, cabinetry, and an assortment of tools. There was no sign of children or anything out of the ordinary. The room was nothing but a vacant disappointment.

Leonard paced the barn, following the light of his cellphone. It beamed across the nothingness, illuminating more hay and more tools. After walking the entire barn twice over, Leonard dejectedly sat on a prickly stack, hanging his head in his hands. This barn and its emptiness had to mean the kids were either elsewhere on the property – perhaps in the main house, in some other hideaway – or in another location entirely, under someone else's care. Maybe Manfred John Phillips III wasn't a kidnapper or a murderer. Maybe he was just a normal man, living his life peacefully as an accountant for his brokerage firm. Maybe he was—

Sixty-eight.

"Janiya." a voice whispered.

It was Two. The sound of her name woke Janiya from her sleep. She didn't know what time it was but figured it was late in the night or very early in the morning, judging by how her body felt.

"Yea?" Janiya answered, rolling over on the concrete floor. Her elbow dug into her ribs, and her head rested on the back of her hand. It was uncomfortably comfortable, the only position in which she could catch any shut-eye.

"I can't stop thinking," Two said.

"About what?"

"About what you said earlier."

"What did I say earlier?"

"When you were arguing with …" Two went silent for a moment, "With him." He motioned. "You said that we shouldn't be here, that we were taken, just like how *you* were taken. Is that true? Do you really believe that?"

Janiya propped herself up on an elbow. She stared through the darkness, finding the outline of Two's fragile excuse for a teenage boy's body. He was staring at her, at least it seemed like he was. His body was pressed up against the edge of the cage. The sound of his voice was timid, scared. He seemed unsure about himself, unsure about everything. He seemed afraid. For the first time since Janiya arrived, one of the other children seemed human.

"I do believe that," Janiya said softly, also wanting to avoid waking the others. "I know it. You weren't born here. Your name is not *Number Two*."

"Then what is it?"

Janiya was taken back by the question. "I don't know. Maybe it's David, or Nick, or Bob."

"Bob?"

Janiya laughed quietly to herself. The sound of the name, spoken like a question, from a child who knew nothing of real life, was funny. It didn't even sound like a real word or a real name. It sounded like some fantasy, constructed by uncles and dads who were playing jokes on their nieces and nephews, sons and daughters.

"That's not the point," Janiya said. "The point is, you should have a life of your own. Children aren't meant to live in cages. No one is. They're meant to run around in fields and parks, playing tag with their brothers and sisters. They're supposed to have moms and dads who care about them, not keep them locked away, feeding them dog food. They're supposed to be loved and to love others. They're not supposed to live like this. This is no life. This is hell, no matter how hard your papa tries to spin it into heaven."

Another silence set in. It seemed like Two was struggling to grasp what Janiya was saying. She peered through the darkness at him. His big white eyes were closed and his head hung toward the floor.

"I know it's hard for you to understand," Janiya continued, "but it's true. Everything that I'm saying is true. You have parents out there who love you. You might have brothers or sisters who would love to have you back in their lives. I know I do."

"What is it like?"

"What is what like?"

"Being out there, beyond the portal, with your family?"

Janiya considered the question, fighting back the swarm of tears that threatened to assault her. The very thought of James and Jamel, Jasmine, Jade, and Mom was torture. Their memory was a guillotine, severing Janiya's mind in two. The pain she felt was tremendous, but she subdued it by continuously telling herself she was getting out of the Goddamn cage and the Goddamn cellar.

"Words can't explain."

"Try."

Sixty-nine.

Jennifer felt the walls of Leonard's apartment closing in around her. She felt trapped, useless. She'd been punching in Leonard's number for the last hour, being sent to voicemail every time. The sound of his voice telling her to *leave a message* on the other end was growing more and more irritating with every missed call. How could he be so stupid? So selfish?

She stared at the wall above the TV, tapping her foot on the ground. She dialed the number again and let her thumb hover over the *call* button. The device pointed towards Jennifer's face, mocking her. She hated being helpless. There was nothing she could do besides stand there and keep dialing. Leonard didn't leave an address or anything to help her find him. He left her with nothing.

"Fuck," she uttered under her breath, canceling the call and seeing her home screen, which was a picture of the sunset over a field by her house. Looking at home, an idea came to her.

Jennifer sped through contacts and found another number. She clicked call and listened to the hollow ring. Each gap between rings was an infinite period of silence like the world stopped spinning momentarily. It rang five times before there was an answer.

"Jennifer?" said Oliver. "Is everything alright?"

"Oliver, where are you?" Jennifer asked, an urgency consuming her words.

"In my truck. Why are you calling so late?"

"Where are you headed?"

"Uh …" Oliver went silent. All Jennifer could hear was the muffled sound of his breath.

"Oliver, just fucking tell me where you're going. Are you going to meet Leonard?"

Oliver hesitated, driving Jennifer into insanity, before answering, "Yes."

"You are? Well why the hell isn't he answering my calls? Where is he? What's Manfred's address?"

"What? Take it easy. I don't know. I don't know why he's not answering. I think his phone is turned off or something. What do you even …? Are you trying to go there?"

"He's alone. Yes, I'm trying to go there!"

"I don't think you should."

Jennifer let out an exhausted gasp in attempt to gather herself. She was tired and frustrated. All she wanted was a fucking address.

"Oliver, tell me the address. I'm already in St. Louis. I can probably be there in less than hour."

"I won't tell you. Not yet at least."

"Fuck, Oliver! Why are you so stubborn? His life could be in danger."

"Yes," Oliver agreed. Jennifer heard what sounded like his truck engine coming to an idle. "That's why I'm not going to give you the address. I'm not going to put your life in danger too."

There was a moment of intense silence. It was so quiet Jennifer could hear the *tick-tock* of Oliver's turn signals.

"Look," Oliver started, his voice as kind and simple as always. "I'll send you the address as soon as I get there. I'm just over an hour away now. When I'm parked and I know the situation, I'll text you. I'm also going to give you a number to call. Leonard gave me a detective's number – the guy who's been working Janiya's case. If anything is awry when I get there, you're going to call him and send him to our location."

"Why can't you just—"

Oliver hung up the phone, leaving Jennifer standing in Leonard's apartment. The walls continued to close in. All she could do was wait.

Seventy

On the foot of his bed, Manfred sat, holding his cock in his hands. It was early in the morning, far past his usual bedtime. Normally he was out by ten o'clock, eleven at the latest, but tonight was different. He was charged with the notion that the prophecy was rolling again, gaining momentum once more. The boy, Robert Banks, had caused a delay, but it was nothing that Manfred couldn't handle. And now, everything had fallen back into place.

Number Three was fiery in the beginning but submitted rather quickly – quicker even than Manfred would have predicted. He originally thought it would take some time to break her, which was why he was so hard on her during his first visit. If he had known she would give in and shut her trap so soon, he would have restrained from tossing her around so much. Though he had to admit, handling her like that was kind of electrifying. He almost didn't want her to break so soon, which was why he was happy she resisted a little during cleansing time. He enjoyed the thrill of putting his hands on her and demonstrating his will. The power he felt when in the cellar was like nothing Manfred could explain. It was, dare he say, Godlike, but he would never admit it aloud. He didn't even enjoy thinking it. He knew that God saw his inner thoughts and instantly felt guilty for making such a comparison.

The very thought of the girl was keeping Manfred up. She was the key to fulfilling the prophecy. The message he had preached earlier in the day was the God's honest truth. Manfred knew it in his heart. The world would soon give way to darkness, and it would be the Four who would restore it. Number Three, the girl from the real world, would be the guiding light for his children. She understood how the world worked, and all of its intricacies, which the other three could not comprehend. She was the key. She was the one who would help save the world.

Manfred massaged himself, thinking of all the good he'd done, knowing there was still more to be accomplished. He had all of his chess pieces in formation, and the weak boy had been weeded out. He could now assume his role as one of the few remaining disciples of the Lord. Feeling currents of energy surge through his veins like some sort of human circuit board, Manfred stood. The girl had been under his care for a few days now and had yet to receive a private message from her papa. Now would be as good a time as any.

The clock turned over to a new hour. As it did so, Manfred went for his robe, one hand still stroking himself. He would go to her. Janiya would finally learn the work of the Lord, in the same way a younger Manfred used to learn.

Seventy-one

Maybe he was—

A noise from near the house.

Leonard shot up from his seat on the hay. He was facing the barn doors, with a clear sightline down the path to the porch. To the reporter's surprise, backlit by a motion sensor light near the grill, there stood a figure. He was moving. Jesus Christ, he was moving. The figure stepped from the porch, headed right towards the barn.

Body fueled by fear and instinct, Leonard rushed to the barn doors. Not knowing what else to do, he slid them shut, trapping himself inside, hoping the man from the house hadn't spotted the gap. Leonard didn't think he could; it was so dark.

The next few moments were critical. He had to think what to do next. He could hide, or he could make for one of the window cut-outs. His first instinct was to bolt for the windows and get the hell out of the barn, so that's what Leonard did. He sprinted to the furthest window and placed his palms on the sill, getting ready to leap through, but right before his legs made to leap, something stopped him. Something inside him said, *Don't.*

Leonard, breathing heavily, stopped at the back edge of the barn. His hands were still on the rough surface of the sill when the doors began to slide open. Without thought, Leonard ducked behind a large stack of hay. In the next moment, the doors were open, and Manfred Phillips was standing in the entryway.

Quieting his breath was a chore, but Leonard tried his best to do so, watching the homeowner from the corner of his haystack. Manfred moved to the wall opposite Leonard and flicked on a light switch, revealing that the man was wearing nothing but a long, purple robe and tight briefs. His hair, which had been slicked back when Leonard saw him on the camera footage, was now thick and stiff in the early hours of the morning. The narrow edges of his face were focused.

What are you doing in here?

Leonard watched, wondering why anyone would need to come to a barn in the middle of the night. Then he remembered he was also in the barn in the middle of the night. He would have laughed, had the situation not been so severe.

Manfred, tall and slender, robe trailing his body like a cape, reached into a cabinet beneath a wall full of gardening tools. From it, he snatched what appeared to be a pill bottle. A moment later, Manfred opened the cap and tossed a handful of pills into his mouth, dry-swallowing them.

Sweat was beginning to fall like spring rain now. Leonard's cotton shirt might have been ten pounds, weighing his body down behind his haystack hiding spot. His legs felt weak. He watched Manfred place the pill bottle back in the cabinet, and he thought about how he could've been out the window, in a place of safety right now.

He longed for his car, parked just a mile or so away. He longed for air conditioning and leather seats and a safety belt. He longed for Jennifer. Goddammit. Why did he even come here?

Doubt and fear ate the edges of Leonard's mind. He was not a fighter. He had never been a fighter. He didn't believe he needed to own a gun and thought that people who did, owned them because they were scared and ignorant. But now, Leonard was scared and wished he had one. If Manfred was the villain Leonard thought he was, then what would he do if he found him hiding in his barn? If Manfred wasn't the villain Leonard thought he was, what would he do? Both possibilities were equally frightening. God, he wished he had a gun. He wished he was anywhere else. He wished—

Stop. It's for the children, you coward.

Leonard wanted to smack himself. He had never felt like this. It had to be the adrenaline of knowing that something life-changing might occur in the next few moments. His skin began to crawl away from his bones as he fought back the urge to flee.

Leonard's internal conflict was interrupted by the sight of Manfred turning to face towards his hiding place. Silently, Leonard turned his back to the stack and crouched. He didn't know why, given the stack stood about a foot taller than his head when upright, but something about crouching felt safer. It felt more hidden somehow.

Leonard listened as footsteps grew closer. Sandaled feet softly slid and shifted the hay and the dirt as Manfred moved towards the stack. This is it, Leonard thought. He looked from side to side, in search of a weapon. There were none. He would have to resort to fists if it came to that. Why hadn't he brought a fucking gun?

Settle down.

The footsteps crept closer. Leonard tried to calm himself. He thought about the children. He thought about how confident he had been when he knew he was going to find them. He needed to find that confidence again. The children's lives were at stake. Cowering in fear wasn't going to help them.

Leonard peered through a slit in the bales. Manfred was about five feet away, headed straight for Leonard, almost like he knew he was there. A few more steps, and then the robed man stopped, his narrow face looking dark.

Manfred turned, facing another stack of hay. There were about ten average-sized bales piled up, looking as ordinary as everything else in the barn. After a brief overhead stretch, Manfred begin to lift the hay. He groaned and grunted as he heaved the bales directly in front of Leonard's hiding place. After a few heaves, Leonard was completely blinded. The piles of hay were stacked directly in front of his slit. He could only listen now.

And the next thing that he heard was the rattling of a chain.

Seventy-two

Janiya was in the middle of explaining her life to Two, telling stories about school and her friends and taking family trips to the zoo, when the cellar door opened. The magnificent light from the room beyond poured into the cellar, temporarily blinding Janiya and her friend. The slender figure of their captor appeared, face hidden in a shadow as the light struck his back. This couldn't be good.

The storytelling ceased as Janiya crept to the back of her cage. She laid back down on her side and pretended to be asleep. The attempt was poor, and she knew it. From his perch atop the stairs, their abductor was like God, seeing all things. He certainly had to notice when she crawled back into her frightened fetal position.

Sounds of creaking wood echoed through the cellar as he moved down the stairs. Janiya squeezed her eyes shut, praying that he would remember that he forgot something on the other side of the cellar and leave again. This wish didn't come true. The wood continued to creak until he was standing in the open space between the four cages. Janiya rolled over and peered through her eyelashes at the man.

This visit, the dim overhead lights weren't turned on. He just stood in the darkness, robe swaying to a still from the walk down, staring directly at Janiya's cage. He was vile. Janiya could see the sharp points of his face even in the dark. His nose was a butcher knife, and his cheeks were stone, cutting through the olive skin that sheathed them.

"Papa," said a voice, undeniably One's, in a revering tone. Janiya wanted to throw something at the boy. He was so fucking stupid.

The captor shooed One away with a hand, saying no words in return. This action made Janiya want to laugh. Maybe it would help the boy realize his ignorance, and lead him to understand how awful his papa was.

"Number Three," Papa said as he walked across the cellar, moving behind some of shelves in the corner of the room.

Shit.

Janiya listened, as her view of the man was severed. There were some clicking sounds and then what sounded like a door swinging open. What the hell was he doing back there?

"I said, *Number Three.*" The man came back into view. The front of his body was in a wash of light. He wore nothing but the robe and boxer briefs. This couldn't be good at all.

"Yes," Janiya responded, her voice consumed with horror.

"I have to show you something."

Janiya retreated onto her knees. There was nothing she wanted less than to be shown anything by this man. Whatever it was, it was going to be bad. She began to think her worst fears were about to come true. She wanted to be sick.

Janiya looked up. He was swaying in front of her cage, fishing the key from his robe's chest pocket. He was a nightmare, standing high above the wires of Janiya's home, looking down upon her with a crooked smile. "Come with me," he said, as the door to the cage rattled open.

Janiya sat still, looking up at his smiling face, her body aching with fear. She didn't want to move. In fact, she couldn't have moved if she tried. She was frozen in terror.

He reached into the cage and grabbed Janiya by the hair, yanking her out onto the concrete floor. The rough ground ripped the skin away from her knees and elbows. Janiya cried out in pain.

"I didn't ask you, did I?"

After gathering herself, Janiya responded, "No."

"No, what?"

"Papa ... no, Papa."

Rage was beginning to mix with her fear. Janiya wouldn't be thrown around like that. She wouldn't be—

He yanked her to her feet by the hair. Janiya cried out again.

"Come," he said, pulling her by the ear to the back of the cellar, away from the rest of the cages towards where they bathed earlier. As they moved, Janiya spotted a lavender light shining through the shelving, coming from one of the strange doors she'd spotted before. Moments later, they were standing in front of an opening that led into a separate cellar room.

This room was not as dark or cold as the room which housed the cages. Its floor was covered with a thick, plush carpet. There were pillows and blankets, and hot lamps covered with purple shades. It was warm and smelled like incense. It was disgusting.

"It is time for your first private message, my dear Number Three." The man pulled his hand from Janiya's ear and ran it down to the small of her back. A soft push thrust her into the room and onto the floor. With a snap of movement, she was on her back, scrambling to press her body against the wall in a defensive posture. He was standing at the doorway still, pulling the robe from his shoulders. He hung it on a rack drilled into the wall near the doorway. It was in this moment that Janiya decided she wouldn't go softly.

As he stepped further into the room, Janiya lunged at him, swinging wildly at his face and his stomach, but nothing landed. Her blows came crashing into the grip of her abductor, and she was almost immediately entrapped in his brutal embrace. He caught both her arms and spun her around, squeezing the breath from her lungs in a fierce hug.

"*That,*" he paused and exhaled onto the back of her neck, "is not how you earn the Lord's favor."

He pushed her to the floor a second time. The life in Janiya's fight left her as her knees hit the floor and her head collided with the concrete wall, tearing flesh from the area just beneath her hairline. A thin streak of blood trickled towards her eye. She wiped it away and began to plead, "Please, don't."

The man knelt beside her. His touch was gentle again as a hand fell to her shoulder. Janiya continued to cry, closing her eyes and turning her head away from her captor. His hot breath kissed her burning skin.

Then there was a voice.

"Papa! Papa! Look out, Papa!"

Seventy-three

The cellar was dark and cold. Three children looked through the steel wires of their cells at Leonard. Each of them contained a set of wide, white eyes and even whiter skin. Their hair was wild, and they reeked of fear. Leonard didn't want them to know that he was also afraid – very afraid.

"Who are you?" a boy asked.

"He is from the world." A girl this time.

"From beyond the portal." A different boy.

"Get away from here, demon," said the original boy. "I've seen you before!"

Leonard held out a hand to try and settle the children. It didn't work.

"Where is Janiya?" Leonard asked, his voice quiet and calm, though his nerves were erupting.

"Don't you tell him," the original speaker commanded.

There was a brief moment of silence and confused staring. Everyone in the cellar was in a state of shock.

"She is back there," the other boy said, fear coursing through his words.

Leonard looked down the hall of the cellar, where a purple light shone from behind some shelving.

"You will burn, Two," the original boy threatened. Then, as Leonard rushed towards the back room, the boy began to shout, "Papa! Papa! Look out, Papa!"

The sound of a door closing rang through the cellar. The lavender light at the end of the hall then disappeared. The only light in the cellar now, was that coming from the barn above. He couldn't see a fucking thing and the barrage of children's voices continued.

Reaching into his pocket, Leonard found his phone and turned on the flashlight. As soon as the white light stretched out across the cellar, a figure emerged. It was Manfred. He was moving fast, lunging forward. Before Leonard knew what was happening, the man's shoulder was in his gut. Leonard dropped his phone with a wheeze, the light skipping across the floor with the object. An eruption of pain surged through his spine as he and Manfred crashed into the concrete floor.

What ensued was like nothing Leonard had experienced before. Having never been in a fight, he didn't know what to expect. It wasn't fast-paced striking and hard blows to the head like he'd seen on TV. Instead, the two jostled on the floor, grunting and huffing for air as they locked each other in a vicious grapple; choking air from each other through squeezing and scratching and clawing.

Manfred gained Leonard's chest and gripped his arms, trying to pin him to the floor. Leonard squirmed and kicked on his back, feeling the weight of the child abuser shift as he bucked. Leonard's lungs worked for oxygen. He was sweaty. Manfred was sweaty. The breath of his opponent was hot and whisky-doused, a foul stench irradiating from his skin. He was vile, but Leonard was too at that moment. Each sought death for his opponent. As Manfred freed a hand, Leonard feared that he might be the one to meet the last cruel fate.

A fist landed against Leonard's chin, and then again on his cheek. The force stung, but his adrenaline was moving. A third punch was coming, but Leonard moved his head at the last moment, causing Manfred to strike the concrete floor. The kidnapper shrieked and instinctively reeled his hand away. Leonard, sensing an opportunity, pulled the man's head down. Once locked in a tight embrace again, disabling Manfred's ability to strike, Leonard sunk his teeth into his cheek.

The copper-like taste of blood filled Leonard's mouth as he ripped a chunk of skin away from Manfred's face. Crimson fluid began to pour over both men. Manfred cried out again, a deep bellow this time. He pawed at the hole in his face and then frantically began to slam his fists down upon Leonard.

"You fucking …!" Manfred screamed, indeterminable words escaped in violent gasps as he delivered blow after blow to Leonard's arms, ears, chest, and face. He was swinging blindly, but effectively. From his position atop, using his larger frame, Manfred possessed a clear advantage. He was dealing a great amount of pain to Leonard, who was doing everything he could to block the punches but was failing.

"You thought you were going to come to my property, to my house?" Manfred stood, sucking for air, and stumbled away from Leonard, who was nearly immobilized from the assault on his face. Both were exhausted. Leonard began to drag his body away from the kidnapper, using his forearms to crawl. "Do you wish to hamper the Lord's will?"

Sweat and blood poured from Leonard as he looked back towards Manfred, who was moving to a shelf in discombobulated steps. From it, Leonard watched him fetch an object, its long, silver blades reflecting light from the barn above. A pair of hedge shears.

Manfred had to stop to suck in oxygen as he turned back to Leonard. His face was torn and bleeding. The sharp angles of his nose and chin were haunting, making him look like the devil's spawn. Leonard knew, as the deranged man stepped over him, that he was about die. He looked up at the open shears and then into Manfred's narrow black eyes, scared for his life.

Leonard's eyes were pleading, not to Manfred, but to anyone, anything at all who could help. He continued away, crab crawling on his elbows, face upright to watch his counterpart. After traversing a couple of feet across the concrete, Leonard was at the center of the cages. He could see the faces of the children looking at him. Their hollow eyes shot between him and Manfred. One of the children was smiling. It was the one who had threatened and called out just minutes before.

Understanding his fate, Leonard felt the urge to cry. He had failed the children. Here was where they would reside for the remainder of their lives because he had failed.

"Look, my children." Manfred exhaled. "This is what I've been warning you about for all these years. Look at the filth before you. This is what becomes of those who live in the world above. They become consumed by wickedness. This man wishes to defy God's will, and now, he must be punished."

Manfred dropped to one knee and casually slipped the shears into Leonard's stomach. The pain was immediate and immense. All of the oxygen in Leonard's body escaped like he was a popped balloon. Not knowing what else to do, Leonard grabbed at the handles of the shears. His palms found Manfred's hands and then his wrists. Face still bleeding, Leonard's murderer grinned, malice coursing through his eyes. Blood began to fill Leonard's mouth as he watched the shears pull away from his stomach. Manfred held them high above his head, readying for a second plunge.

Closing his eyes, Leonard attempted to make peace with his reality. His last moments were going to be in this cellar, with the children he had failed all staring at him while he was murdered. They would go on living in cages because Leonard wasn't strong enough to save them. God, he wished he was back in his apartment with Jennifer. He didn't want to die here.

Running through his final thoughts, Leonard braced for a second stabbing. There was a fire in his belly that couldn't be extinguished. He didn't want more holes, but the reality was inevitable. Leonard closed his eyes as the shears began dropping towards him, but before they entered his body a second time, a loud crack rang out across the walls.

Leonard's ears sang as his eyes opened, revealing that the side of his murderer's head was now missing. Blood oozed from the gaping hole, pouring out like a slow river as Manfred's lifeless body slumped on top of Leonard. The shears went clamoring against the concrete as they slipped from his hands.

Everything was warm. Leonard's stomach felt like it had been ripped out of his body. His face stung from being pelted. There was a bloody ringing in his ears from the violent blast of a pistol's report.

The last thing he saw was the faces of the children before everything went black.

Seventy-four

"Leonard. Leonard! Are you alright?" Oliver ran to his friend's aid. He rolled Manfred's limp body over and saw the gaping holes in Leonard's stomach, pumping out blood in thick spatters. The children were shouting and crying. One of them in particular, a boy, was hollering threats and insults at Oliver, cursing him to the grave. He paid the child no mind. They would be rescued in due time. First, he needed to attend to the dying man on the floor – to his dying friend.

Oliver knew almost nothing about first aid, especially for stomach wounds, so his first instinct was to press his hands against the opening. Warm, sticky blood covered his hands and seeped through the cracks between his fingers as soon as he forced them against the wound. Oliver grew frantic, having not the slightest idea what to do. The only thing crossing his mind was that he needed to keep Leonard alive until emergency services arrived. He had texted Jennifer, telling her to call the detective as soon as he entered the barn and saw the cellar door opened.

"Help's on their way," he assured.

"The girl," said Leonard, his voice but a broken whisper. "Locked … in the back."

"What? Keep quiet." Oliver ordered. He looked at the children, whose eyes were large and confused. They were weeping, and their little bodies shook, each of them hysterical. The raging boy rattled his cage while a girl rocked back on her heels and pressed her hands against her ears. It was chaos.

"Don't worry," Oliver said gently, hands still pressed against Leonard's stomach. "It's going to be alright. It's all going to be alright."

"You demon!" The boy shouted as his fingers wrapped white around his cage's mesh. "You murdered our papa!"

Oliver, slack-jawed, just looked at the child. It struck him that the kids loved the man who Oliver had just put a bullet through. They considered him a father, a *papa*.

"Where is the other girl? Where's Janiya?"

"There's a room in the back," another boy said. "Where Papa takes us to deliver his personal messages. She is in there."

Oliver shook his head. "Leonard, can you keep pressure against this?"

Leonard nodded and weakly brought his hands to his stomach, coughing and splattering blood over Oliver's cheeks. Wiping off the blood, Oliver took off down the hallway, passing by some shelving that was illuminated by the barn light and a phone's flashlight. Oliver grabbed the cellphone and found the door. He ripped it open and saw a little girl, crouched in the corner of the room, shaking in fear.

"Janiya?"

The little girl sprinted to Oliver and wrapped her arms around his waist. She was crying, and also smiling.

"It's okay," Oliver said. "It's alright now. We've got you. I've got you."

The girl couldn't stop crying. She held Oliver in the tightest hug he'd ever received. The embrace reminded him of the time Becca hugged him, while they watched as her mother was lowered into a grave. Becca's was a hug derived from grief, a powerful emotion, but Janiya's was sourced from something on the opposite end of the spectrum.

"Come with me," Oliver said, resting his palm on her shoulder, gently guiding her towards Leonard and the other children.

The others were still crying, visibly shaken by the sight of their dead papa on the floor. The angrier boy never stopped screaming. Every word he spoke caused the entire cellar to rumble like an earthquake was shifting the Earth beneath the concrete floors.

"Hey. Hey, now. It's alright," Oliver told the boy, but he didn't listen. The child just kept on, and the cellar kept on, shaking and rumbling. The force almost seemed to be magnifying with each word, each insult, in some unexplainable way. Oliver wasn't sure if he was imagining it or not.

Janiya was moving on her own now, towards the other girl's cage. In her hand was a key, which she used to unlock the cage. Next, Janiya unlocked the boy's cage, the one who wasn't shouting and hollering. As soon as the door swung open, the boy crawled out and sprinted towards the crying girl. Oliver watched as he wrapped his arms around her, hugging her in the same fashion that Janiya had just hugged Oliver.

"It's going to be alright," the boy told the girl. A smile extended the length of his face, which gleamed with the drying streaks of tears. The girl nestled into his chest and hugged him back. Oliver turned his head, letting them have their moment.

"I don't think we should let this one out," Janiya said. The sound of her voice was like hearing a memory. Oliver had heard it before, in his dreams, but now it was real life. It was such a strange feeling.

"Why not?" Oliver asked.

"Listen to him. Look at him. He's insane. He actually believes all the shit that asshole told him."

The boy continued to scream, and the light which poured in from the barn seemed to flicker. Oliver was stunned but shook it off, knowing he had to be imagining things. It had to be a side effect of the trauma.

"Devils!" shouted the boy. "All of you."

"Easy, boy," Oliver calmly said. "It's okay. Everything is okay."

The boy turned his head, allowing his white eyes to meet Oliver's, sending shivers up his spine. This boy was otherworldly, reminding Oliver of Robert Banks. Looking at the child made Oliver just as uncomfortable. It was a strange feeling, being terrified of a thirteen-year-old.

"Maybe you're right," Oliver spoke to Janiya. "Leonard, how are you doing?"

"I'm still here," Leonard choked out and spat up more blood. He looked bad, but there was nothing Oliver could do until the medical services arrived.

"You're going to be alright," Oliver said as he knelt beside his friend. "Here, let me take over."

Once again, Oliver pressed his hands against Leonard's stomach. It was warm, but the rest of Leonard's body was growing cold and stiff. Oliver could see that his face was already swollen from his fight with the kidnapper. There were small slashes on his cheeks and forehead from fists colliding with them. One eye was completely swollen shut.

"Let me out!" the boy shouted.

"Shush, now!" Oliver commanded.

The other boy said, "Yea, come on, One, calm down."

"Silence, Two." He looked at Oliver. "I said, let me out. I demand you let me out!" With the boy's words came an eruption of sound that sent Oliver flailing to the concrete beside Leonard. Janiya and the others went tumbling over as well. Oliver looked up, watching as the wires of the boy's cage exploded from their structure, splintering through the air like tiny javelins.

"What the hell?" Oliver said as a burst of pain shot through his body. He looked down as the boy rushed out of his cage, loping towards the huddle of men on the ground. Children's screaming erupted again as Oliver found three long splinters of steel lodged into his body. One stabbed through his chest while the others punctured the organs under his ribs.

"One, no!" shouted Janiya. "Stop!"

But there was no stopping the child. He had the hedge shears in but a second. And another second later, the blades found a home beside the splinter in Oliver's chest.

The vision in Oliver's eyes began to fail as his body shook in a violent, uncontrollable spasm. He slumped and stared at the bloody gardening tool in the boy's hands, in a state of disbelief that this was how his life would end.

As the room around him collapsed, Oliver thought about Becca. Her red hair, wispy and free, falling over her freckled face. Her smile when she caught a fish. Her little overalls, soaked from puddles. Her Chuck Taylor's muddying up the couch. The way she loved her mom. The way she said, *I love you, Dad.*

"Er ... hello," a tired voice said, followed by a drawn-out yawn. "Detective Baumgartner."

"Detective Baumgartner," Jennifer rushed, "My name is Jennifer Tennyson. I'm—"

"Who ...? Why are you calling so early in the fucking morning? How did you get this number?"

Jennifer exhaled. "It doesn't fucking matter. I have information about the Peters case. Now you need to shut the hell up and listen to me."

"Janiya Peters?" he said and groaned. "What is—"

"I know where she is. And you need to get there immediately. There are lives in danger. Multiple lives."

"Hold on. Hold on." Baumgartner ordered. Jennifer listened as he made a series of rustling sounds like moving out of bed. "Where is she? How do you know where she is? And why are you saying *lives*? How many—"

"Just fucking listen. You need to get to 2340 West Redbird Lane immediately! There are children being held in a cellar. There are men trying to get them out of it. There's a fucking murderer who is going to try and stop them. So you need to move. I'm only calling you because I was told to call you first. I'm calling 9-1-1 now."

"Alright, alright. 2340 West Redbird Lane. I'm going to check it out. Don't ..." a crashing sound came like Baumgartner had dropped his phone. A moment later he said, "Don't. I'm on it. I will send people. Don't worry about calling anyone else."

"What? Why not?"

He hung up, offering Jennifer no answer. She was standing in Leonard's kitchen, sweating with anxiety. *Why the hell would he tell me not to worry about calling anyone else? It's not like it's going to hurt.*

She stood there a moment in a stunned silence. She was scared for Leonard. She was scared for Oliver. She was scared for the children.

"Fuck him," she said, dialing 9-1-1.

Seventy-six

Deputy Michael Voss, a two-year veteran of the St. Louis County Police Department, was the first to arrive on the scene. He walked a long stretch of darkness to the barn door, the red-and-blues of his cruiser cycling across the trees and the night air. Through the doors of the barn, yellow lights lit up yellow hay on the floor – the same floor that had a four-by-four-foot opening in the far corner. Screaming and shouting echoed out through the hole in the ground, sounding like the voices of children.

His mustached lip pursed, and his brow furrowed. Voss grabbed the handle of his pistol, a standard-issue Glock 22 he'd never used outside of the range. He hoped to God he wouldn't have to use it in the next few moments.

The officer shivered as the soft ground of the barn gave way, just a little, underneath his black boots. The voices grew louder as he came nearer to the hole. Every noise startled him, even the familiar sound of the radio on his hip when it shot off, alerting the officer that more cars were coming, as were medical services. That was good, Voss thought, hoping that he wouldn't be hitching a ride in one of the incoming ambulances.

"Hello?" the deputy shouted as approached the hole. "This is Deputy Voss, with the St. Louis County Police Department. What's going on down there?"

"Help!" a child's voice shouted in return.

Voss ran to the opening and glanced down, his eyes passing over a flight of stairs to take in a scene of absolute chaos. Three men lay on the floor in pools of blood. Three children lay beside them, piled up on a fourth child who was screaming and crying. There were cages and bloody gardening tools. There was a pistol on the floor near the debris of what looked like an exploded dog kennel. And there was the putrid stench of death.

Deputy Voss reached for his radio and attempted to called in a report, but the signal was jammed. *What the ...?*

Shocked, scared, and confused, the officer began to hear the distant *chug-chug-chug* of a helicopter echoing through the air.

"What is that?" one of the children asked, piercing Voss with a set of milk-white eyes. For a moment, it seemed the officer was staring into the pit of hell.

"I don't know," Voss said, still standing atop the cellar door. "It's ... it's all going to be alright."

The officer started down the rickety stairs, when the sounds of footsteps and jangling gear alerted him from the barn's doors. Voss turned, facing the entryway, where a team of six men came funneling through. Each wore body armor and held rifles that bore long, cylindrical suppressors on the ends.

Voss opened his mouth to speak, but before a word could escape him, the soft and sudden *pffft* of a suppressed bullet ripped through the air and into his head.

Seventy-seven

He awoke to the sterile, white walls and lights of what seemed to be a hospital bedroom. Hanging over his bed were unknown medical tools and electronics, whizzing and whirring as tubes like tentacles hung through space and found themselves lodged in Leonard's arms. Every inch of his body ached, including his throbbing head. His mouth felt like a desert, dry as the Sahara. Never before had he needed water so badly.

After a few painful moments of coming back to life, Leonard began to realize that where he thought he was, wasn't where he thought was. He wasn't in a St. Louis hospital ward at all. Everything in the room was … different. Nerves beginning to erupt, Leonard attempted to sit up, immediately finding he didn't possess the strength to do so. His stomach felt like it had been plucked from his body, leaving behind nothing but a gaping hole. That was when Leonard began to remember what happened in the cellar. That was when he remembered being stabbed by a pair of shears.

Leonard winced and clutched his gut. Just the thought made him surge with pain. It also made him curious. He pulled up his gown and saw an enormous X of thick black stitches running the length of his recently shaved stomach. He looked like he'd received a transplant in some backstreet organ lab.

The sound of a door opening took Leonard's attention. As the gray steel was slung open, a woman of about thirty walked in, wearing a long, white doctor's coat. Her face was plain but pretty, and a little fierce. She kind of reminded him of Deputy Williams back in Clyde County.

"Mr Beard," she announced, looking down at a clipboard. "It seems you've finally come back to us."

Leonard looked her in the eyes, brown and dark, then gazed past the doctor into a hallway, wondering where it went.

"My name is Dr Haller." Her voice was shrill and disconnected, sounding more like she worked a toll booth than an operating room. "How are you feeling?"

Head on his pillow, neck craned, Leonard replied in a hoarse voice, "Okay. But I could use some water."

Dr Haller smiled. "I'm sure you could, but unfortunately, we can't have you swallowing anything right now." She motioned to the scars extending over Leonard's belly. "All of your vital nutrients are being fed to you through some of these tubes. I know it is a bit uncomfortable, but you will have to wait at least seventy-two hours before consuming anything."

Leonard groaned. "Where are the kids? Where's Oliver?"

The doctor sat on a backless chair and rolled up to Leonard's bedside. She began turning knobs on the medical equipment and then fetched a needle and a small bottle of dark liquid from a drawer adjacent to the bed. She drew the liquid from the bottle and flicked the end of the needle before jamming it into a cannula inserted in Leonard's right arm.

"You will find out everything soon enough, Leonard." Dr Haller injected the liquid into the right forearm. "Does that hurt?"

Leonard shook his head, finding it a strain to speak.

"That's great. You're doing great," the doctor encouraged. "You know, you've been out for almost twenty-eight hours? That's a long time to be under."

Leonard smiled an awkward smile. He was confused. The fact that he didn't know where he was, and that this doctor wouldn't tell him where Oliver and the kids were, was a bit unnerving.

"That should help with the pain. In about five or ten minutes, you'll feel like you're floating above the atmosphere. How's that sound?" She spoke to Leonard like he was a child. "Now, I know you're probably a bit perplexed, maybe even a bit scared, but you'll find your answers soon enough. For now, just get some rest, and try not to move too much. Don't want to pull those stitches now, do we?"

Seventy-eight

Jennifer sat on Leonard's couch, holding her phone, shaking as she watched the morning news. The TV showed the familiar faces of Leonard and Oliver, as well as two faces she didn't recognize, those of a dead police officer and the man called Manfred. An STKN anchor was in the process of explaining that Leonard and Oliver broke into Manfred's house, and a fight ensued. Apparently, the story was that Manfred killed Leonard and Oliver in self-defense. The officer died by a stray bullet upon arriving on the scene.

Jennifer stood and sent her coffee mug through the television. A spiderweb of cracks shot across, separating the screen in a fractured array of bright colors. She was furious, knowing that Leonard and Oliver were being slandered. Something, someone, was covering everything up for some reason. They didn't just *break in.*

The apartment fell silent, leaving Jennifer standing near the couch, breathing in heavy gasps. She was sweating, boiling over. The reporter mentioned nothing about the children, or a cellar, or anything like that. How the fuck could there be nothing else? How could all four of the men have died? Nothing about the report made sense. It seemed far too convenient that every person on scene died, leaving no one alive to make a statement.

What were they hiding?

Jennifer began to cry, sinking back into the couch, defeated and exhausted. Her mind was on the verge of imploding. She didn't know what to believe. Everything in her wanted the report to be false, but why would it be? There was no reason for the news station to hide the information from the public. It didn't make sense, but nothing made sense lately.

After what seemed like an eternity of sitting, thinking, texting Baumgartner for information, and dry-sobbing, Jennifer found herself beginning to believe what the reporter was saying. Leonard was dead, murdered by a man who was just protecting his home. And Oliver was dead too. And a police officer was dead. And the kidnapper was—

The door to Leonard's apartment sprang open with a sharp blast. Jennifer lunged from the couch as four figures poured in through the opening, pointing weapons towards her chest. She tried to scream, but before she could, a hand was over her mouth and a needle was in her neck.

Seventy-nine

A red sun fell over a massive Clyde County sky. Six-wheeled diesel trucks and old beaters formed a cavalcade of remembrance along the winding county road that led to the Saint Clara cemetery. The wheels had stopped moving, parked now, and the drivers all stood around an open hole, which bore six-feet into the fertile, Southern Missouri dirt. Everyone was teary-eyed, even those who weren't quite friends with the dead man.

All eyes were on Becca, whose heels were firmly planted in the soil. Her pale, freckled skin popped against the black dress that draped to the dirt near her ankles. The strawberry hair atop her head was tied into a bun that more resembled a crown. She reigned strong, a symbol of power before the court of black-clad onlookers. Everyone expected her to cry, to break down, to call out to the sky in anger, but the girl did none of these things. She just stood still, eyes closed, head facing towards the gray clouds, waiting for the preacher to finish his words, as then it would be her turn to speak.

"Thank you all for coming," Becca finally said, voice rivaling the freight train that chugged by in the distance.

Becca carried on with a series of words she wouldn't remember afterwards. The speech fell from her lips as though she was a drone, being spoken through by some distant operator. She felt nothing, numb to her core. All that crossed her mind was that she wanted to be away – far, far away. She needed to put miles between her and Clyde County, the place that reminded her of all she'd lost.

After the speech, the orphan crept through the crowd. Hands fell upon her shoulders and whispers of, "I'm so sorry," met her ears as she weaved between the somber townsfolk. Becca could only nod and say that it was alright, though it wasn't. She thanked them for coming as they tried to console her. Even when Sheriff Farnswell, who seemed partly to blame for her father's burial, stood before her and offered his condolences, Becca accepted. She shook her head and brushed by, rushing to get away.

As the casket began to lower into the ground, Becca sprinted to her father's Ranger. Once behind the wheel, she threw the truck into gear and drove. She had no destination in mind. Becca just knew that she needed to speed away, to escape the sight of her father being put to rest, mere feet from where her mother already lay. The sight was too much to bear.

The crowd of people in the rearview began to fade to a blur as Becca put a few miles between them. Windows down, she listened to the hum of the wind and watched the twisting road, hoping this would be the last time she ever saw the place that had taken everything from her. She wanted to cry; she wanted to feel that rich sense of emotion, the sting of grief, but couldn't. All she'd felt since hearing the news about her father was a bone-numbing anger. He died, and so did the reporter, without ever finding the kids. *Home defense* is what the detective and the news reports labeled it. It didn't even seem real.

Becca slammed her fist against the steering wheel. As she pulled her red palm away, a light, brighter than any she'd ever seen, emerged in the truck's mirrors. Through the open windows, she could hear a steady *clank-clank-clank*, followed by an otherworldly blast of sound that shook the steel of her truck. The horizon she had just left behind was then engulfed in towers of flame.

Eighty.

Russell Keating adjusted his tie and brushed his hair with his fingers before walking through the door. "Hello everyone," he said, eyeballing three candlestick-white children, one of whom was chained to a steel chair. A black girl of about the same age was also present, sitting next to a wheelchair-bound black man. "How are you all feeling?"

"Where are we?" questioned the man in a weak voice. His name, Russell had been told, was Leonard Beard.

"Don't you worry about that, Leonard." Russell smiled and closed the door behind him. The sound of a steel bolt slamming into a lock rang through the room. The children looked scared, their little bodies trembling slightly. Three of them wore protective glasses to shield their eyes from the bright, artificial lights. "You will all learn, in due time, where you are, and why exactly you are here. Just know," Russell smiled again, "that you are here because you are very special."

One of the girls, Janiya, shifted in her seat. The other girl, whose name was discovered to be Maria, clutched the chainless boy's hand. This boy was named Caleb. The other one, the safety risk, was named Jonah. This at least was what their parents called them, before they had been abducted by the maniac who now resided in a grave.

"What do you mean, *special?*" asked Janiya.

"I think you have an idea of what I mean," Russell shared, walking the room, eyeing each child steadily, firmly. "But if you don't, you will certainly find out very soon."

377

Janiya shifted again and looked at Leonard, who was still too weak to say or move much.

Russell continued, "I just wanted to be the first to cordially welcome you to our facility. I know the last few days have been rough. It is hard leaving the life you know and entering into something completely new. Janiya, you should know a thing or two about that. Perhaps you've been of aid to your friends?" The question was rhetorical. Russell went on, "I can promise you all that your lives here will be like nothing that you experienced in that madman's cellar."

"Shut up you liar, you dem—"

Russell snapped, and a small shock flowed through Jonah's raging body, quickly silencing the boy.

"I know you might be angry, but you must know that everything Manfred taught you was a lie. Well," Russell stopped to consider, "at least, it was stretching of the truth."

"How do you know what he taught us?" Caleb asked, his voice small and fragile.

"He had a camera system in your cellar. I know everything about what went on there. Your papa couldn't have been more wrong about you all being chosen by God to fulfill some divine prophecy." Russell laughed in mockery of the dead man. "But he couldn't have been more right about you all being special. He was right in you being connected. He was right in saying that you will change the world."

Janiya shrunk back in her chair. Russell watched as her thumbs began to tumble over one another. Caleb squeezed Maria's hand even tighter. Leonard just watched, eager to hear what Russell had to say.

"Now is not the time to discuss everything in detail. Like I said, you will all find out very soon what your purposes are." Russell smiled one last time and began back towards the door. With a computerized click, a light flashed green overhead, and the deadbolt released. "I know that you will come to love this place, and you will find a great respect for the work we do here."

Russell left the room, his place taken by one of the facility's head caretakers. A voice called, "Mr Keating, Sec-Def is on the phone for you."

Russell turned and saw a low-level agent holding a satellite phone. The commander of the Department of Scientific Research for Advanced Defenses took the phone, shooing the agent away with his hand.

"This is Keating," Russell said into the voice box as he walked through the labyrinth of hallways that lay six stories beneath the Earth's surface. The new subjects in his custody sparked the commander's interest in examining some of those who were further along in their progress. The four children and Leonard were like babies, who had just opened their eyes for the first time. They were clueless of the magnitude of their existence.

"How are the new research subjects doing?" asked the Secretary of Defense.

"They're doing fine. In fact, I just gave them their welcoming brief."

"Very good," said the slow voice on the other end of the phone. "And I take it everything on the outside is being handled? Judging by the media stories, it seems that all is in fine order."

"Yes, everything is in order. One of my best agents has been in St. Louis, keeping everything at bay."

"Baumgartner?"

"Yes, Baumgartner. He arranged a train carrying explosive materials to the Clyde County power plant to derail near Oliver Brady's funeral procession. He and a small team are awaiting the derailment, standing by to eliminate any survivors. All those involved in the Banks investigation will be taken care of."

"Very well." The Sec-Def sounded pleased.

"And we have another girl, Beard's little fling, en route to the facility as we speak."

"Hmm."

Russell waited anxiously. He never enjoyed these conversations.

"Very well. Make sure you keep a firm handle on this situation, Keating."

"Will do. And I'll have a full report on your desk by close of business tomorrow."

The phone call ended, leaving Russell alone, staring through a floor-to-ceiling window that led to Rion and Julianna Sanderson's room. The twins, sixteen years of age now, sat on the floor, meditating. The commander stood a moment, before rapping his hand against the glass, three times.

Julianna looked up, while Rion continued his ritual. The girl, who Russell had known since she was three, smiled at seeing the commander. Her ice-blue eyes gleamed, blinking rapidly, as was her unique manner of communicating through the glass. Russell blinked back, then nodded his head.

Julianna, who was sitting cross-legged, extended her arms, making her appear like a tiny windmill on a windless day. She closed her eyes and tilted her head to the ceiling, her face contorting as the veins in her neck pulsed and strained. A fraction of a second later, her body was gone, disappearing from the room, leaving Rion alone in his meditative state.

Russell turned around in the hallway, facing where the girl now stood. She was breathing heavily and beaming with pride.

"Very good, my dear," he said, placing a hand on Julianna's shoulder. She truly was a masterpiece of hard work – her beautiful, raw power, the result of the dedicated research of countless American scientists. "Run along now, darling."

The girl took off down the hallway, skipping towards the recess facility to join her friends.

Made in the USA
Monee, IL
05 December 2020

50899952R00225